WAGONS HO!

DELORES TWITCHEL

PublishAmerica
Baltimore

First printing

At the specific preference of the author, PublishAmerica allowed this work to remain exactly as the author intended, verbatim, without editorial input.

ISBN: 1-4241-2684-3
PUBLISHED BY PUBLISHAMERICA, LLLP
www.publishamerica.com
Baltimore

Printed in the United States of America

DEDICATION

Dedicated to the Lord,
to my husband Les.

Special thanks to
Alan Mueller, Joyce Scrivner, and Kent Scrivner
for their help.

CHAPTER ONE

"The graduates will please stand to receive their diplomas," the dean of the newly founded medical school invited. The graduates began filing past the lectern to receive the coveted piece of paper that proclaimed them a doctor of medicine. "Doctor David Duvall," the voice continued.

David, powerfully built, muscular, strong, and towering above most of his classmates, reached for the diploma with one hand and shook the hand of the dean with the other. "Congratulations, Doctor Duvall," said the dean.

His blue eyes gleaming, his smile showing even white teeth, he answered, "Thank you, sir," and made his way back to his seat. His high cheekbones and patrician nose clearly made him the most handsome man there. Many a girl envied his wavy dark blond hair.

David felt a great sense of accomplishment, of achievement. He felt a special satisfaction when the dean had called him doctor. Although he felt as prepared as man could make him, he still realized how little knowledge he had. He knew the great physician was the Lord and his hand did all healing. He would simply be the Lord's instrument.

He had given the matter of where he would practice medicine much thought, and last week he had made his decision. He had decided to go to Oregon and had signed up to go on the wagon train leaving the first of May from Independence, Missouri.

He dreaded the confrontation he knew he would have with his mother. He knew he would have trouble convincing his mother he was doing the right thing. Mrs. Duvall would want him to stay home in Boston and join his father's practice, but David felt he had been called by God to go out West.

His father had served the elite of Boston for twenty-five years and had made a fortune doing so; however, David felt that a doctor should help all people needing him, not just the affluent of his father's practice.

So lost in thought about his coming confrontation with his mother, it seemed only a few seconds until the graduation ceremony was over, and graduates were receiving congratulations from family and friends. David made his way to his parents.

His father, as tall and muscular as David, was a handsome gray haired man. He was the first to speak, his blue eyes sparkling with pride. "Congratulations, son," his father said shaking David's hand, patting him on the back, then ruffling his dark blond wavy hair, a habit that he had to show his approval since David was a child. "I know how glad you are to have your schooling behind you. I'm not so old I don't remember how exhausting it was to stay up nights to study or sit with patients and to catch sleep as one could. Now you can get on with the rest of your life. I know that we're going to have a great time working together."

David didn't reply, but smiled at his father. Instead, he turned to his mother, a tall regal woman. Her dark hair was salt and pepper. She had vivid blue eyes, which could pierce the heart of anyone who disagreed with her. She had been an outstanding beauty in her day. Her demeanor spoke of wealth and authority. "Son, you don't know how proud I am of you. I can hardly wait for you to get home to stay. I know you and your father will be very happy working together," Mrs. Duvall said, embracing her son.

"Yes," David said, feeling disloyal. "Well, that is something we have to talk about when we get home," David answered her, looking first at her, then at his father.

Doctor Marcus Duvall looked puzzled and Mrs. Duvall said, "What can there possibly be to talk about? Everything is all arranged."

"It will wait until we get home," David answered her, knowing she didn't like to be crossed. "I'm ready to go now, if you are."

"David, you aren't going to be difficult, are you?" Mrs. Duvall asked, smiling at her son. She really didn't believe for one moment that David could possibly want something different from what the family had planned.

David didn't answer, but linked arms with his father and mother, and started with them to their carriage. He wished he didn't have to hurt them. With David walking between his parents, it was easy to see where he got his good looks. "What did you think of the ceremony?" he asked, trying to avoid developing the situation until they were home. He wanted to be well away from prying eyes and ears when they discussed his future.

"I was very impressed, especially when you received top honors in your class," his father said, swollen with pride. We're very proud of you."

"Yes, son, we certainly are," Mrs. Duvall said, squeezing his arm. Soon they reached their carriage, and David helped his mother into it. When all three were settled, David took the reins, and they started the drive to their elegant home.

"I've asked some friends for dinner tomorrow night. Mr. and Mrs. Stanford and Alice are coming. You know how Alice dotes on you."

"Yes, Mother, I know, but the feeling is not mutual, as I've told you many times. I wish you hadn't invited them. When you keep inviting them, you just encourage Alice."

David dreaded the coming dinner. Mrs. Stanford and his mother always made sly innuendoes about Alice's addition to the family. Alice was just as bad. She never missed an opportunity to lay her hand on his arm or cuddle close to him. Her excuse was that she was cold or afraid of something or other. Although Alice was a very pretty girl with flaming red hair and green eyes, she left David cold.

"But, David, she would make you such a suitable wife. You need someone of the Stanford's standing in the community."

I guess she thinks if she parades Alice in front of me enough, I'll succumb to her charms. Not in a million years would I let myself be tied to anyone like Alice. She is totally self-centered, selfish and spoiled, David thought.

"Mother, I'm going to say this once and once only. When it comes to picking a wife, I'll do my own choosing with God's guidance," David told his mother, his blue eyes icy.

"Good for you, son," Marcus Duvall interjected. "Leave the boy alone, Maddie."

Mrs. Duvall tossed her head in condescension, crossed her arms over her chest in anger, but didn't reply. It was a sure sign that she was preparing for battle. She only adopted that stance when the fireworks were ready to explode. They traveled the rest of their journey in an uneasy silence.

Reaching the large brick house, David helped his mother from the carriage, and the three of them went up the steps leading to the black painted door. The door opened into a large walnut paneled hallway. A large crystal chandelier hung from the high white plastered ceiling. Several doors led off the passageway. Without stopping, Mrs. Duvall headed for the massive staircase on one side of the hall.

"Just a moment, Mother, please. I have to talk to you and Dad. Please come into the sitting room and sit down."

Frowning, his father ran a hand through his hair, something he always did when perplexed or upset. *What can possibly be ailing the boy?* He wondered.

Sucking in a deep breath, with nostrils flaring, Mrs. Duvall threw her head back in the haughty way that she always did when she was upset or trying to make someone feel inferior. She was very proud of her position as one of Boston's leading society matrons, and many times she had made others, whom she considered beneath her, feel inferior. "Oh, very well," she said ungraciously, "But I don't see what there is to talk about. Things *are* settled. Besides, I have to get ready for the Stanford's' visit tomorrow evening, and while we are on the subject of the Stanford's, I think you'd do well to reconsider Alice. Alice is a very lovely, young woman. You could do much worse," she said, sniffing in disdain as she turned toward the sitting room.

Although David loved his mother very much, he was aware that she was not always nice, especially when she didn't get her way. David ignored her comments and stood aside for his parents to precede him into the room.

It was stylishly furnished with matching blue damask-covered couches and walnut tables. Elegant red glass lamps sat on the tables on either side of the couches and by the two wing chairs covered in a blue floral pattern on a white background. Filled bookshelves lined the wall on either side of a walnut mantle adorning a huge fireplace. Paintings of ancestors and colorful landscapes decked the white painted walls. Blue velvet draperies and white lace panels covered the large windows. A deep blue carpet completed the furnishings.

Although the whole house was beautiful, this room was David's favorite. He had spent many happy hours here as a child and young boy reading the many volumes filling the bookshelves in the room and playing games with his father and cousins. His parents had always seen that he had everything he wanted, so it was going to be very difficult to go against their wishes to go to Oregon.

His parents sat on one of the blue couches, while David choose one of the chairs. When they were seated comfortably, Mrs. Duvall said, "Now, what is so important that you have to tell it *right now*?"

David took a deep breath and quickly let it out, then began. "Mother, Dad, you aren't going to like what I'm going to say." Both parents looked alarmed. "I'm not going into practice with you, Dad."

Both parents began to talk at once. "But, son, why?" Doctor Duvall asked.

"What do you mean, you're not going into your father's practice? Of course, you are. What's gotten into you, David?" his mother asked belligerently. "We have had this planned all your life."

"I'm sorry to disappoint you both, but I feel God is calling me to go to Oregon. I've signed on a train going the first of May."

"What! Ridiculous! I simply won't have it," Mrs. Duvall, her voice rising to a shriek.

"What do you think you can do in Oregon that you can't do here, son?" Doctor Duvall asked quietly. He was unable to hide his keen disappointment, but he was willing to listen to David.

"I just think that I could help more people there than I can here," David replied. "I have felt God's calling for some months now."

"Oh, I feel faint," Mrs. Duvall, said in a die-away voice. "Get me my smelling salts." David's mother always felt faint when she wanted to bring one of her family into line. It had never failed to bring the culprit to heel.

"Mother, you know that you are perfectly all right," Doctor Duvall voiced sternly.

David tried in vain to hide a smile, which infuriated his mother.

Changing tactics, in a voice that shook, she said, "Well, don't think that you will get one penny from us if you go." Shaking her finger at David, she warned, "I'll see you don't if it is the last thing I ever do," her voice becoming more shrill. She was quickly working herself into frenzy.

"Now, Mother, don't say anything more that you'll be sorry for," Doctor Duvall told her. "You can't live David's life for him."

"I'll be sorry? He's the one that should be sorry! The very idea, going to a wilderness," she said disgustedly. "If he stays here, his future is decided. He'll be a man of wealth. Out there, he'll be *nobody*. He'll have no money, she said to the room in general."

"Mother, I believe you are forgetting the inheritance Grandmother Duvall left me. It's a fortune all by itself. If I didn't want to, I wouldn't have to work a day in my life and still have more money than I could ever spend," David replied, looking sad. He felt bad about hurting his mother, but God's will for his life came first. "Surely, you want me to do God's will?" he asked gently. He had known for a long time that his mother was not close to the Lord. He always prayed that she would find the peace that only God can give.

Mrs. Duvall made no reply.

Doctor Duvall cleared his throat and said, "Mother, I know you are disappointed, so am I, but David has to lead his life as he sees fit, especially since he feels it is God's calling."

"I can see both of you are against me," Mrs. Duvall cried. She jumped up, running from the room. She raced up the stairs and down the hall to her bedroom. The two men heard her door slam.

Doctor Duvall looked at David and shrugged his shoulders in resignation.

"I'm sorry to hurt both of you. How long before you retire, Dad?"

"I planned to retire at the end of this year. By then you'll be settled. Why?"

"Oh, I just thought that you and Mother might consider coming to Oregon too. That is what I'd like, so that we could be together."

"It would take some doing. I don't think your mother would give in to go easily. Let's work on it. I'd like to be with my son. If we pray enough, maybe God will change her." He extended his hand to David. The two men shook hands to seal the bargain.

"Great, Dad. You've always been able to do more with her than anyone else, and prayer works miracles."

Mrs. Duvall refused to come down to dinner that evening, complaining of a headache. She always developed a headache as a last resort when things didn't go her way. Many times she had won sympathy and ultimately her way with her husband and son when suffering a painful headache. This time neither of them went to comfort her.

CHAPTER TWO

The gray shades of predawn gave way to the first golden rays of the April sunshine. The earth stood clothed in garments of the rebirth of spring. Trees were adorned in their new green leaves, and the lush green of the grass hid the last of the dead blades from last year. Jonquils and tulips created riots of color in flowerbeds and along walkways in the town. The early morning breeze promised a warm day.

Lexie Fletcher fought through layers of sleep to wake to the early morning sounds coming from the kitchen downstairs. She knew her father would have gone to work. He always left for the office early on Fridays. She heard the sounds of the kitchen door closing and then the clanking of the stove lids on the kitchen cook stove. She recognized the sounds. Her mother was adding wood to an already vigorously burning fire.

"Lexie, it's time to get up," Sarah Fletcher, Lexie's mother, called from downstairs. "Breakfast is almost ready."

Lexie stretched her arms above her head and looked around her room. Powder blue wallpaper with clusters of pink and white flowers adorned the walls. Pristine white woodwork matched the white ceiling. Frothy lace curtains fluttered in the breeze coming through the two open windows.

She reached up and took hold of two of the spindles on the walnut bed that her father had made for her and pulled, stretching again.

Her father had been a furniture maker before coming to Missouri. He had made her walnut washstand for her too. He had carried the mirror for the washstand packed in quilts and feather bedding all the way from Tennessee when they had come to Missouri ten years ago.

Blue, pink, and white braided rugs that she and her mother had made were scattered on the dark oak floor.

Lexie looked about her. She loved everything in her room. Her parents had redecorated it for her on her eighteenth birthday in February, almost two months ago. Now it looked like a young woman's room, not a young girl's room as it did before. She wished they would acknowledge that she was an adult in other ways.

Lexie tumbled out of bed with her usual exuberance and stretched to her full height of five feet one inch tall. "Coming, Mother," she called. She walked over to the walnut washstand and poured some water from the pink and white floral-patterned porcelain pitcher into its matching basin. Quickly, she splashed the cool water onto her face. "That ought to wake me up," she said. Picking up the blue hand towel, folded neatly on the washstand, she dried her face.

Looking into the mirror, she saw just an ordinary face and well proportioned body, not the beautiful image staring back at her. Soft curly black hair framed a perfectly oval face. Black arching brows rose above the deep blue eyes that faced her. She saw rose-colored lips and cheeks and thought to herself, w*ell, not the best, but that's the way God made me. If only I didn't have such rosy cheeks and lips.*

Scrutinizing her face, she remembered the day of her eighth grade graduation. Sarah had made a sky-blue silk dress for her. It was a beautiful dress and brought out the blue of her eyes. On promotion day, she had dressed and come downstairs, only to be met by her mother's baleful glance.

"Lexie Fletcher, you go right back upstairs and wash that stuff off your face!" she said angrily.

"What stuff?" Lexie asked, perplexed.

"That paint on your face. Where did you get it?" she asked accusingly.

"Mama, I don't have any paint on my face," Lexie said.

Her mother took her arm in a firm grip and marched her over to the cabinet where the water bucket and wash pan were. She poured a dipper full of water into the pan and proceeded to scrub Lexie's face. Lexie began to cry. "Mama, I don't have anything on my face."

Sarah looked carefully at the cloth. Nothing was on it. "Oh, my land, my darling daughter. I feel terrible. You *don't* have anything on your face. I thought for sure you had put something on your eyebrows and your cheeks and lips, but you haven't. It must be the blue dress that brings out your natural color. I'm sorry, honey. I should have believed you. Please forgive me. I never noticed how you've changed lately, how beautiful my little girl has become."

Mamma and Daddy act like they still think I'm the little eight-year-old that I was when we came here from Tennessee. So many times they still treat me like a little girl. I wonder if they'll ever realize that I've grown up. Here, I've been eighteen since February. Before I know it, I'll be a prune-faced old maid, she thought. She felt both frustrated and helpless when it came to convincing them she should be treated as an adult.

Lexie examined her face closely, looking for a blemish that wasn't there. Though not a vain girl, Lexie did want to look nice. She felt it was necessary for a girl to look nice to catch a husband, and she wanted to get married, but she had begun to wonder if God wanted her to remain single. She had no gentlemen callers for several months.

Lexie had thought that perhaps Carson Fullbrite had been the one God had chosen for her. He had come calling for several weeks. He had even asked her to marry him. Before she said yes she asked if he was a believer. She was disappointed to find he wasn't a Christian. She was not going to tie herself, no matter how she felt about a man, to a nonbeliever. She had been taught since she was a child that to be married to an unbeliever was to be unequally yoked, which was forbidden in the scriptures.

Carson had told her that he didn't believe in God and that nothing would make him change his mind. When he saw that Lexie was determined to have nothing more to do with him, he pleaded that he would attend church with her if she would just marry him. Finally, he

16

told her that he loved her so much that he had considered telling her that he had become a believer, but he found that he couldn't bring himself to lie to her. Then, when she still didn't respond, he became angry, ranting and raving, calling her a fanatic.

Lexie wondered now how she ever thought he could be the one to be her life's mate. It was amazing how changed he seemed. She was glad that she found out what a temper he had before he had convinced her to marry him.

Although several young men had wanted to court her before she started dating Carson, since they had broken up, Lexie had been seeing no one. She often wondered why no young men came calling any more.

Finding no blemishes, Lexie considered once more her rosy cheeks and lips. *I wonder if other people think I paint my face. If Mother thought I'd painted it, other people probably do too. They probably think I'm a loose woman.* Lexie shrugged away the unpleasant memories and laughed to herself, thinking how ridiculous it was that she could be considered a loose woman. If anything, she was just the opposite.

She pulled her lavender striped cotton nightgown over her head and tossed it onto the bed. From the closet, she took a navy blue skirt and a white blouse. *I'll bet my students get tired of seeing me wear skirts and white blouses to school,* she thought while she dressed. *I wonder what they would think if I dressed up today. No, it would be silly to dress differently. I won't make any changes today,* she decided, pulling a blue skirt over her head.

Buttoning the last button on her blouse, she reached for her hairbrush and began brushing the shiny black curls that clustered around her face. *Oh, well, today is the last day this year that they will have to see me, and who knows where I'll be next year. I hope I will be right here at the same old school because Mother and Daddy surely won't let me go to another town to teach. Enough of that kind of thinking,* she chastised herself. *Here I am being ungrateful. God has given me the best parents in the world. Father in Heaven, I thank you again for the good parents you have given me. Please forgive my unkind thoughts. In Jesus' name, I pray. Amen.* She laid the brush down on the washstand and ran a hand under her hair, fluffing it away from her neck.

"I guess I look like a typical schoolmarm," she said aloud, making a face at herself in the mirror and grinning mischievously. An only child, although her parents had wanted more children, she sometimes was lonely and voiced her thoughts aloud to herself, a habit she had carried with her since childhood.

She walked over to the bed, sat down and pulled on her stockings and shoes. Getting up from the bed, she folded her nightgown neatly and put it under her pillow. She fluffed her pillow, and with a few smooth strokes, made her bed. She walked back to the washstand for one last check of her appearance. Glancing once more into the mirror, she flipped a curl into place, shrugged, thought *I guess that will have to do*, and turned toward the stairs.

Feeling exuberant, knowing this was the last day of school and that she had successfully completed one year of teaching, she fairly skipped downstairs. Coming into the kitchen, she called, "Good morning, Mama! Isn't it a beautiful day for the last day of school?" Whirling around, she continued, "Look at the great sunshine God gave us after all that rain we've had for the last month. He knew the kids needed sunshine for the last day." She stopped and raised her eyebrows, thoughtful for a second, then said, "I can't believe today *is* the last day. It seems that school just started. Doesn't this year just seem to have flown by?" She walked over to the wash pan and began to wash her hands.

Standing at the cook stove an older version of Lexie turned, looked at her daughter, and smiled. "It certainly seems to have flown to me," she said. Sarah Fletcher didn't look her forty years. She had her daughter's blue eyes, rosy cheeks, and lips. Only her hair was different. It was not as dark as Lexie's. It had just a hint of red. Her face was still unlined, and her hair had only a sprinkling of gray. As petite as Lexie, her figure was still neat and trim as that of a young girl. Tom Fletcher, her husband, called both Sarah and Lexie his two girls.

"I wonder if there will be a big turnout for the promotion day ceremonies?" Lexie asked, looking over her shoulder at her mother.

She dried her hands and took a seat at the table.

"Unless too many of the kids' dads are working in the fields, there probably will be," Sarah said, as she stood waiting for the eggs in the heavy frying pan to finish cooking. She deftly turned them over and reached over to another frying pan to turn ham.

"Do you think I should have dressed up in my Sunday best today?" Lexie asked, looking down at herself.

"No, I think you look just fine, as you always do. Here, have an egg and some ham," she said, turning from the stove, bringing the food to the table. She deftly scooped browned ham and a fried egg onto a plate, added a biscuit, and set it in front of Lexie. Next she placed a jar of strawberry preserves before Lexie's plate.

Lexie sat down at the table and bowed her head to ask the blessing. When she had finished, Sarah poured both of them a cup of coffee and sat down at the table.

"Guess I'd better hurry if I'm not going to be late for class," Lexie said, watching the breeze gently blow the white cottage curtains at the window of the yellow and white floral wallpapered kitchen while she sipped her coffee.

"It's so pretty out today, I think I'll work some in the garden before I come to school. That garden is the best looking one that I've had in years," Sarah said, looking out the window too.

"Oh, Mamma, you always have a good garden. I wish I were half the gardener you are," Lexie said, stuffing egg and ham into her mouth and washing them down with the freshly brewed coffee.

Sarah smiled her thanks. "You'll learn. It took me a long time to learn. It's a good thing your daddy had patience with me. I remember one time I hoed down radishes that had come up. I thought they were weeds."

Lexie laughed and said, "Oh, you didn't. What did Daddy say?" she asked, quickly swallowing her breakfast. She always enjoyed the stories of Sarah and Tom's life together.

"Well, he would have said a lot more than he did, but I started to cry. You know he never could stand to see me cry," Sarah said in a satisfied manner.

Lexie said longingly, "I hope I find a husband who will love me as much as Daddy loves you. You two remind me of honeymooners."

"I'm sure you will. It's my greatest hope for you in this life, after the peace that comes from the Lord, of course," Sarah said.

"I know," Lexie said and got up from the table. She walked over to the white painted cabinets and picked up a huge platter of cookies.

She deftly wrapped the platter in a white linen dishtowel. "I hope this will be enough cookies to go around. If I only knew how many people would be there, it would sure help. I keep worrying that everything will go wrong today. Oh gosh, Mom, I almost forgot about my dirty dishes. I'm so excited about today." Lexie turned to the table to collect her dirty dishes.

"Never mind about the dishes. I'll get them. Tell you what, I'm going to make some more cookies this morning," Sarah told her. "If you see that you are going to need more, I can bring them when I bring the tea. Just send one of your students to tell me. Oh, never mind sending someone, I'll just bring more when I come."

"Great! Mama, you're the best mother in the whole wide world. I thank God for giving you to me," Lexie said, kissing her mother on the cheek. She felt guilty about her earlier critical thoughts. "I'd better leave now, so I'll have plenty of time to get things ready for the ceremonies."

She let herself out of the house, carefully balancing the platter and other school necessities on her arm and hand as she closed the door, and started down the street. Lexie walked the half-mile from her home each day to the school.

Each morning during cold weather, she had built a fire in the big pot-bellied stove in the corner of the one room school. Two of the fathers supplied the school with enough wood to keep everyone warm, and two of the older boys fed the stove during the day. On especially cold days, Lexie had taken a pot of beans and let them cook on the stove. By lunchtime the beans were done, and the children were very grateful for the warm food. Lexie always made sure that God was given thanks for the food that she brought.

Reaching the school, she set the cookies down to unlock the door.

Sunshine inside the room greeted her and displayed the newly cleaned and polished desks and shiny slate chalkboard that had been installed last fall.

Lexie and the students had spent yesterday afternoon cleaning out desks and shelving books. The little girls had dusted every thing in the school. The boys had cut the grass outside and washed the windows. The older girls had helped Lexie scrub the floor and chalkboard. Lexie looked around her with deep satisfaction.

She had enjoyed this year. She had taken over the teaching position when the regular teacher had to take a leave of absence for health reasons. She felt she had done a good job with the students. They worked hard, and she and they got along well together.

Lexie didn't want to see anyone suffer, but she hoped somehow that she would be able to teach again next year. *If only he would move and find another school* she thought. She thought the only thing better than teaching would be to be married to a good Christian man, but she guessed she would just have to wait for that. She sure hoped God didn't want her to remain single, but she thought He might since no one seemed interested in her.

Picking up the cookie platter, she walked inside and set it upon her desk. Next, she went to open the windows to let in the fresh spring air. She rearranged some books on her desk.

"Good morning, Miss Fletcher," Katie Brown said cheerfully, as she came through the open door. Katie, a lively girl with brown hair and brown eyes, smiled at Lexie

"Good morning, Katie. How are you this morning?"

"Oh, I'm fine." Her round face broke into a grin. "I'm so excited about today. I hope I don't forget any of my speech," Katie said, smoothing down her pink and white print cotton dress. Before Lexie could answer, she continued, "Do you like my dress? I got it for my tenth birthday last month."

"It's a beautiful dress, Katie, and you look lovely. As for your speech, I'm sure you'll do just fine."

"Thank you. I sure hope my speech is good. I've been working real hard on it. Is there something I can do to help you get ready for this afternoon?" Katie asked.

"You know, I believe we are completely ready, but if you would like me to listen to you rehearse your speech, I'd be glad to do so."

"Oh, would you? I'd like that. You could tell me what I'm doing wrong," Katie said. Lexie sat at her desk and listened carefully to Katie laboriously go through her speech.

"Katie, that was fine." She watched as crimson flooded Katie's cheeks. "You know the whole thing very well. There is only one thing that you could improve." Ignoring the downcast expression on Katie's face, she continued. "Put a little expression into your delivery. What I mean is, say it like you are just talking to us instead of saying memorized lines," Lexie told her.

Katie brightened, thought a moment then said, "You mean like this?" She took a deep breath, smiled tentatively, and began to deliver the speech again.

When Katie finished, Lexie said, "Precisely. That was great! Your parents will be so proud of you." She felt that all children needed to be encouraged, and Katie was no exception. She was a perfectionist. No half measures for Katie. Everything had to be just so, and Lexie wanted to alleviate her stress.

Other students began trickling into the building as Lexie listened to Katie. Each student quietly took his seat and sat listening attentively, in sharp contrast to the excited faces. Each girl's hair was braided neatly or combed into long curls while boys had heads of hair slicked back with olive oil or hair tonic. All wore their Sunday best clothes. For the girls it was brightly colored calico dresses, and the boys wore chambray shirts and woolen or broadcloth trousers.

Lexie looked out over a room full of freshly scrubbed faces. "Good morning, everyone." With a smile, Lexie greeted them when Katie finished her delivery.

"Good morning, Miss Fletcher," came their reply.

Rising from her chair as Katie took her seat, Lexie walked around to the front of her desk and stood leaning against it, thinking *what a sweet group of children these are.*

"Thank you for helping me, Miss Fletcher," Katie said, sitting down primly in her seat.

"You are very welcome, Katie. Would anyone else like me to listen to your presentation for your parents?" Lexie asked, smiling at her students. "They won't be here for another two hours, and I think we have everything ready for them. We could rehearse and still have plenty of playtime. By the way, I want to compliment you again on how nice our school looks today. All of you did a great job getting ready for today. Everyone of you looks super nice too."

Several children raised their hands to ask for help with their speeches. Lexie patiently listened to each person, giving supportive criticism when needed.

After listening to the speeches, the students went outside to play. Lexie cautioned them as they left the schoolroom not to get dirty. A chorus of 'we won't' answered her.

Sarah Fletcher arrived first, bringing more cookies and two huge jugs of tea. She enlisted two of the older boys to help her carry in the food that was sitting in her buggy. They placed the tea and cookies on Lexie's desk to be eaten later. Lexie saw Tom Brown, a tall skinny seventh grader, raise the cloth and peek at the cookies. Tom always looked hungry, so she didn't say anything to him.

Soon parents began to arrive. Most of the parents were farming people. Just three families lived in town. It seemed that all parents were present. Lexie was pleased to see that all of the board members also were in attendance. She welcomed the parents warmly.

First, everyone stood and recited the Golden Rule, and then The Lord's Prayer. Next, came a poem recited by Tom Brown. Rebecca and Amanda Green, twin third graders sang a duet. Both twins looked so much alike with the same blue eyes and blonde hair that it was difficult to tell them apart. Every student had a part in the program, and applause was thunderous for all students. When the last student had performed, Lexie handed out certificates of promotion to students in grades one through seven and diplomas to the two eighth grade students. Each student was applauded loudly as he received his certificate or diploma, so that each one felt special when he sat down.

When the final applause died, Lexie stood and said, "Ladies and gentlemen, that concludes our program. I hope you enjoyed it as much as the students and I did as we prepared it. I want to thank all of you for coming today and for helping me to make this school year so successful. Students," she continued, turning to them as they sat in their seats, "thank you for working so hard, and for being such good students this year." Turning back to the adults sitting on benches along the wall, she said, "I also want to thank my mother for bringing the cookies and the tea," Lexie said. "We couldn't have graduation without those," she said, beaming at Sarah.

Parents and students met these words by rising to their feet and applauding both Lexie and her mother. When the applause died down, Lexie smiled and said, "Now, let's have some refreshments. Zeke, will you and Martin please pass the cookies to everyone? Rebecca and Amanda, please pour the tea. Betsy and Polly, please hand the tea to everyone, and, Sally, please hand out the napkins," Lexie requested. She watched as the students, pleased with the opportunity to help, swiftly went about performing the duty assigned them. Rebecca and Amanda poured tea into tin cups that Lexie had borrowed from her church for the special occasion. She kept a close eye on what all of the children were doing as she walked around visiting with each parent until everyone was served, telling them how well behaved and studious their children were.

While everyone was eating, a first grader, little Timmy Blair popped a whole cookie into his mouth. Timmy was small for his age. He had brown hair, and his brown eyes sparkled like deep, dark pools when he was being mischievous. The older boys always teased him about the freckles on his face. Lexie had reprimanded them sternly when they called him 'turkey egg.'

His cheeks bulging with the cookie, he asked, "Miss Fletcher, are you going to be back next year? I sure hope you will. I don't know how we could get along without you if you don't come back. You're the greatest teacher ever," he said, brown eyes sparkling.

"Well, Timmy, I don't know yet. The school board will decide that," Lexie said.

"Well, by golly, I want you back next year!" Timmy said forcefully, smacking his hands together for emphasis.

A chorus of "Me too!" answered him.

Lexie was pleased that the children wanted her back. She was doubly glad that the board was there to hear them say so. "Let's just wait and see. Just remember that I've really enjoyed being with you this year, and I'd *like* to be with you again next year," she said, smiling.

After everyone finished eating, they seemed to be enjoying themselves and were in no hurry to leave. They visited with their neighbors, talking about their children, their gardens, and church. Then a discussion arose about rumors of a wagon train going to Oregon.

"I heard there are four families from here going to Oregon on this train," Paul Abernathy, one of the farmers, said. He was a small, shy man, who looked as if a good puff of wind would blow him away. He rubbed his hands against his brown woolen clad thighs as he spoke. It was unusual for him to speak out publicly. His ruddy complexion had turned a nice shade of red when he finished.

"That's true. One family that I know for sure is going is the Bates family. I hear the Oliver's are also going," Sam Brown, a wheezing, heavy-set man with salt and pepper hair said. Lexie wondered if the corncob pipe that he carried in his shirt pocket caused the wheezing.

Lexie listened with one ear to what they were saying, as she made the rounds, telling each child and his parent's goodbye. One by one the families began to leave until only the school board members were left. Their children scuttled outside to play.

Sarah had been cleaning up the room, packing away the leftovers and the cups and plates that were to be washed and returned. Students had picked up the cloth napkins and deposited them in a brown paper bag. Sarah had told them to put the bag in her buggy, and she would take them home with her for washing.

"Lexie, I'm going home now. Do you have anything you want me to carry for you?" Sarah asked, picking up the last of the food containers that she had brought. "I'll take the cups and plates with me."

"Thanks, Mom, but I can manage. I'll be along soon."

"Well, I'm going then. I'll see you at home." She told everyone goodbye and went out the open door.

25

When Sarah had gone, the board members looked at one another, and Mrs. Flora Hopkins, a small-boned woman who was president of the board, cleared her throat twice as though dreading an unpleasant task. "Lexie, dear," she said. "The board and I want to compliment you on how well you've done this school year."

"Thank you," Lexie replied. She had a strong feeling that she wasn't going to like what was coming.

Mrs. Hopkins, a kindly woman, owner of the general store, looked uncomfortable and said, "We think you've done wonders with the students, and I wish we didn't have to tell you this. As you know, Matthew Thomas went on leave of absence because of health reasons. Well, the board had its regular meeting last night before the summer break, and Mr. Thomas attended. He told us that he is much better, and that he will be able to resume his duties in September," Mrs. Hopkins said.

Although Lexie tried to steel herself, her stomach tightened into a knot. She couldn't keep the disappointment from showing on her face.

Seeing the look of disappointment on Lexie's face, Mrs. Hopkins, sensitive to the needs of others, said, "Lexie, dear, you don't know how badly we all feel about this. If there were some way we could keep you, we would. We have watched you grow from a young child to a very fine adult. You are a sensitive and caring young woman, and we do hate to let you go."

The other board members nodded in agreement. Mr. Sam Brown, a tall, stooped, lanky farmer with thinning auburn hair said, "We really do hate to lose you. You are a fine teacher and a fine person."

"Well, thank you. Naturally, I'm very disappointed, but I wouldn't want Mr. Thomas to be ill just so that I could continue teaching. And I did know that the possibility existed that I might have to leave at the end of this year." She felt she didn't have the courage to say more. "I certainly will miss the children," she ended softly. She was beginning to feel worse as each second ticked by. *I hope they leave in a hurry, or I may disgrace myself and bawl like a baby, although I really don't want a job at Mr. Thomas' expense.* Lexie swallowed the lump that rose in her throat and said, "I want to thank all of you for letting me teach this year." She attempted to smile, but it was a pitiful attempt, wavering and dying.

Silas Martin, a self-satisfied man, overweight, and wearing a black broadcloth suit that looked as if he were ready to spill out of it, spoke up, "I hope you aren't too disappointed. You're young, so it shouldn't be too hard for you to find another teaching position." He was a pompous man who thought a pat on the shoulder would solve all problems, and if it didn't, just ignore it and it would go away.

"Yes, I'm sure you're right. I also want to thank all of you for being so kind," was all Lexie could manage.

Lexie looked around at the now spotlessly clean room, handed over the key, and picked up her things. Each board member shook her hand when leaving, and she turned the knob, which locked the building. All left in separate directions. Lexie, the last to leave, turned for one final look at the school building. *It's not as if I were going away. It's just going to be different.* A tear slipped down her face, followed by several more. From time to time as she walked along, she wiped away the tears. She hadn't felt this dreadful since she and Carson said goodbye so acrimoniously. She had been devastated at the things he had said to her, wondering if some of them could be true.

Her mind became a turmoil of scattered thoughts. *What of the future? Will I ever find a husband?* Although Lexie loved her parents' home, it couldn't take the place of a home of her own. She wanted a home and a husband to love her. She told herself that she would feel better tomorrow, but the thought didn't persist.

As she walked along, she was reminded of a time when she was seven. Her family had a small orchard in Tennessee. Lexie had decided one day to climb the biggest tree in the orchard. It was an old apple tree. Lexie was always a passive child, so it never occurred to Tom or Sarah to warn her about the danger of climbing. Lexie was especially lonely that day. The white fluffy clouds hung low in the brilliantly blue sky. Lexie felt that she could almost reach them if she got just a little closer. She had no trouble scrambling up the old gnarled tree trunk and onto the branches above. She climbed to the top and sat on one of the branches. The clouds still looked as far away to her as they had when she was on the ground. After a while, she got tired of sitting on the hard branch and decided to climb down. Looking down, the earth seemed a long, long way down. About that time, Sarah called, "Lexie, what are you doing?"

Lexie replied, "I'm out here. I'll be there in a few minutes." She was not about to tell Sarah where she really was. Sarah went back into the house, and Lexie started down. She looked down and froze. After a few moments, she decided it wasn't as frightening to climb down, as it would be to face Sarah's wrath for being in the tree. Very carefully, she started down. She timidly made her way from the top branches and had gone several feet when her foot slipped off the branch. With the additional weight on the branch she was holding in her hand, it broke, tossing Lexie to the ground.

Lexie would never forget how she felt falling through the air and then the feeling of thudding onto the hard ground, the breath knocked out of her. Lexie thought that feeling of falling, unable to catch herself, was the same feeling that she felt today, a helpless, falling, sinking feeling.

Luckily, she was only bruised, scratched, and shaken in her fall from the tree. Her parents had never disciplined her for climbing the tree. They were too thankful she wasn't hurt. They thought she had been punished enough in the fall. Lexie only hoped that she would recover as quickly today. Somehow, she didn't think it possible.

Reaching home, she called to her mother. "I'm home. I don't have a job any more," she added in a wavering voice. Suddenly the tears became a deluge.

Sarah Fletcher heard her daughter's unrestrained sobbing and guessed what had happened. She quickly came from the kitchen and put her arms around Lexie. "Oh, honey, don't cry so. It'll be all right. Remember that God is in control. He has a plan that we can't see right now. There will always be another teaching job, or you could help your dad at the newspaper office."

"But I don't want to work in a newspaper office," Lexie said, holding tightly to Sarah. "I want to teach. You know Daddy will never let me go to another town to teach this fall. He'll say I'm too young when here I am eighteen and almost two months. You remember how both of us had to plead with him to let me go to Miss Adam's Academy for Young Ladies, and that was only thirty miles away," Lexie managed to get out between sobs and hiccoughs. She was so unhappy she didn't notice how wet her tears were getting Sarah's dress.

Sarah, ignoring the wet feeling, could see that Lexie was working herself up to be sick if her unhappiness wasn't quelled soon. *She's right. Tom won't let her leave. How hard it is to be young.*

"Yes, I remember very well, but give God a chance. Have you prayed about your feelings?"

"Yes, for months now, and I've gotten no answer."

"Then just remember that God works with His own timetable. He wants what's best for you. If you are not supposed to teach, something better will come along," she said encouragingly.

"The only thing better than teaching, that I can see, would be to have a husband and a home of my own. I've prayed about that too. Just think nearly all the girl's my age here in town are already married. Alice and Joan are mothers. I certainly don't see *any* indication that any young man is interested in seeing *me*, much less marrying me."

"If you are worried about being an old maid, forget it. Why are you so worried about getting married anyway? You have plenty of time for marriage. God will send the perfect husband for you in His good time. You don't want second best, do you?"

"You know I don't. It's just that it's hard waiting. If I have to wait, I want to teach. I love teaching and the children. I've prayed and prayed that somehow I could stay without hurting Mr. Thomas, and now everything just seems to be falling apart. My life seems to be in a shamble. Before Carson and I broke up, quite a few of the fellows seemed interested in courting me. Now, no one calls," she said.

"Yes, I don't understand that either, but, honey, you just have to remember that God is in charge of all things. Remember the scripture that says, "*And we know that all things work for good to them that love God, to them who are called according to His purpose.*" Now dry those tears. It's almost time for your daddy to come home. You don't want him to see you crying."

"I'll try. I'll really try, but it's not going to be easy," Lexie said, as she walked over to the wash pan and splashed cold water on her face. "Now," she said, drying her face on the sunny yellow hand towel. Summoning up a wavering smile, she continued, "I'm ready for anything," knowing full well she didn't mean a word she had said. She only hoped she convinced her mother.

Sarah was not fooled for an instant. "That's my girl," Sarah told her lovingly. She was careful not to let Lexie see how much her heart ached for her daughter. She knew how great Lexie's disappointment was and how badly she wanted to spread her wings and leave the nest. She said a quick prayer that God would ease Lexie's unhappiness and that she would find true love as she and Tom had.

CHAPTER THREE

"Hi, I'm home! Where is everyone?" Tom Fletcher called. Even if Lexie and Sarah were sitting right in front of him when he came in, he still greeted them the same way. His next statement was always, "How are my two girls?"

Forty-two-year-old Tom was still as robust as a much younger man. He always teased Sarah about graying hair when he didn't have a gray hair in his jet-black hair. Sarah always came back with, "What do you expect, when I have to put up with you, you tall, handsome galoot?" This conversation always ended with hugs and kisses and reassurances that no matter if Sarah's hair were orange with large green dots, he, Tom, would still love her forever. It had been that way for both of them since the night they met at a party twenty-three years ago.

When Tom got home from the skating party the night he met Sarah, he woke up his mother and told her he had met the girl he was going to marry. His mother dryly asked him if the girl he was so interested in knew his plan. He told her no, but that she soon would, and he had remained single-minded in his pursuit of her until they were married six months later. Sarah always told him that she had to marry him just to get some rest because he had just worn her down.

Sarah never told Tom until after they had been married for two years that she had told her mother much the same thing the night they met. She told him that he hadn't had a chance because she prayed almost incessantly that God would give him to her. Tom was elated to hear her say that.

Tom was a good husband and father, loving and kind. He was a good provider for his family. They never wanted for anything that was in his power to give them. His one fault was that he didn't want Lexie to grow up. He knew she would soon marry when she did.

He had some very bad moments when he thought she might marry Carson Fullbrite, not only about her leaving home, but because Carson wasn't a Christian. He could tell by Carson's attitude about life in general that he wasn't a Christian long before Lexie knew. He definitely wanted Lexie to marry a man who knew God. He also thought she was too young to get married, that she was only infatuated with being in love. He wanted her to share the kind of love he and Sarah had, the kind that grew daily.

For the past ten years, ever since he had moved his family from Wilton, Tennessee, to Centerville, Missouri, he had owned and operated the town's newspaper, *The Herald.* He always laughingly attributed his muscular frame to working so hard on the paper, just gathering the news. The exercise he got from just gathering the news was enough to keep him fit, he always said. "Hunting up news for the next addition, not to mention the many times a day I have to get up and down at my desk, keeps me fit." Sarah always told him to stop acting silly.

Tom often thought about how Sarah didn't want to leave her family to move to Missouri, but she had been happy after they came. At least, he thought she had been. If she wasn't, she never let him see.

Today when Tom came home, Sarah was in the kitchen peeling potatoes for dinner. "Hi, honey," she said, stopping work on the potatoes and raising her face to his for a quick kiss, as he stooped to kiss and to hug her. Despite the potato water on her hands, she clung to him for a moment and got another kiss for her efforts.

"Where's Lexie? I've got great news for you two," he asked rising to his full six foot two inches, throwing out his chest, and looking very pleased with himself.

"She's upstairs. I hope your news *is* good news. She's heartbroken.

Matthew Thomas is able to resume teaching next year," Sarah said.

"I'm sorry that she is upset, but that won't matter when she hears what I have to say," Tom said, running a hand through his black hair, his cornflower blue eyes sparkling. He walked to the stairs in the living room and called to Lexie, "Lexie! Honey, come down here, I've got good news for us!"

Lexie looked in her mirror. She had hoped that Tom wouldn't notice that she had been crying, but her nose was still red and her eyes were puffy. *He'll be able to tell. I don't want him to think that I'm a crybaby.* With drooping shoulders, she walked despondently down the stairs and went into the kitchen where Sarah and Tom were seated at the table. She stopped just inside the door, feeling totally dejected.

"Hi, Little Bit," he said, calling Lexie by his favorite name for her. "How's my girl? I hear that school board didn't keep a good thing when they had it," he continued, attempting to lighten the atmosphere. He carefully observed the ravages of the tears.

"Oh, Daddy, don't joke. I wanted to stay so badly. You don't know what teaching means to me. I'm so miserable I don't know what to do." Completely dejected, she walked listlessly over to the table and sat down.

"Nonsense," he said gruffly. "Now perk up. I've got something great to tell you, and I don't like to see those pretty blue eyes that you got from me all red and puffy."

"Why, Tom Fletcher," Sarah said, shaking a wet finger in the air at him. "Everyone knows that Lexie has my eyes. They're as blue as yours," she said, trying to lighten the situation.

"Now don't get your dander up. I'll concede that she got them from both of us. How else could she be so beautiful?" he asked, following Sarah's lead.

"Oh, you two," Lexie said, attempting to smile. "You're too much. Either one of you would be glad for me to have the other's eyes."

"She knows us pretty well, Tom," Sarah said, grinning. "Now, why don't you tell us about your great news?"

"All right, here goes." He paused for effect, looked from one to the other and said, "I signed us up to go to Oregon on the first wagon train of 1843. It's leaving the first day of May."

"You did what!" Sarah almost shouted, jumping up from the table, almost overturning it. Water from the potato pan splashed all over the floor. She felt as though someone had hit her in the stomach.

Lexie's mouth dropped open. She jumped up from the chair. "That's supposed to be good news?" she squeaked. "What else can go wrong?" she asked, throwing up her hands in defeat.

Ignoring the water on the floor, Sarah shrilled, "How could you do such a thing? Well, I for one won't go traipsing off to Oregon," she said angrily. Doubling her fists and placing them on her hips defiantly, she said, "I left my family to come out here, and I hardly ever get to see them. My brother is the only family I have left, and I don't intend to go farther away from him than I am now. It's been three years since I've seen him as it is. You can just go without me. I won't go," she said, tears gathering in her eyes. She turned on her heel and charged over to the door to leave the room.

Before she could leave, Tom said, "Darling, Sarah, I thought Lexie and I were your family." Crestfallen, he looked at her with sad eyes and said, "Yes, Ruth, I know. Remember how you've always quoted me that scripture, *"Whither thou goest, I will go, and where thou lodgest I will lodge." Thy people shall be my people, and thy God, my God. "*

Tom pushed himself away from the table and crossed the kitchen, his very demeanor one of dejection. He went outside and quietly shut the door, more telling than if he had slammed it behind him.

Totally deflated, he felt as if he had lost something very dear to him. He felt anger rising, and tried to control it. His next thoughts were *why didn't she tell me. I had no idea she was so unhappy.* He couldn't bear seeing Sarah unhappy. *I need to think of what's best to do.* He walked briskly down through the yard and into the field beyond.

Stricken, Lexie and Sarah looked at one another. "I didn't realize he would be so hurt. I'll have to go after him. He's right, and I'm wrong. I'm supposed to be submissive to my husband. Watch dinner and don't let it burn," Sarah said over her shoulder and let herself out the door. "I don't know how I can bear to go, but I'll have to do it."

She went racing through the yard and into the field after Tom. It

34

really didn't matter where they lived as long as they were together. Only Tom's happiness mattered to her. She couldn't bear losing him.

"Tom, Tom! Don't go. I'm sorry," she called. "Wait for me!" She raced down through the field back of their house after him. "Tom, darling, Tom, please wait! I can't keep running," she called breathlessly.

Tom stopped, turned, and then sprinted back to her.

Unused to running, her lungs felt as if they were bursting. "I'm sorry. Please forgive me. You were right. I did promise you that I would be like Ruth, and I will be. I promise," she said, bending double, trying to catch her breath. She raised a hand to brush tears away from her face. "I'm sorry that I hurt you," she said brokenly.

Tom, reaching her, caught her in his arms. "I love you, pretty woman," he said, kissing her passionately. "Sweetheart, I'm sorry that I hurt you too. I shouldn't have taunted you. I didn't realize that you'd been so unhappy here," Tom said, wiping away her tears. "Why didn't you tell me?" He moved his head back to look at her, still holding her tightly.

"Oh, Tom, I haven't been unhappy. I just get lonely for my family," she said, snuggling into his chest, trying to explain her feelings to him. "Please try to understand. Robbie's family is all I have left except for you and Lexie. But never forget, although I miss Robbie, I'd be totally and completely miserable without you. I love you."

"If it means so much to you to stay here, we won't go. Your happiness means everything to me. But I have to tell you, I've made arrangements to sell the paper, and I can't go back on my word," Tom said. "Please believe me, my greatest desire is to please you. Can you forgive me for acting like a jerk?" As Sarah nodded yes, he continued, "You've let me make the decisions for our family so long that I never really thought you'd might disagree. Never, *never* forget, I love you, too."

They stood basking in their love for one another until Sarah asked, "What will you do in Oregon? How will we live?"

"Start another newspaper," Tom replied. "Shall we go, or stay here?"

"We won't stay here, we'll go. We'll go," she repeated, "but if we do, how will Lexie ever find a husband? You do want to see her happily married, don't you?"

"Honey, there are probably four times as many men out there as there are women. The only problem will be of choosing which one she wants. I looked through the list of people signed up to go and there were at least thirty unmarried men going on *our* train. No telling how many others are already there." he said, hugging her tightly.

Sarah moved back a fraction within Tom's arms and said," I just want her to be happy. I want you to be happy, too."

"I am happy. No one else could have made me happier," he said giving her another hug. "Honey, I didn't tell you all of the good news. The rest might make you feel better. When I was looking through the list of people signed on, I saw a Robert and Leona Whitfield and two children, Robert, Jr. and Peter, signed up to go. *And,* I have a letter in my pocket addressed to Mrs. Sarah Fletcher from Gunter's Gap, Tennessee," Tom said, pulling a letter from his back pocket and handing it to her. "I wouldn't be surprised to hear of a trip going to Oregon in the letter."

Sarah, looking radiant at the news, took the letter from him and tore it open with fingers that shook. "It is from Robbie and Leona!" she said, as she continued to read. "I can hardly believe what I'm reading. They *are* going to Oregon. They say they will stopover here to visit us on their way. They'll be here next week," she said, her eyes devouring the words. Raising her eyes to Tom's well-loved face, she said, "Won't they be surprised to find that we are going too? Since my baby brother is going, sweetheart, I'm glad to be going now. But will Lexie be glad?"

"I think she will. Maybe not at first, but she will be soon. I truly feel God is leading us there. That's why I signed us up to go in the first place."

"Let's go tell her the good news. I'll re-read my letter later," she said, putting the letter into her skirt pocket. Together the two walked arm in arm back to the house.

Lexie sat at the table, staring into space. Her mind was in a whirl. Desolation reigned supreme in her heart. *What else can go wrong?*

First, school, now this. I don't want to go to Oregon. Days and days of travel to nothing, just wilderness. Whatever possesses Daddy? How can he ask us to leave our beautiful home here? She looked around the familiar room, loving every corner of it.

Tom and Sarah came into the kitchen. The first thing they saw was Lexie's woebegone look and the tears streaming down her face.

"Daddy, if you and Mother are going to Oregon, I want to stay here. I just don't want to go thousands of miles to a wilderness. I'll never forget that corduroy road that just about bounced my insides out when we came here from Tennessee. Do I *have* to go with you? I want to be a teacher. Fat chance I'll have out there," Lexie said without stopping to take a breath or waiting for an answer. "I want to get married, someday, before I get too old. What chance will I have for that?" She furiously wiped away the tears that kept coming.

"I'll get you a crutch and a cane, old lady," Tom said dryly. "Yes, you do have to go with us," he said adamantly. "You won't find any corduroy roads going to Oregon. There will only be wagon trails to follow. As for teaching, you'll have just as good a chance to teach out there as you will here. You are too young to set off by yourself, and that's final. Besides your mother and I want to keep you with us as long as possible," he added gently.

Again tears welled up in Lexie's eyes, but she didn't argue. "Are you sure that we have to go, even if it makes Mother and me unhappy?" She still had hopes of dissuading him.

"Very sure. It's all settled," Tom said. "Your uncle Robbie's family is going too. Your mother is eager to go, now that she knows they are going. She will get to see them all the time."

Lexie made no reply. She just sat there, pulling at her skirt, her mind whirling. *I guess it's all right if I'm unhappy.*

"When do we leave?" Sarah wanted to know. "Are we taking all our household goods? I won't leave my grandfather clock or my cherry wood highboy. Oh, and my mother's china. I'll not leave that."

"We have to be in Independence two weeks from Sunday. We'll take only necessities, and the things you mentioned. Oh, and anything Lexie can't bear to part with. We'll be better off than many people going. We'll have three wagons to take our things. I spoke for them today. We can have other things that we want made after we get there. If I need to, I can make most of them. Don't forget, I'm still pretty handy with a hammer and a saw."

"Two weeks? What are we to do with our things here?" Sarah asked, agitatedly.

"We'll have an auction the day before we leave. Don't worry, honey. It will be okay. Trust me," he said, trying to calm her.

"My goodness, how will we ever get ready, Lexie?"

Lexie felt resigned to her fate and replied bitterly, "I don't know. I guess Daddy will have all the answers."

"Yes, I guess I have, young lady," Tom replied darkly. "Please allow me to know what is best for our family."

Lexie sat clenching her teeth and looking at her clasped hands in her lap. She didn't remember her father ever answering her so sternly.

"One day you'll thank me for this. As for wilderness, more people are going to Oregon all the time. On this train that we're taking, there is a minister, and a doctor. Several carpenters are going. Then, we'll have the newspaper as soon as I can get one started. I even heard that a banker is likely to start another bank there within the year. The rest are farmers. It will seem just like home before you know it."

Yeah! I'll just bet. Lexie looked at her father, then at her mother. Both of them looked so pleased, she couldn't bring herself to say anything more. She didn't think it would do any good anyway.

"Well, tomorrow will take care of itself," Sarah said. "Let's get on with today. Lexie, would you please finish peeling the potatoes and put them on to cook? I'll open a jar of green beans and fry some sausage. Tom, please open a jar of applesauce for me, and we'll have dinner ready in no time."

The three of them bustled around the kitchen. Even though the atmosphere was strained, and Lexie had a hard time swallowing the tears, the three of them soon had dinner on the table, and they sat down to eat. As was their custom, they joined hands and bowed their heads. Tom gave thanks for the meal.

"Heavenly Father, we thank you for this food and all the other blessings that you have bestowed on us. We ask that you continue to bless and keep us, and that you lead us safely to our new home. Father, please make Lexie happy about going. In Jesus' name, we pray. Amen.

Lexie couldn't restrain a sob. She sat, so upset that she just pushed the food around on her plate, pretending to eat.

"Lexie, you aren't eating very much," Sarah said. She felt elated now that she knew Robbie, Leona, and the boys were going. She wanted Lexie to be happy about it too.

"I'm not very hungry. I guess I had too many cookies." Sarah knew better, but she made no further comment. From time to time, Lexie couldn't control a sniff or a hiccough. Tom and Sarah pretended not to notice.

When the meal was over, Tom said, "I'm going out to look at the garden. Maybe some of it will be ready before we go."

"I think I'll go with you," Sarah said. "Do you want to come, Lexie?"

"No, thank you. I'll stay here and do the dishes." *I don't know why they want to look at the garden. They know we'll be gone before it is ready to eat.* She stacked the dishes and carried them over to the cabinet. She filled the dishpan with hot water from the teakettle sitting on the stove. She added slivers of lye soap. It didn't take her long to wash, rinse, and dry the dishes and to put them away.

Just as Lexie finished putting the last dish away, Sarah and Tom came in from the garden. Lexie said to them, "I think I'll go to my room and read for awhile." She didn't feel that she could cope with trying to make conversation. She certainly didn't want to argue with her father tonight, and she most assuredly *didn't* want to talk about Oregon.

"All right. You have had a long, hard day. Sleep tight," Sarah said, kissing her cheek.

Lexie didn't even say goodnight to Tom, but went into her room and picked up her Bible. She sat on her bed and began to read the twenty-seventh Psalm. Her heart was so heavy, she couldn't concentrate on what she was reading until she got to verse 14. It seemed to jump out at her. It read, *"Wait on the Lord: be of good courage, and He shall strengthen thine heart: wait, I say, on the Lord."* Lexie looked at the verse a long time.

I'll try, Heavenly Father. I'll try. Lexie closed her Bible and laid it on the table by her bed. She knelt by her bed to pray. Most of what she said was a jumble of things. Some would have made no sense to a human ear. It didn't even make sense to her. All of it was a mixture of wanting to teach, wanting a husband, and not wanting to go to Oregon. This was mixed together with pleas for forgiveness for being such a baby and an unthankful child. She was so muddled that she couldn't even complete a thought.

She couldn't remember a time when she felt such black despair. Finally, she rose from her kneeling position, quickly undressed, and climbed into bed. By the time she lay down, her feelings completely overwhelmed her. She cried herself to sleep.

For the next week, the Fletchers' house was the proverbial beehive of activity. Robbie and his family stopped on their way to Independence. They spent one day and night before moving on. After the short visit with the family, Lexie and Sarah got down to the business of sorting clothing and household items they would take with them. They began to pack everything into trunks and kegs. Some items would be stored in boxes in the bottom of the wagons.

One morning the Fletchers had a visitor. When Lexie answered the door, her best friend, Olivia Green stood waiting to be admitted. Olivia stood almost a head taller than Lexie. Her long blond hair gleamed in the bright sunlight. Green eyes matched her name. Always spirited, this morning excitement fairly oozed from every pore of Olivia's body.

"Come in," Lexie invited gaily. "Have you found a new boyfriend?" she teased.

Olivia came inside, grabbed Lexie and hugged her. "Guess what? We're going to Oregon too!"

"I don't believe it!" Lexie cried, hugging Olivia and dancing both of them around in a circle. "This is the best news I've heard in weeks. Maybe it won't be so bad having to go now. When did your family decide to go?"

"I'm not sure," she answered, her green eyes sparkling. "Everything was all settled when they told me last night. Listen, I can't stay. I promised Mother that I'd just tell you and come right back to help her get ready. We haven't even started to pack," she said and headed for the door. "Ohhh! I'm so excited. I can hardly wait. Just think of the men we'll meet," she turned to say.

Lexie followed her friend out to the porch, told her goodbye. "I wouldn't count on that if I were you," Lexie said, unable to keep the sarcasm from her voice.

Olivia laughed and said, "You'll see."

"Come back as soon as possible and tell me all about your plans."

"Okay, I will."

Lexie stood waving until Olivia had fairly skipped past several houses down the street. With hands clasped in front of her chest in excitement, Lexie went back to help her mother pack and to tell her the good news.

They worked long, hard hours everyday. The two women took one day to make soap to take with them. Tom couldn't see why they needed to *waste* a day to do that. When Tom told Sarah that she was wasting a day, she hit the roof.

"What do you plan for me to do laundry with?" she asked. "It's not like I can run to a store to get soap. I don't think that you'll want to wear dirty clothes all the way to Oregon."

"I'm sorry, honey. Don't get mad. I just hate to see you work so hard," Tom answered, winking at Lexie.

Lexie was amused at her parents. Tom was putty in Sarah's hands, but sometimes, she thought her dad just said things to rile her mother. He always said that after a fight, it was so nice making up. Soon things were smoothed over between her parents, and the last day in their Missouri home arrived.

Because they were well to do, and could afford it, everything was loaded into three covered wagons they were taking with them. Tom had hired two young men in town who wanted to go to Oregon, but had no means to go. One of them was to drive one of the household wagons. The other was to drive the wagon for the printing press and other equipment for the newspaper. The family would drive the third wagon containing necessities for the trail.

That night as Lexie went to bed, she looked around the room that she adored. Biting her lips to keep from crying she thought, *tomorrow night, we'll be sleeping in a covered wagon. This is my last night here.*

She had her daily time of Bible study and devotion that she always had before climbing into bed. She wondered if she could continue to have daily devotions on the trail. She decided that she would find time some way. She was a long time going to sleep that night. Her mind was in a whirl. Her thoughts were now mixed about going. She didn't want to go, but since Olivia was so thrilled about going, perhaps she was wrong to want to stay in Centerville. Everything was going to be so different. It seemed she had just shut her eyes when Sarah called for her to get up.

The auction started promptly at nine o'clock. By one o'clock in the afternoon, Lexie had seen all their precious possessions sold. Even the house was no longer theirs. Their new life had begun.

CHAPTER FOUR

"Wagons ho!" cried the wagon master. The huge white-covered wagons of the train began to move out in stately splendor. The trek from Centerville was behind them. Wagons from all directions had converged on Independence to form the train. Each family was assigned their particular spot in the train. It was a long train. Almost five hundred people were making this trip.

The weather had cooperated beautifully. It was a warm, sunshiny day. Everything looked so fresh and green. The lush, green foliage of the trees swayed gently in the spring breeze. Excitement and conviviality permeated the air. Friends and neighbors lined up on the street in Independence to wave goodbye and wish the pioneers Godspeed on their journey. Last minute hugs and kisses were given and received, and then the pioneer families were on their way.

Since wagons were loaded to their limit, it made it easier on the teams pulling them if women and children walked. Others wanted to walk just to avoid the jouncing of the wagons. Some of the people who came to see them off walked with them for a while, but finally turned back. Children bubbled with excitement. A few were shedding tears for friends and family left behind.

It would be a long grinding walk. Lexie wondered how long it would take for their shoes to wear out. She was thankful that it wasn't necessary for her and Sarah to walk all the way. They had decided that

Sarah and Lexie were to help drive part of the time. Taking turns riding the horses, walking, and riding in the wagon wouldn't be as tiring as it would be if they had to walk all the way. Tom wanted his family to be comfortable.

Lexie's family was about midway in the train. Her father had told her that Doctor David Duvall's wagon was right behind them. He said that he didn't know where Olivia's family was. The people in front of them were named Blake. They had no children. They were an older couple. Tom guessed them to be about fifty-five. He said that he had found Robbie and his family. They were close to the front of the train. Sarah immediately set out to visit with them.

"Just about how far will we be going?" Lexie asked. She knew it would take them from four to six months, depending on how fast the train traveled and whether or not they had unexpected delays. Because she had been in such a bad frame of mind, she had not even bothered to ask before. She had kept hoping that something would change her father's mind about going.

"It's about 2,000 miles to Oregon. We'll be going a little farther, so I'd say less than 2,100 miles," Tom replied. "We are going to a little town called Stringtown. It's already settled. I understand there are about five hundred people already living there."

"That's a funny name for a town. Are you sure it's not Springtown?" Lexie wanted to know.

"No, it's not. I'm *sure* it's Stringtown. It was named that because the first houses there were strung out in a line on either side of one street. Do you really think I'd start out without knowing where we are going?" He said, offended that Lexie would question him.

The wagons rumbled along the beaten trail until they were outside the city limits of Independence. "Today, we're getting a late start, but tomorrow everyone will be awakened at four o'clock. We'll be expected to be ready to leave at six o'clock in the morning," Tom said.

The sun rose higher, and the temperature climbed. Hour after hour dragged on. Women and children walked slower and slower. Sarah returned at noon when the train stopped for an hour to water the animals and eat a cold lunch. They called lunch nooning. Tired women hastily laid out food and packed it away after the meal. They were hoping to get a few minutes rest before starting on.

Lexie soon got tired of the jostling of the wagon. "Could I ride one of the horses for awhile?" she asked. I'm so tired of this wagon."

"I guess that will be all right, if you keep close to the wagons," Tom said.

"Are you going to try to find Olivia, darling?" Sarah asked.

"Yes, I want to look for Olivia's family. May I do that?" Lexie was taking no chances of making her father angry, so that he would refuse to let her ride in the future.

"Well, just don't get too far away," Sarah said.

Soon Lexie was on the horse, riding toward the front of the train. She didn't find Olivia's family. She waved to Robbie and his family. She asked them how they were, but didn't stop. She rode back the way she came. Keeping her horse to a walk, she was able to observe people in wagons, as well as people walking or mounted as she was.

Like her mother, most of the women and girls were dressed in calico or gingham dresses and sunbonnets. They would stay cooler dressed that way. Men and boys were dressed in a variety of ways from nice suits to faded wool or cotton trousers and chambray shirts.

She waved gaily to Sarah and Tom as she rode by. On this first day out, not many people were visiting together. In the days to come, they would get to know one another better.

As she passed the doctor's wagon, she noticed that the driver didn't look much like a physician. He was wearing an old felt hat, almost covering strawberry blond hair, faded woolen trousers and shirt, and scuffed cowhide boots. A red bandana, which clashed with his hair, was tied around his throat to complete his outfit.

"Good afternoon, doctor," she called.

"Oh, I'm not the doctor. I'm just a driver. My name is Abe Williams," came the reply.

"I'm glad to meet you, Abe. My name is Fletcher, Lexie Fletcher. Our wagons are right in front of yours."

"Right pleased to meet you, miss," Abe returned.

Just then a large man came riding up. He wore a black broadcloth suit, and white shirt. A black felt hat was perched on top of his dark blond head.

"Are you looking for me? I'm Doctor Duvall. Is someone ill?" he said, bringing his horse to a halt. Not only did his clothes set him apart from most of the other men of the train, but so did his self-assured demeanor.

"Oh, no, I was just being friendly. I thought Abe was you," Lexie replied. She felt foolish because she had said anything. "I'm looking for the Greens' wagon. Do you by any chance know them?" she said, reining in her horse.

"Yes, yes, I do. I met them this morning. I'll ride along with you and show you where they are." *What a gorgeous girl!* David was almost bowled over by Lexie's fragile beauty. *She's so tiny. She looks as if she'd break if you touch her, but she handles that horse to perfection. She must be a lot stronger than she looks.*

"Thanks," A dimple broke forth with her smile. "My name is Lexie Fletcher. Our wagons are right in front of yours. Whoa, boy," she said patting the skittish animal on its neck, handling him with ease.

"I'm very pleased to meet you, Miss Fletcher. My name is David Duvall." David turned his horse around and the two animals fell into step together. *I can't get over what a beautiful girl she is. She looks a perfect example of young womanhood.* "So you wanted to become a pioneer woman and live in the Wild West?" he said, as the two of them kept the horses walking back down the trail.

"No, nothing like that, I'm afraid. My folks made me come. They said I'm too young to stay in Missouri by myself. I'm a teacher, and I wanted to stay at home. My folks said no. I just hope I can find a teaching job when we get to Oregon." Lexie wondered why she was babbling so much to a complete stranger; however, he didn't seem like a stranger to her. For some reason, she felt comfortable and safe with him.

"You probably won't have any trouble at all," he said looking at her intently. He felt he couldn't take his eyes off her. He was mesmerized by her looks, her smile. Her hair was a riot of curls framing her pretty face. "Don't you have something to wear on your head? That sun is getting awfully hot today. I don't mean to be critical. That's the doctor in me speaking," he said smiling apologetically.

"Sure I do, but I hate wearing any kind of hat or bonnet." *What a gorgeous hunk of man. Wonder where he is going to settle?*

"Have you been teaching long, Miss Fletcher? If you'll pardon my saying so, you don't look old enough to be a teacher."

"This was my first year. I just hope it won't be my last. What about you, doctor? How long have you been practicing?"

"I don't even have as much experience as you. This will be my first practice."

"What made you decide to come west?"

"I could have gone into practice with my father in Boston, but I felt the Lord was calling me to come west to help others." David wondered if Lexie was a Christian. *Well, there is just one way to find out. I'm not going to let myself get interested in a girl who doesn't know the Lord.*

Before he could form the question, Lexie said, "It's good to know there are other Christians to travel with. Have you decided where you will settle?" Lexie asked?

"I'm going to a small town called Stringtown. A lawyer friend of mine is already there. He says that it's a very nice place to live."

"That's where we're going to live. If enough families are there, maybe I'll have a chance to teach after all." Lexie couldn't hide the excitement in her voice.

"That's great. Perhaps we'll be neighbors," David said.

Just then David noticed the Greens' wagon. He had stared at Lexie so intently that he had almost passed by the wagon without seeing it.

"Here we are, Miss Fletcher. I'll see you later," He tipped his hat and wheeling his horse around, cantered off in the opposite direction.

Waving goodbye, Lexie turned in the saddle and called after him, "Thanks for showing me the way."

"My pleasure," he said, turning to look at her and wave in turn.

"Hi, Mrs. Green! Where's Olivia?" Lexie greeted Mrs. Green, as she rode up to the wagon.

"Here I am," Olivia called, sticking her head out of the wagon.

"Let's ride awhile," Lexie called to her friend.

Disappointed, Olivia answered, "I'd love to, but I can't. My dad has our only horse."

Lexie pulled her horse to a stop and dismounted. "Then we'll walk together."

Many families brought just enough oxen or horses to pull their wagons, but some of the more affluent families brought extra horses to ride. Everyone on the train had been told that many horses and oxen would die along the way. It was necessary for the travelers to have extra animals to replace their teams if they were needed.

The Fletchers had been told that it was easier for oxen to pull the wagons than for horses to do so; therefore, they had oxen to pull the wagons and horses to ride.

Olivia swung down from the wagon, which was not easy since Mrs. Green didn't stop the wagon, only slowed it down. Lexie turned the animal, and they began walking in the direction the wagons were traveling.

"Isn't that doctor the most handsome man you ever saw?" Olivia asked.

"Well, maybe. Close anyway." Even though Olivia *was* Lexie's best friend, Lexie was not about to tell her *how* impressed she was with David.

"What did you talk about?" Olivia asked.

"Oh, he wanted to know how long I'd been teaching, and I asked him about his practice. He also said that he is going to live in Stringtown. So are we," Lexie said nonchalantly. Her eyes gave lie to the tone of voice she expressed.

"You don't fool me, Lexie Fletcher," Olivia said, shaking a finger at Lexie. "You were bowled over by him. Drat it all. With your looks, probably no one else has a chance with him. It just doesn't seem fair that you met him first. That is, assuming he's not married. Is he?"

"Oh, don't be silly. You met him first. You'll have as much chance as anyone, if he is single. I don't know whether he's married or not. I couldn't just ask him. Besides, he was probably just curious, as I was. He was probably just trying to make new friends," Lexie said, trying to put her friend at ease. Crossing her fingers childishly, she hoped that

Olivia was right. She had the sudden thought that if he were not married; she wished he could be Mr. Right. The thought grew as they walked along. She had never felt as comfortable with Carson as she had with David after just one meeting. She longed to see him again, soon.

"Did you ever think that both of us might find a husband and be married before we get to Oregon?" Olivia asked.

"Not in my wildest dreams," Lexie replied. The image of David remained firmly in front of her eyes. "I'm just waiting for God to send me the right man. Doctor Duvall is a Christian. I know because he said he felt God had called him to come west to practice." *A doctor, a Christian, and good looking. What more could a girl ask?* Lexie thought.

Lexie didn't fool Olivia at all. She had seen that look in Lexie's eyes too many times when Lexie was bent on getting something. Olivia decided to pursue other interests, leaving David to Lexie.

The girls walked on, talking about the life they were going to be living for the next few months. All the while Lexie held the image of the handsome doctor in front of her. Finally, Lexie said, "You haven't told me where your family will be stopping. Please tell me its Stringtown."

"Yes, it *is* Stringtown. We'll still be able to see each other just like always. Dad says there will be a lot of work for a carpenter there."

They continued talking about what they would do as soon as they reached their new home. Olivia wanted to get a new house before anything else when they arrived. Lexie wanted to find a school where she could teach. She would leave housing to her parents.

Finally, Lexie said, "I must be getting back to help Mother with supper. We probably will stop before long. It must be getting late. Gosh, my feet hurt." She said goodbye to Olivia, and the two started in separate directions. Lexie wasn't far from her family's wagons, so she didn't mount her horse. She led it to their wagon and tied the horse to the back of it.

Approaching the front of the wagon, she saw her father driving. "Where's Mother?" she asked, looking around for Sarah.

"She went inside to lie down. She has developed one of her bad headaches." Sarah had suffered from extremely bad headaches since she was a child. Her vision was sometimes affected, and she became nauseated.

"Should we get Doctor Duvall to give her something for it?"

"Perhaps we should. If you'll take the reins, I'll go see if I can find him. I couldn't stop the wagon to look for him while you were gone."

"I'm sorry, Dad. I should have come back sooner. The doctor wasn't at his wagon as I came back." She didn't tell Tom that she had met him on the trail. Lexie took Tom's extended hand and climbed up to the wagon seat. She took the reins while Tom went to look for the doctor.

The sun was getting well past midway in the west. Lexie knew it was getting time to plan supper. She would have no trouble fixing it, for Sarah had taught her how to cook when she was barely thirteen. She and Sarah had packed together, so she knew where to find everything that she would need.

It wasn't long until David and Tom approached the wagon. "Doctor, my wife is lying down inside the wagon. Lexie this is Doctor Duvall. My daughter Lexie, Doctor. Excuse me, I'll just go tie up our horses," he said turning the animal around.

"We met on the trail this afternoon," David said, dismounting. He handed the reins to Tom. Tom thought it strange that Lexie hadn't said she had met the doctor.

David tossed his medical bag upon the wagon seat, and hoisted himself up into the wagon. "Well, Miss Fletcher, I didn't expect to have the pleasure of seeing you again so soon," he said as he climbed aboard. Without waiting for a reply, he continued, "Your father said your mother is feeling quite sick." Tom had already told him that Sarah had a bad headache.

"I didn't expect to see you either, and yes, she has a bad headache."

David raised the canvas flap attached to the oiled wagon covering and climbed into the back of the wagon. He gently completed his examination of Sarah and declared that she had had too much sun for the first day out. "That's what triggered this headache. You need to become accustomed to the sun gradually, and be sure to keep your head covered when you are outside," he told her. He gave her some headache powders and told her she would feel much better after a good night's sleep.

Sarah told him that she was sure she would feel better directly. When asked if his family was with him, he told her that he was traveling alone. Hearing he was alone, she invited him for supper that evening.

"If I don't feel like cooking, Lexie will do it. She is a wonderful cook. She should be, I taught her everything I know and some things I didn't know," she said. Sarah always tried to keep a sense of humor despite her pain.

"I'm sure she is," David replied, "and I'd be delighted, except for the fact that I have a driver that I have to feed."

"No problem. I take it he has no family with him either?"

"No, I'm afraid he doesn't."

"Bring him too. The more, the merrier."

CHAPTER FIVE

"Wagons make circle," came the call of the wagon master. Although a small, gray-haired man, the wagon master, Jacob Smythe, still commanded respect. In contrast with his small stature, his voice was loud and carried well. He had learned to project his voice at an early age, so he could be heard through much of the train.

This was his third trip to Oregon. What he lacked in stature, he made up for in determination, and he was determined to have everything done correctly. He had made sure that each driver had a copy of his rules. With his brown eyes snapping, he assumed an aggressive stance. He told everyone, in no uncertain terms, that if the rules were not followed rigidly, the driver would be kicked off the train.

The wagons began, one after the other, forming the tight circle they would make each night. Following the wagon master's directions, the first wagon turned to the right to start the circle, and the second wagon turned left, so that the wagons met at the center of the circle, which he had drawn out. The wagons stopped front to back, right next to each other, forming a tight protective enclosure for the people and for the livestock. Each night the livestock were herded inside the circle. With livestock inside the circle, they would be safe from wild animals or Indians.

As soon as the circle was completed, an industrious scramble of children and some adults began as they searched for wood to build campfires to cook the evening meal. Tom told Lexie that he would gather the wood for their fires. He said it would be easy to find wood by the trail tonight since heavy forests surrounded either side of the trail. Soon he returned with enough wood to last all night and some to spare. He carefully stored the extra kindling inside one of the wagons. For an emergency, he said.

While he was gone, Lexie unpacked the cooking utensils and metal plates and cups the family would need. Soon campfires were dotted along the trail. Busy wives began the nightly ritual of unloading kitchen utensils to prepare their evening meal. Cooking over a campfire was not a pleasant chore for tired women. Lexie felt sorry for all of them who had walked from early morning. Besides cooking, dishes would have to be washed, and beds had to be made. Some travelers had tents to erect. In the morning, everything had to be repacked and stored away.

The last rays of the shimmering sun rapidly dissolved into the gray dusk of evening while Lexie worked industriously preparing the meal.

By the light of the campfire that Tom had made, David and Tom sat talking while waiting for Lexie to get the meal ready. David held up one side of the conversation, but at the same time, he kept a vigilant watch of Lexie.

"Doctor Duvall, how much do I owe you for your call today?" Tom inquired.

"You don't owe me a thing. Having a delicious meal that I don't have to fix myself is payment enough. While we're talking about meals, do you know of some lady who might be willing to fix meals for my driver and me? I have plenty of supplies to contribute, and I am more than willing to pay well for meals. Cooking is not my strong point. I can hardly boil water."

Tom looked thoughtful for a moment, and then said; "Sarah and Lexie probably would do it for you. The two young fellows that are driving for me are going to have meals with us."

"That would be fabulous. Would you ask them for me?"

Lexie, listening while she quietly stirred corn meal into the cornbread batter she was mixing for the meal, said, "He won't need to ask. Of course, we will. It won't be that much extra, and if you have supplies, we won't run short of food." *What an opportunity to get to know him better. At least, I know that I'm going to love mealtime on this trip!*

She poured the cornbread mixture into a Dutch oven. She walked over to a long metal rod with a hook on it that Tom had attached to the side of the wagon. She swung it away from the wagon as if opening a gate. She hooked the bail of the Dutch oven on it and swung the rod out over the fire. Tom also had made a fold-up table, which he had fastened to the wagon. He had laughingly said he wanted them to have all the comforts of home.

David watched Lexie's hands deftly slice meat into strips and peel potatoes and onions. She sliced the potatoes and onions, putting them and the meat into a three-legged frying pan that sat up over the campfire. She put salt and pepper over the whole thing and set it over the campfire to cook. He followed her every movement as she turned the ingredients in the frying pan. *How graceful she is. She has a sensual air even when peeling potatoes. Her every movement is perfection. No woman could be more feminine. She is so dainty and fragile looking. I've never seen anyone as small as she is so perfectly shaped. Besides being so lovely, what an asset she would be to any man: intelligent, and kind. Lord, I know that I just met her, but I certainly feel drawn to her. Could she possibly be the one you intend for me, or am I meant to go alone? If it's your will that I marry, please let it be her.* A peaceful feeling seemed to sweep over him after his question to the Lord, but he didn't receive an answer.

Lexie became aware of David's scrutiny of her. Immediately she became all thumbs. A rosy flush, not caused by the fire, spread over her neck and face. She noticed that she had missed slicing one potato. She picked up a knife to slice it, fumbled and dropped the potato on the ground. She nervously bent over and retrieved it, briskly washed it off, quickly sliced it, and tossed it into the frying pan. *I'm acting like an idiot. He's only looking at me because there is nothing else to do.*

David noticed how ill at ease Lexie had become, and it only endeared her more to him. *Quit staring, or you'll make her a nervous wreck,* he chastised himself. "I'll go get Abe and be right back," David said. He needed a few minutes to think. *How could one girl, that I just met, affect me so strongly? I never believed in love at first sight before, but I do now.*

Abe was sitting at David's wagon, so David was gone only a few moments. He and Abe walked together to the Fletcher's wagon where they sat down on two kegs that Tom had unloaded from the wagons. This time David determined that he would observe Lexie without being so obvious. It gave him special satisfaction to note that Lexie did nothing to try to attract his attention. *She certainly is not like Alice, who is always trying some ploy to attract my attention to her in one-way or another.* The thought of Alice, a very unpleasant one, gave him pause. *If God hadn't called me to Oregon, I think I would have gone anyway, just to get rid of her and my mother's plans.*

Tom was aware of David's watching Lexie and was amused by his apparent attraction. He sobered when he was reminded of how he had felt when he first met Sarah, the love of his life. He wondered if Lexie knew how David felt. More than that, he wondered if the attraction was mutual. His Lexie was revealing nothing.

The sounds of other families' snatches of conversation began to fill the early night air as they gathered together for the evening. Children could be heard laughing at play, and somewhere a baby was crying. Blazing campfires were sending the clean, pure odor of wood smoke into the air. Kerosene lanterns added much needed light. Even the clink of pots and pans could be heard, making a homey symphony of sound. Soon delicious smells were wafting through the air. Overpowering was the smell of coffee. Everyone was going to eat well on the first night out.

The three men at the Fletcher wagon enjoyed talking to one another. Tom told them all about the newspaper business, and David told them about medical school. Abe, who was barely eighteen, told them of his dream of having a farm in Oregon. Long before the three men were ready to end their conversation, the meal was ready.

Out of the night, the two Fletcher drivers, Ben and Samuel Bradford, twin brothers appeared as if on cue. Twin giants, they were so much alike with light brown hair, dark brown eyes, and olive skin that Lexie wondered how anyone could tell them apart. They were even dressed alike with dark brown trousers and tan shirts. Lexie thought they could be called the tan twins.

Lexie dipped generous portions of cornbread, beans, the crisply fried potato dish, and cooked dried apples onto plates and handed them to each man. She took the enamel coffee pot from the fire and poured cups of strong black coffee and handed them around.

Everyone sat on kegs or campstools, which Lexie's father had made. Each held his plate on his lap because the forty-inch folding table that he had attached to the side of the wagon was too small for all of them to sit around.

Walking over to the front of the wagon, Lexie called to Sarah. "Mother, supper is ready. Do you feel like coming out here to eat, or do you want me to bring you a plate?"

Sarah's head appeared in the opening, as she said, "I'm coming out there. Doctor Duvall, your medicine has worked wonders. I feel fine now." Both David and Tom hastened over to her, one on each side of her. They held her arms, as if she were a piece of delicate porcelain, helping her down from the wagon. Tom settled her on a campstool next to his. Lexie gave her mother a plate, and everyone bowed their heads while Tom gave thanks for the meal. After the prayer, each of them sat enjoying the food and quietly talking about the events of the day.

"Mrs. Fletcher, you surely had an apt pupil in your daughter. This meal is delicious. Miss Fletcher, you are a wonderful cook. I'm really enjoying this meal," David said.

Abe, who sat munching on the delicious food, said, "Boy, I haven't had a meal as good as this since my ma died. I lost both my folks to cholera when I was twelve," he stated between bites. "Got sent to a home for orphans." Abe just stated a fact. He wasn't asking for pity.

"It surely is good," Ben interrupted. Samuel just nodded in agreement.

Lexie felt red creep up her neck. She thanked the men and sat down to eat.

When the meal was finished, Ben slapped his knees, got up and announced. "Well, I guess I'll be going. Thanks for the good eats."

Abe, and Samuel followed suit. They thanked the Fletchers for the meal, excused themselves, and went their own ways.

Tom, Sarah, and David sat talking quietly about sleeping arrangements. "Abe and I are going to sleep under the wagon, unless there is bad weather, and then we'll sleep inside a tent we brought or inside the wagon," David told them.

"*Roughing it* is not for me," Lexie said. "I'm sleeping inside."

After a few more minutes of idle talk about the trail, Lexie rose from her seat and began to clear away the dishes and leftovers from the meal. She was stacking everything on the fold-down table when David got to his feet.

Lexie thought he was going to leave, but instead he turned to Sarah and said, "Mr. and Mrs. Fletcher and Miss Fletcher, I can't thank you enough for your hospitality. You don't know how much it means to me not to have to cook for Abe and myself. Now, I'm going to help Miss Fletcher with these dishes."

"Doctor Duvall, you don't need to help. I can do them easily," Lexie said.

"Please don't argue with your doctor," David said smiling widely. "I'm a dab hand at dishwashing. When I was little, dishwashing was one of my mother's favorite forms of punishment. Believe me, I got plenty of practice," he said dryly. "I *really* hated dishwashing."

As he intended, all three Fletchers laughed wholeheartedly. Lexie prepared the water and handed David a dishtowel. "Okay, you asked for it," she said smiling.

"Another thing. Since we are going to be seeing one another like family, do you think all of you could call me David? Seems a lot friendlier to me, especially since you are taking the place of my family by feeding me."

"Then we're Tom, Sarah, and Lexie," Tom stated.

When the dishes were finished, and everything was packed away, David seemed in no hurry to leave. He handed Lexie his dishtowel. He went back to his seat and sat down. He had hardly gotten settled when a tall, lanky man came hurrying up to the Fletcher's wagon. He wore the typical woolen trousers and chambray shirt that most of the men wore and a brown leather vest over his shirt. He wore no hat, unusual for the men of the train.

"Evening, folks. My name is Jeb Howard," he said in a rush. He spoke rapidly as if emotionally upset. "Could you by any chance tell me where that doctor's wagon is? I heard there is a doctor in this here train."

"Evening, Jeb. I'm the doctor. My name is Duvall," David said, getting up from his seat and extending his hand to Jeb Howard.

"Thank goodness you're here." Jeb said, shaking David's hand. "My wife stepped in a prairie dog hole or some kind of hole and hurt her foot and ankle. I can't tell if it's broke or not. It's all swelled up," Jeb said, running his hand through his brown hair in a nervous manner. "She's a hurtin' somethin' awful."

"My wagon is right behind this one. It will just take a moment to grab my bag, and I'll be right with you." David quickly excused himself to the Fletchers and hastened off into the night.

CHAPTER SIX

The sound of gunfire ripped through the air. Lexie jumped convulsively, sat up in bed, and looked out at the murky light. Her heart was racing double time. Her breath came in shallow gasps. "Oh!" she gasped, and then realized where she was. When she regained her breath, she said, "Mom, are you awake?"

"Yes, dear, I'm awake. Who could sleep through all that racket?"

"I think those guards enjoy waking everyone up so rudely. I'll never get used to that gunfire every morning. It almost scared me to death. Couldn't they just ring a bell or something?"

"If those guards didn't fire those rifles to wake everyone, there's no telling when we would get started."

"But at four o'clock? Surely people could get ready if they woke us at four-thirty."

"It takes awhile to get animals sorted and whatever else they do. Then there is breakfast to get and everything to repack," Sarah said. "I guess Tom will be coming back shortly," she said stretching and stifling a yawn.

Guards kept vigil over the train each night, guarding people as well as animals. Each able-bodied man was to take a turn. Only David was exempt, despite his protests, because he might be called out at any time for medical reasons. "You'll be much more use to us if you just tend to the sick," Mr. Smythe had told him.

Tom's first turn as guard had been last night. The wagon master was adamant that the train should never be left unprotected.

"We'd better get cracking," Sarah said, getting up. "The men will be here soon for breakfast."

"Okay, I'm up," Lexie said, as she tumbled out of bed. She quickly pulled on her clothes and climbed out of the wagon. While Sarah dressed, Lexie put more wood on the embers of last night's campfire and took the pot of beans that had cooked all night off the fire. They would have them for their evening meal, along with some stewed dried fruit and cornbread. She measured out rice and water into a kettle and put it on to cook. She added cinnamon, sugar and some butter to the mixture. It didn't take long for the kettle of rice to be cooked and fluffy. By the time she had the rice dished up the men were there waiting.

Each one added milk to his cereal. Tom had arranged to buy milk from the Ralph Crawford family. With their two cows, they were going to furnish both milk and butter for the Fletchers. Mrs. Crawford said there would always be enough butter because she just put cream into a can and hung it from the side of the wagon and the jostling of the wagon would churn the cream into butter. They would have plenty of sweet buttermilk to drink too.

The Fletcher crew wasted no time eating, and the men left to hitch up the wagons while Lexie and Sarah did dishes and packed everything away for the day's journey.

By six o'clock the wagons were rolling. There had been a small altercation when the owner of the wagon that traveled first yesterday was told he had to go to the last place. He couldn't understand why the wagons had to rotate positions. The wagon master handed him a duplicate set of the rules. A copy had been given to all drivers when they signed up to go. Defeated, the driver agreed to move, and the change was made.

Quite a few farms were still along the trail, but they became fewer all the time. Trees were plentiful, and the grass on either side of the trail was still green. The hot sun of summer had not done its damage yet. The trail was sometimes rough since sprouts had sprung up in the trail because of its disuse since the previous year.

By the second day, the train had reached the Missouri River. The wagons took three days to be ferried across. Those nights a circle of wagons adorned each side of the river.

Lexie went down to the ferry to watch the wagons and animals being loaded to cross the river, but there was so much yelling and cursing that she went back to their wagons. Since she didn't want to stay at the river to watch the crossing, she helped Sarah with some cooking and baking.

When she was finished with the work, she went inside the wagon and pulled out a book from a number of them stored in one of the pockets sewn into the canvas cover of the wagon. She sat on the wagon seat so that she would have a backrest while she read. The noise and excitement at the river interfered with her concentration, so she put the book back into the pocket inside the wagon.

She wished David would ride by, but he didn't. She felt restless and didn't know why. At times she felt as if she were hanging over a cliff. She knew she should be able to shake off such feelings, but she felt powerless to escape them. She didn't even want to be with Olivia, which certainly was a change. They had been almost inseparable ever since the Fletchers had arrived from Tennessee. She didn't see much of David because he stayed at the river most of each day helping people with wagons and animals get across.

Then Mr. Clarence Anderson, an elderly man, was injured when a wheel came off his wagon and fell onto his leg. His leg was crushed with the impact of the wheel. His screams could be heard all the way back to the Fletchers' wagons before he lost consciousness.

Clem Abbott and Henry Blakemore, both muscular men, heaved the wheel off the injured leg. Mr. Smythe sent two of the men to find David, who came at a run. He examined the unconscious man and knew within minutes that the leg would have to come off. Rising to his feet and putting his arms around Mrs. Anderson to comfort her, he said, "Mrs. Anderson, Mr. Anderson's leg is crushed. It's going to have to come off. I'm terribly sorry."

Mrs. Anderson brushed away the tears running down her face. "Will he be all right then? I can stand almost anything except losing him."

"Conditions aren't good, but I'll do my best. Mr. Smythe, would you get some men to find some boards and some saw horses or barrels to make a table. Mrs. Anderson we need quilts and a sheet to cover the table and plenty of hot water.

"Folks, if you are not helping, please leave the area. We don't need any distractions, but we could sure use your prayers," David said.

In a short period of time Mr. Anderson was placed on the table, and David with his instruments sterilized, began the surgery. Mr. Smythe took care of the anesthetic for David. With no skilled help, even though people were willing to do what they could, the operation seemed to take a lifetime to David. Finally, he pulled the flap of skin that he had left over the wound and stitched it into place.

"Well, barring infection, he ought to do," David said. "Where's Mrs. Anderson?"

Lexie, Sarah, Olivia, and Mrs. Green had taken Mrs. Anderson inside the wagon and sat with her during the ordeal. The women prayed constantly for Mr. and Mrs. Anderson, for David, and for the men helping him.

When the surgery was over, the men carefully laid Mr. Anderson inside the wagon. David took Mrs. Anderson aside and explained how to care for her husband.

For the next four nights, David sat up all night taking care of him. He slept in snatches during the day while Mrs. Anderson, Lexie, and Sarah cared for Mr. Anderson. Each evening, he took on the responsibility of getting Mr. Anderson's team unhitched. He also saw that the Anderson wagon was taken safely across the river as well.

Lexie thought David was wonderful to help others the way he did, giving so untiringly of himself, but the days became a time of loneliness for her. Everyone was so busy that there wasn't much time for socializing.

Lexie felt the only highlight of the time was when the minister, John Case, came by. He was a very handsome man, broad shouldered and tall. His blond hair was rather long, touching his collar. He had piercing gray eyes. A small scar at the corner of his right eye didn't mar his good looks. He invited the family to come to Wednesday night devotions. Of course they accepted.

Finally, it was time for the Fletcher and Duvall wagons to be ferried across the water. David came to tell Sarah and Lexie they would be crossing in just a short while.

"Where's Tom?" Sarah wanted to know. "He surely doesn't want me to drive this thing onto that ferry?"

"No," he said to tell you that he would be here in plenty of time to take it across.

"Good," Lexie stated. "I, for one, am frightened enough without having to worry about Mother's getting us on the ferry." She laughed as she said it, but the laugh sounded hollow in her own ears.

"Tell you what, Lexie, why don't you cross with Abe and me? We'll put you in the middle, and keep you safe," David said.

"Sounds like a good idea to me," Tom said, walking up to the others. "Then I can give my full attention to Sarah."

"You make me sound like a package you have to deliver. That I'm totally incompetent or even worse a coward," Sarah complained.

"A very precious package, dear," Tom, replied, helping her up onto the wagon. He turned to look at Lexie to see what she was going to do when David spoke.

"Lexie? Are you going to come with me?"

"All right, if you think I should."

Instantly David's face was wreathed in smiles. He walked her back to his wagon and helped her to climb up. Abe was already aboard. Lexie forced a smile as she and Abe greeted each other.

"Hi, Abe. Looks like you are going to be stuck with me."

"Always a pleasure, Miss Lexie," Abe replied. "Always a pleasure."

In just a short time, Lexie watched Sarah and Tom's wagons roll onto the ferry. Despite her brave words, Sarah thought that she would be frightened, but was surprised to find that she wasn't. She had simply put her trust in God and Tom, as His instrument, to see them safely across.

Their crossing was uneventful. Lexie watched their wagons climb the river's bank on the other side and let out a sigh of relief. Sarah climbed down from the wagon, bowed to Lexie, David, and Abe, and then waved to Lexie. Lexie returned the wave with a trembling hand.

David saluted her. Abe just grinned.

When David was sure that the Fletcher wagons were safely across, he climbed up on the seat by Lexie. "All right, we're ready to roll," he said, smiling at her. Abe flicked the reins, and the wagon began to roll down the slight embankment onto the ferry. Abe was careful to leave room for the other wagons crossing with them.

As the ferry began to move across the water, Lexie's face turned a pasty white. She covered her face with her hands and bent over, hiding her face in her lap. She began to shake alarmingly. "Hey, girl," David said, suddenly realizing her fear. He gently raised her up, put an arm around her shoulders, and pulled her to him. Her fear only endeared her to him. "Nothing to be afraid of," he crooned, as if talking to a small child while holding her tightly.

"I'm sorry that I'm such a baby, but I'm terrified of water. I almost drowned when I was little, and I can't seem to shake this fear that I have."

"Do you swim?" David asked.

"Yes," Lexie said, nodding her head. "But just a little, not really enough to count. I couldn't swim this river."

"What happened to make you so fearful?" David asked. He hoped that by getting her to talk, she would forget her fear.

"I was wading in a creek near our house before I learned to swim when I stepped into a large hole. It was very deep, and I couldn't get out. I panicked and of course swallowed half the creek before Daddy reached me. He pulled me out. I've been terrified ever since," she said not taking her eyes off David. He made me learn to swim, but I hated every minute of it. Besides hating it, I was scared to death each time I went into the water.

"We'll have to see if we can't remedy that," David told her. "Look where we are. We're at the other side." He thought he had distracted her from her fears very well.

Lexie, who had been giving David all her attention, looked at the bank swiftly approaching, gave a big sigh of relief, and said, "What a ninny you two must think me. I feel like a fool."

"You have a very understandable fear. You know what is always said about falling off a horse? You need to get right back on to conquer your fears. The same could be said about swimming," David said, still holding her tightly. *Lord, please let me have this woman for my wife. She becomes more precious to me daily.* "Someday when we have time, I'll teach you to swim so well that you won't be afraid."

Abe, who had been quietly attending the wagon's progress felt impelled to say, "Miss Lexie, I'm not very bright, but I know that nobody thinks you're a fool or a ninny. What happened to you would scare anybody." As Lexie turned to look at him, red color suffused his face, and he became silent. That was a long speech for Abe to make.

"Abe, what a nice thing to say," Lexie declared, realizing his discomfort, and attempting to put him at ease.

"Now that we've got that settled to everyone's satisfaction," David said bowing to Lexie, "Miss Fletcher, may I help you down from this humble carriage?" David said, laughing good-humouredly. He jumped down from the wagon. When Lexie had scooted to the side of the wagon, he enclosed her tiny waist with his hands and lifted her down.

"My goodness, you're tiny. I can get my hands around your entire waist." David told her.

"I'm no different from most girls," She answered. "Thank you for taking me with you. I'll go stay with mother. I know you want to help others get across."

Lexie wondered how David was going to teach her to swim. She stood watching him as he waved and walked away. It was unheard of that a single man, not one of the family, would teach a single girl to swim. It just wasn't done. Did that mean that he wanted to be more than a friend? If so, he certainly wasn't forthcoming in telling her.

CHAPTER SEVEN

That night a large number of people gathered for Bible devotions and to give thanks for God's care of them thus far. Olivia and Lexie walked together to where the devotions were to be held.

As they were walking along, a very pretty girl jumped down from her wagon. She had dark brown hair and dark brown eyes. Her complexion was a beautiful peaches and cream. Her womanly form fit perfectly in a blue and white striped dress. The dress had short puffy sleeves. A high neckline sported a round collar. The full skirt fell in soft folds to her ankles. "Hi, are you going to devotions?" she asked.

"We sure are," Lexie replied while Olivia just nodded her head up and down.

"Mind if I walk with you? I'm Millicent Bond."

"Of course we don't mind. Come on. My name is Olivia Green and this is Lexie Fletcher. Why haven't we seen you before?"

"Oh, I've been ill and unable to get out much."

"I'm sorry," Lexie, said, "are you all right now?"

"Sure, I'm fine."

The three girls linked arms and walked on, talking about family and their trip. Millicent told them she was an only child. Her father was a farmer who had an itch to move to less crowded spaces. She also told them that she was engaged to Johnny Perkins. She held up her left hand to show them the diamond and sapphire ring on her finger.

"I guess you could call us childhood sweethearts. We grew up together. Johnny used to pull my pigtails when we were little. Whoever would have thought we would fall in love. We are going to be married as soon as we reach Oregon. Johnny is already there, waiting for me to come," she said proudly.

Each of the other two expressed their good wishes for her and Johnny. Secretly they wished for someone who loved them too.

"I wonder how you know for sure you are in love, a love that will last a lifetime?" Lexie pondered. "Wouldn't it be awful if you married one man and then fell in love with another?"

"Oh, you don't need to worry about that," Millicent replied. "When the right man comes along, you'll know it."

"That's what my mother says," Olivia said.

As they reached the place where the crowd had gathered, Millicent said, "I'm sure glad I met you two. It was beginning to be lonely by myself all the time. I know we'll be good friends." The other two told her how glad they were to make a new friend too.

"We walk together every day. We'll pick you up to walk with us." Lexie said.

The three worked their way to the front of the crowd. It was a large crowd because many of the families on the train were God-fearing people. "I'm so short I won't be able to see a thing if we don't get up front," Lexie said. Millicent who topped Lexie by only an inch agreed.

Olivia just looked smug, and then said, "It's too bad about you short people and the trouble you have. I *never* have a problem seeing."

"Let's get her for that," Lexie said.

"You bet we will. What shall we do, beat her with a wet noodle?" Millicent asked.

"That's it. That's what we'll do." Lexie agreed. She heard a faint titter from behind her. Turning around, she saw several people had heard their conversation and were smiling or trying to keep from laughing aloud.

"Pay no attention to us," she said, red creeping up her face. "We're not always this silly. Sometimes we're worse," she added, dimpling adoringly. At this remark several people did laugh aloud, and one man clapped his hands. "You tell 'em, honey," he said. The three girls laughed uproariously.

The girls had a hard time controlling their giggles until everyone became quiet when the minister John Case walked to the front of the crowd. With hands extended he waited for the crowd to get quiet.

When the area was quiet, he said, "I want to welcome you to the Lord's service. Let's begin with prayer." Every head bowed and eyes closed as the young man led them in a prayer of thanksgiving and supplication for a safe journey. The topic of discussion was the journey of the Israelites from the land of Egypt and God's careful care of them. It was a vivid description of God's blessings so freely bestowed to man.

Olivia had a difficult time keeping her mind on the subject of discussion. She could only concentrate on John Case. Lexie thought Olivia must be enjoying the sermon, she was so enrapt.

After the devotion and prayer time, people gathered for a time of fellowship. Several girls Lexie's and Olivia's age stood talking quietly with Lexie and the other two girls when John Case came over to them.

"Good evening, ladies. I hope you enjoyed the message tonight," he said. With both hands in his pockets, John flexed his muscles, shrugging his shoulders, as though he were tired. He smiled through even, white teeth.

"Oh, Brother Case, it was wonderful," gushed Sophie Lewis, an overweight girl with protruding teeth. Her black tangled hair hung down her back almost to her waist. The top of her head looked as though birds had been nesting in it.

"Yes, I thought it was very inspiring," Lenora Johnson said. She was a very attractive girl of above average height and voluptuous figure. Her fiery red hair and green eyes spoke of a volatile disposition.

Lenora knew that she was attractive and used that attraction to her benefit whenever she could. With a false southern accent she spoke, "Ah swear, Ah could just listen to you all night," she said, batting her long lashes.

Always looking to be the center of attraction, she unobtrusively began edging out the other girls in order to stand closer to John. Sophie, who wanted John to notice her, frowned deeply and elbowed Lenora hard. Since Sophie was a hefty girl, and she put force behind the nudge, Lenora stumbled. She quickly regained her balance. She sent Sophie a look that would shrivel a lesser girl. Sophie seemed impervious to the look.

Lexie thought it was hilarious that the two girls were practically fighting over the young minister. She glanced over at Olivia to see if she saw the two girls. Olivia remained quietly in the background with an enthralled look on her face. She hadn't taken her eyes off John Case. Millicent was having a hard time to keep from laughing. The two looked at one another conspiratorially and grinned.

John had not missed any of the byplay. *Oh, oh, beware, Case. A couple of man-eaters, if I ever saw any. I'll be very careful around them.* John told himself. "Thank you ladies," he said, smoothing down his blond hair ruffled by the spring breeze. He looked at Olivia closely. He liked the blue of her eyes, the long blond curls, her womanly body, even her small turned up nose.

Olivia had taken just one look at John Case and immediately had fallen in love with him. She stood tongue-tied and rooted to the spot. *Why can't I think of something clever to say? I feel so stupid,* she thought.

John was certainly not indifferent to Olivia. *Now there's a girl I intend to get to know better. She's quiet and unassuming. She's a real lady. Her glorious blonde hair makes me want to run my fingers through it.*

Lexie might as well have been on the moon for all the notice John gave her. It amused her to see how quickly the two were smitten. Now she understood why Olivia had seemed so engrossed in the message.

John talked with the girls for a while until Sophie and Lenora's parents joined them. Each of them expressed how much they enjoyed the good sermon, collected their girls and left. Both girls kept looking back over their shoulders to look at the three left behind.

Sophie caught Lenora's eye and quickly stuck out her tongue at her. She was so interested in letting Lenora see her displeasure that she stumbled and would have fallen if her father had not quickly grabbed her arm roughly. "Look where you are going, not at that young man," he warned.

"Yes, Poppa, I will," she said, resigned.

"Olivia, we had better start back to our wagons too," Lexie said. "Looks like Mom and Dad are visiting with Uncle Robbie and Aunt Leona again. That could take all night."

"Yes, I'm sure you're right," Olivia said dreamily, her eyes never leaving John's face. She had not an inkling of what Lexie had said.

"In that case, I'll walk you back," John said, extending his arm to Olivia. The two walked off leaving Lexie and Millicent to trail behind them. The two girls looked at one another and giggled. Not once did John and Olivia look back to see if Millicent and Lexie were following.

"What was that you were saying about knowing the right man when you saw him? Olivia fell hard, didn't she?" Lexie asked.

"She sure did. I think she went down for the third time," Millicent gurgled.

Lexie told Millicent goodnight when the two reached her wagon and hurried on to catch up with John and Olivia.

John was all Olivia could talk about for days. It seemed the feeling was mutual because the two became inseparable. Lexie remembered Olivia's remarks about finding a husband before reaching Oregon. It looked as if she might be going to have one.

"Mom, Olivia is smitten with a man," Lexie announced.

"Oh, with whom?" Sarah replied casually. "Not David surely? It would be too bad if both of you set your caps for him." Sarah had noticed how interested Lexie seemed in David.

"Mother! How can you say a thing like that? What makes you think I'm setting my cap for him? I'm sure I don't treat him any differently than I do the other fellows." She quickly changed the subject. Without giving Sarah a chance to answer she continued, "No, Olivia's smitten with Brother John Case, and the feeling must be mutual. At Bible devotions, he didn't even realize that I was on the planet. Just think our feisty fun-loving Olivia might become a preacher's wife. You should have seen them. Olivia was completely bowled over. She was literally struck dumb, and for Olivia, that's quite a change. She usually does the bowling over, and she never knows when to be quiet."

Lexie was happy for her friend, but she missed her time with Olivia. In fact, she was quite bored. She didn't like trying to read while the wagons were moving. The motion made her queasy and at night there was so much work to do that it got dark before she had a chance to pick up a book and read much. She did well just to do her daily Bible readings some days. Millicent was no help for she had contracted a fever and had to stay in bed until she recovered.

David and Lexie's parents wouldn't let Lexie visit Millicent for fear of her catching the fever. David was at a loss to know what caused the fever. "You know that doctors know a lot more about the human body and its ills today than in the past, but there's so much that we don't know. We just have to depend on the Lord to help us. So I think it best to keep Millicent in isolation."

Lexie knew that he was right, but she was used to having a lot of friends to visit. She wished she had found someone who would love her as Olivia had. She wondered again what David had meant when he said he would teach her to swim. Did that mean that he was really interested in her, or was he just being the kindly doctor that she knew he was? One moment he seemed really interested. The next he would revert to being just a good friend. She longed for each evening to come so that they could be alone together for their nightly walk. Maybe he would give her a clue tonight.

Sarah wasn't much help in alleviating Lexie's boredom either. She was completely taken with being able to visit with Robbie and his family and spent much of each afternoon with them. She said she was making up for lost time and didn't seem to notice how lonely Lexie was feeling. Lexie still took rides daily, but usually by herself, and she constantly wished herself back home. Whenever she had thoughts of pity for herself, she felt ashamed. Poor Millicent was in much worse shape. I can be thankful that I'm not ill. *At least I get to see David most evenings*, she thought.

CHAPTER EIGHT

Two days after the train left the Missouri River it came to Fort Leavenworth. Stopping there gave people a chance to purchase any items that they had forgotten to bring with them or needed to replenish.

The drivers of the wagons were becoming expert at making the nightly circle, so that no time was wasted in its formation today. They easily followed the marked path made by Mr. Smythe. Animals were quickly unhitched and taken to the holding place. Wood was hurriedly gathered for campfires.

They arrived early afternoon, and since they were tired of being on the trail, excitedly prepared for a celebration. Women did some much needed baking while the men went into the fort to gossip and buy any needed supplies. When the men returned, they relayed the news that everyone was invited to an old fashioned hoedown after supper. All over the camp, a festive air prevailed. Men, women, and children donned their Sunday best clothes. Harried mothers, who were trying to make refreshments to contribute for the dance, admonished children to keep clean.

Lexie dug through her trunk and found a sky blue dress. It had a close fitting bodice, a square neckline trimmed in blue lace, and large puffy sleeves. The skirt was bouffant and ankle length. Her mother always told Lexie she looked like a dream in it.

Lexie just hoped that David would think so, too. She realized that she was spending too much time thinking about David, but she seemed unable to help herself. *I'm headed for a big disappointment*, she kept telling herself. She was disappointed that he hadn't asked her to go to the dance with him.

Sarah and Lexie put the finishing touches on the evening meal, and no time was wasted in consuming every morsel. There was no offer of help with dishes tonight, as the men left to get ready for the evening.

David left with them, but he turned around and came back to Lexie, who was helping with the cleanup. Lexie always felt excited by how handsome a figure David made. His carriage and self-assurance alone made him a striking young man. His tall, trim good looks caught the eye of all the girls. *I wonder if some of the girls would faint if they saw him flex his muscles.* She stifled a giggle at the mental picture of David flexing his muscles for the girls that her thoughts conjured up. *I guess I am just as bad* as *they are.* She only hoped that he was as interested in her as she was in him. Tom had always said that Lexie could charm the tusks off elephants. She just hoped she could charm David.

"Lexie, are you going to the dance tonight?" David asked, walking over to her. His eyes searched her face. He longed to reach out and touch her.

"I plan to go. Why, did you need me to do something for you?" she asked, looking up at him smiling, her left dimple showing adoringly.

If she keeps looking at me like that, I won't be responsible for the consequences, he thought. "I certainly do. I need you to escort me to the dance tonight," he said with a crooked smile. *I wish I knew how she feels about me. She becomes more important to me each day. I never dreamed I could feel this way about a slip of a girl.*

Why, he seems bashful. Surely, as good-looking as he is, he's never had trouble getting a date. "I don't think I can do that." Seeing the dejected look that appeared on his face, she said quickly, "*But,* I'd be happy to let you take *me*," she told him smiling enticingly.

A look of relief and something else she couldn't define, came over his face. He started to reach for her, caught himself, and instead shoved his hands into his pockets and said, "It's a deal. I'll get changed and be back for you before long. I need to check on Millicent before we go."

David left, thinking how hard it was getting for him to hide his feelings from Lexie, never dreaming she didn't have a clue about them. Lexie scrambled into the wagon to put on her finery. When she was finished with the final touches, she climbed down from the wagon, whirled around and asked her parents who were sitting on campstools reading from the light of the fire, "Well, how do I look?"

"Exquisite," Sarah said, looking up from the book she was reading. "You'll be a great success tonight." She closed the book and rose to her feet. "I'd better get dressed, now that you are out of the wagon." She climbed into the wagon and closed the flap.

Tom, who pretended to be taking a long time to look up, smiled and said, "My beautiful girl, you'll be the envy of every other girl at that dance. Maybe I'd better take a stick with me to beat off the boys." At Lexie's indignant look, he laughed whole-heartedly and said. "Now I'd better get in there and get changed. Your mother can probably make room for me."

"I heard that. I can always make room for you, my darling," Sarah cooed.

Tom looked at Lexie, wriggled his eyebrows, and grinned wolfishly, but wasted no time before scrambling into the wagon.

Lexie sat watching the stars. Breathlessly, she waited for David's return. Deep inside herself, she felt something exciting was bound to happen tonight. When she was with him, she felt as if she had come home from a long journey. When they weren't together, she felt lost and lonely.

Tom and Sarah's softly spoken intimate speech intermingled with Sarah's giggles from within the wagon didn't help either. Lexie longed for a love like theirs with David. She thought about the scripture in Hosea 2:19 which promised, *I will betroth thee unto me for ever; yea, I will betroth thee unto me in righteousness, and in judgment, and in loving-kindness, and in mercy.* Lexie realized that the Lord was speaking in the scripture, but she had always longed for a comparable love in a man. She thought of Millicent whose love was so far away. *She must miss him dreadfully. I'm sorry that she will miss the party tonight.*

Tom and Sarah soon left for the party, after assuring themselves that Lexie would be all right by herself until David came for her. Sarah carried the cake that she had spent most of the afternoon preparing. Lexie watched them walk out of sight. Tom had his arm around Sarah as if they were still young sweethearts.

Lexie waited and waited. Her thoughts turned back to Millicent and how she would miss the dance. She decided that Millicent probably wouldn't care. She wouldn't want to go to the dance without her Johnny. Still David didn't come. She sat tapping her foot impatiently. Impatience turned to disappointment. The longer she waited, the more disappointed she became. *How could he just leave me sitting here?* She asked herself. She was just about ready to go take off her dress and go to bed when David, looking distressed, came hurrying up to the wagon.

"Gosh, I'm sorry, Lexie. I was just about ready to come for you when I had to go dress a cut for one of Matt Taylor's girls. It took a while to stop the bleeding."

"How awful. How did she get cut?"

"On a piece of broken crockery. It was a clean cut. I don't think she'll get infection. After I got her squared away, I had to check on Mr. Anderson. Please, forgive me?" Without giving her a chance to reply, he continued, "I've got some good news. Millicent's fever has broken, thank God. She'll soon be on the mend."

"Of course, I forgive you," she said, her disappointment evaporating. "I realize that your job comes first," she smiled tenderly at him. "You wouldn't be half the doctor or the man you are if it didn't," she said getting up from her seat. "Oh, David, it's great to know Millicent's better."

"Yes, it is. Thank you for understanding. You always know just the right thing to say."

"You are pretty good at that too. When may I see her?"

"I think she'll be able to have company by the end of the week"

They stood looking at one another for a moment, and then Lexie said in a subdued voice, "I thought you had forgotten me."

"Lexie, you are so beautiful," he said, taking her hand and whirling her around so that he could see all of her. "There's no way I could ever forget you or your family. All of you have been so kind to me. Here, take my arm, lovely lady," he said crooking his arm. Lexie completely missed the longing in his eyes.

Lexie perked up at his words, turned toward him and made a slight curtsey. She took his arm, and they started off into the night. The wagons looked lonely, as nearly everyone was inside the fort. They talked in a desultory manner while the sound of the instruments: a banjo, fiddle, and guitar, resounded in the air. The pungent odor of dust competed with the music.

"Did you ever see so much beauty?" Lexie asked, looking at the stars, liberally sprinkled in the sky. "The stars almost seem close enough for one to reach up and pull them down," she said, raising her arm toward the sky.

Looking at her, David replied, "Never, and I don't ever expect to see anything more beautiful."

Lexie turned to look at him, thinking his statement a strange answer. She could see only a serious look on his face. She turned away from him, looking at the path again. *I wonder what he meant by that? Surely he's seen other things as beautiful as starlight.*

"I'll bet you dance every dance tonight," David said, breaking into her thoughts, "so I'm putting in my order now. Will you dance at least every other dance with me? More if possible?"

"Of course, I will, if I don't choke to death on that dust people are kicking up," Lexie said, thrilled with the prospect. She found it hard to speak in a normal manner, to keep the exuberance from her voice. She had wondered ever since that first day when she had met him how it would feel to have his arms around her. She shivered in anticipation.

"Are you cold?" David asked, pulling her closer to his side.

"No, just excited," she answered forthrightly.

Just then three young men came up to them. "Hi, Doc, Miss," a thin, gangly young man greeted them. His face contrasted vividly with his body, for it was a round face. "I see you got a girl," he said to David. "Hope we can find one too." The other two grinned and nodded to them.

"Hi, fellows," David said. Pointing out each man, he introduced him. "Lexie, this is Caleb Taylor, that one is Zeke Williams, and this one is Taylor Moore."

All three were physically fit specimens dressed in their Sunday best. They had changed from the woolen trousers they usually wore for navy broadcloth trousers and white cotton shirts. Each one had his hair slicked down, an unusual thing for them to do, and they had dispensed with the usual hat.

Although David's background was different from the other three men, a deep friendship among them was budding. "May I present Miss Lexie Fletcher?" The three men greeted Lexie and immediately asked her for a dance.

"Each of you can have one, but I claim every other dance," David said emphatically.

"Fellers, wouldn't you know he'd beat us to the best lookin' girl around?" Taylor asked, not altogether joking.

Lexie felt herself blush. David took her hand and squeezed it. Still holding her hand amid much laughter and jovial conversation, the group of young people approached the gate to the fort.

A large barren space in the middle of the parade ground was filled with people dancing or just standing around talking. Bursts of laughter filled the air. At one end of the open space, the musicians stood playing exuberantly. Close to them were three tables covered with cakes and cider. Already a line of people was waiting to be served by the ladies of the fort. Children playing tag darted in and out from among groups of people talking. A group of four teenage girls stood in a huddle, looking at several teenage boys, giggling at everything the boys did.

The fort was a rough looking place, made of logs. No painted houses adorned the fort. A few rough-sawn benches graced the area, so that the elderly people in the train could sit down. Others were sitting on wagon tongues, kegs or crates. A few men sat on the ground. Many were standing in clusters eating and talking, and a few were standing alone as if afraid to become part of the festivities.

Lexie heard a squeal, and Olivia came charging up to her, tugging John along behind her. "Isn't this fun?" Olivia gushed. "I never thought we'd be having a celebration tonight. Where have you been? John and

I have already danced five dances." Although a minister, John saw nothing wrong with dancing. He thought it was good exercise.

"Olivia, honey, slow down. Give her a chance to speak" John told her. His loving look belied his chiding words.

"It is entirely my fault we're late," David said, not explaining the reason.

"Olivia, it's wonderful. David said Milly can have visitors by the end of the week."

"Great. Isn't it strange how you can miss a person so much that you have known such a short time?"

The friends visited for a while, and Ben, Abe, and Sam came by, each towing a well-dressed girl with him. Abe's girl was Sara. Ben introduced Betty, and Sam introduced Sally. After introductions were made, the couples visited the refreshment tables. When they had eaten, they walked to the dance area. The ground was bare and dusty. Kicked up by the high-spirited dancers, swirls of dust gathered on shoes, trousers, and skirts.

David led Lexie onto the bare ground. The three musicians were playing a waltz. As he took her into his arms, Lexie looked up at him and smiled. For just a moment David let his mask slip, and Lexie caught a loving look from him that almost took her breath away. In just an instant, the look was replaced with a smile of friendliness; however, he wanted to be much more than a friend. *I've wanted to hold her in my arms ever since I met her. She feels so good. This is where she belongs.* He pulled her a little closer, as he whirled her around in the dance. He was finding it more difficult to keep his desire for Lexie under control. She was feather-light and followed his steps perfectly.

Did I imagine that look? Is it possible that he could really care for me? Lexie wondered. She felt very shy in his arms. *This must be the nearest thing to Heaven on this earth,* she thought, as she deftly followed his lead. She felt as if she were floating. Because she felt shy, instead of looking at him, she focused on the third button of his shirt.

They danced silently for a few moments. Then David tenderly asked, "Is something wrong with my shirt? Although I enjoy looking at the top of your head, I'd much rather look at your beautiful face."

Color suffused Lexie's face. She quickly looked up at him smiling. "No, of course not. I'm sorry. It's just that you are so tall," she prevaricated. "I almost have to crane my neck up to look at you when you are so close."

David didn't believe that was the real reason but let it ride. In answer, he pulled her closer. "That's better," he said looking down at her. "Are you having fun?" he asked, his eyes never wavering from her face.

"Yes, very much. Are you?" she said, still looking up at him.

"I never enjoyed an evening more," he said. Lexie hoped that it was because they were together. They finished the dance, and the next selection was a Virginia reel, quickly claimed by Clem.

When David wasn't dancing with Lexie, he stood on the sidelines watching her. A group of girls, about Lexie's age, soon surrounded him. Lexie could hear them trying to gain his attention when she and her partners were close by. She had a hard time paying attention to what her partners were saying and watching what was happening with David.

She was pleased to see that he always politely answered the girls, but showed no interest in asking them to dance, even though he received some strong hints. He kept his eyes on Lexie, never letting his eyes wander from her. Some of the girls got discouraged and went looking for greener pastures when he showed no interest. However, a few of them waited and approached him each time he didn't dance with Lexie.

Lenora Johnson, the fiery redhead from prayer service, was one of the pushy hangers-on. She kept trying to slip her hand inside his arm to hold on, but without being too obvious, he managed to free himself every time. One time he pretended to swat a bug away; another he reached up untangling his arm with hers to scratch his forehead. Lenora, not only tried to monopolize him, she tried to dominate the conversation. She was a beautiful girl and knew that she made an impressive figure.

Lexie felt the green-eyed monster jealousy taking hold of her senses even though David was doing a fine job of brushing off the unwanted attentions. *I'd like to scratch her eyes out. Why couldn't I be just few inches taller?* Lexie thought. Instantly, she felt ashamed of the strong feelings Lenora roused in her. *Heavenly Father, forgive me for acting so unlike a Christian.*

David kept his word about wanting every other dance. No sooner had the music stopped than he claimed Lexie for the next dance, leaving a bevy of pouting girls and disappointed young men. He whirled Lexie into waltzes, square dances, and Virginia Reels. They had just finished a waltz and were walking back to the edge of the dance area when suddenly a tall full-bearded man, wearing buckskin shirt and trousers, stepped in front of Lexie. His warrior-like stance showed him a man to be reckoned with.

Lexie was looking up at David. She was fanning herself with her hand, speaking to David about how warm it was. She didn't notice the man approach until he was right in front of them.

"My dance, I think," he said evenly. Lexie looked up into the face of Carson Fullbrite, a face frozen with hatred. "Carson Fullbrite, what are you doing here?" she exclaimed in surprise. "I didn't know you were on this train."

"Coming after my girl," he answered, smiling rakishly. His eyes looked like hard burning coals in his face. "I caught up with the train this afternoon. You really didn't think I'd let you get away, did you?"

He ignored David as he reached for Lexie's hands, but she quickly thrust them behind her. A gleam of insanity filled his eyes. Carson had never felt such a need for anyone as he did Lexie. He couldn't stand the thought of not having her. He determined he would have her one way or another. More than wanting her, he hated the way he felt, but something compelled him to pursue her. He couldn't seem to help himself.

Frowning, Lexie told him," If by any slight chance you mean me, forget it. I am not your girl. Please let us pass. As you can see, I have an escort, and you're in our way." Lexie was upset by Carson's appearance. She thought she had seen the last of him.

Carson was a tall, handsome man. He had coal black hair and gray eyes. His muscular build attracted even the most beautiful of girls. His parents had spoiled him, giving him whatever he wanted, and so he had never learned self-restraint. He knew the power he held over women. As a result, he was a man who didn't accept being thwarted easily.

Shaking his head from side to side, barely keeping his temper under control, he spoke. "Still as stubborn as ever, aren't you, and I guess you are still the same little Bible thumper, too, aren't you?" he added sarcastically. His gaze never wavering and paying no heed to David, he said, "You'll come around," he added arrogantly. "Now let's dance," he said, grabbing her arm in a brutal hold. Lexie could see the muscles tense in his arms.

"Carson, why do you come around here after all this time?" Lexie asked, jerking her arm away. "Did you really think I'd change my mind after the things you said to me? I meant it when I said I didn't want to see you again." Lexie was beginning to tremble in her agitation.

Ever since Carson stepped in front of them, David felt anger stir within him. Seeing Lexie's stress only served to build it. "Sir, I don't know who you are, but I think you'd better leave and quit upsetting Miss Fletcher," David said, quietly interrupting, his voice cold steel, his muscles tightening. He was doing his best to control his rising anger. He took Lexie by the arm and gently pulled her behind him. His quiet demeanor was in direct contrast to Carson Fullbrite's agitation.

Turning his eyes on David and thrusting out his chin, Carson drew himself up to his full height; his hands doubled into hard fists. He was trembling in his fury. His anger matched David's. With shoulders thrown back and chest thrust out, he said mockingly, his brown eyes black pools of hate, "And just who might you be, her father? I think you'd better stay out of this, if you know what's good for you."

David thought quickly. He was sure that Lexie didn't want anything to do with this man who seemed to upset her severely. David replied caustically. "I'm the man Lexie is going to marry, so I believe I'm very involved in this discussion," he said, putting his arm around her, holding her tightly. He hoped Lexie didn't contradict him because no way was he going to let this man have her. She was his soul mate. She belonged to him.

It was a good thing Carson was looking at David and not Lexie. Her mouth dropped open, and she let out a ragged breath of surprise, quickly looking up at David.

Carson leaned forward, his face monstrous in his fury. With his face almost touching David's, he said, "Oh, yeah, mighty sudden wasn't it? Or, Lady," he asked aggressively, "Were you just leading me on?"

David could detect the smell of alcohol on his breath. He turned from David toward Lexie. Without waiting for an answer he continued, "Just when is the happy day?" It was obvious that he didn't believe David. He had been watching Lexie, and David. They had acted more like friends than lovers to him. But he realized that he could be mistaken. He knew that Bible thumpers were a different breed. Turning the blast of his anger on Lexie, he ground out, "Lady, you sure work fast, or is this just a ruse to get rid of me?" He shifted his squinting eyes back to David. "Has she even told you about me?" He kept shifting his weight from one foot to the other; his hands still doubled into fists.

Lexie was at a loss as to what to reply. She turned to her anchor in the storm. She sent David a look of entreaty. David's response was quick. As tightly as he had her anchored to his side, he pulled her closer to him and said, "We haven't set a date as yet. We're still making plans," he said without blinking an eye. He sent up a quick silent prayer for forgiveness "I'm sure if she thought you were important, she would have told me," he said, adding salt to the wound. "We have no secrets from each other. Besides, this is not the time or place to be discussing this. Excuse us, please." He stepped around Carson, taking Lexie with him.

As they walked off, they heard Carson say, "I think it's a pretty sad affair when a man can take a fellow's girl away from him just because he's not around for a few days." Adopting another tactic he asked loudly, "Did you know she led me on for months, and then dropped me just because I don't believe in her God?" he said unwilling to let the matter rest, following them while speaking to their backs.

"Maybe with you, pal, that's not important, but it is to Lexie, and it is to me," David interrupted, not bothering to turn around to look at Carson.

Lexie had felt the muscles in David's arm bunching and knew that he was ready to fight. Looking over her shoulder at Carson, she knew that he was ready to square off. "Carson," Lexie implored, "why are you trying to make trouble?" She pulled David to a stop. Turning around, she continued, "You know very well that I'm not your girl. You know I told you months ago that we were through. I haven't *even seen* you in months, and I don't want to see you now." Turning back to David, she said, "Please take me back to our wagon. I can't stay here," she implored, trembling visibly. David could see the tears welling up in her eyes.

David relaxed, and said tenderly, "Certainly, darling, come along." He turned to Carson, and said gently, making the threat more ominous than if he had shouted, "You, my friend, had better not bother her any more, or you will answer to me." He put his arm around Lexie, and they walked off into the night.

"Time will tell, time will tell, who bothers who," Carson replied nastily.

Carson stood with fists on his hips, white with tension. His uppermost thought now was getting even with both, Lexie for rejecting him and David for interfering and trying to take his woman. He would see both of them punished. He continued watching them as they walked away.

Hips swaying provocatively, Lenora Johnson approached Carson. "Are you having trouble with your girl, Carson?" She had made it her business to find out all the names of the single men traveling on the train, and she had decided at the dance that she was going to have Doctor David Duvall for her husband. Olivia could have John Case. She didn't want to be a minister's wife any way. That would be too confining, like living in a fishbowl, she thought. She would use whatever means it took to get David. She was never one to miss the main chance. As for Lexie, she could just go hang.

"Well, what's it to *you*, if I am?" Carson answered sourly.

"Oh, for one thing, I'd sure like to be the one Doctor Duvall has his arm around. I know that you want that Fletcher girl. Most everyone here now knows it too. You sure didn't bother to hide your feelings. Maybe we could work together to change their plans to our advantage?" she informed him conspiratorially. "With two of us working together, it shouldn't be too hard to break them apart."

Carson stood looking at her from head to toe, carefully taking in her red hair, green eyes, and over-ripe figure. Another girl would have been mortified at his obvious stare, but it didn't seem to bother Lenora. "Maybe we could at that," he said, a wolfish grin on his face. "Maybe we could." He was never averse to using anyone as a means to an end. "You have all the right equipment." A smile of satisfaction spread over her face. Carson took her arm. With heads together, the two walked off into the night.

As soon as Lexie and David had walked far enough that Carson wouldn't be able to hear, Lexie turned to David and said, "Whatever made you say such a thing?"

"David hugged her to his side and said lightly, "What thing? Oh, you mean about our engagement?" At Lexie's nod, he continued. "Couldn't let my favorite cook be intimidated by him, now could I?" He had hoped to ease the situation, but Lexie still looked troubled.

"Thanks, but what are we going to do?" she asked snappily, not sounding grateful at all.

David felt strongly that God had answered his petition that Lexie become his wife. He had made up his mind to marry her, if *she* followed God's will. And come floodwater or drought, he intended to see that she would. *If I didn't think she needed more time to get used to me, and the idea of marrying me, I'd carry her off and marry her out-of-hand right now,* he thought.

He knew exactly what they were going to do. First, he planned to have a private talk with Tom tomorrow. He also intended to find out all about Carson Fullbrite and what he had meant to Lexie. "Just let things ride for awhile, and then we'll decide what to do," he told her.

"All right, if you think it's best," she said, not at all sure, but hoping he would convince her. By this time, they had reached the Fletcher wagons. David turned Lexie to him, enfolded her in his arms and their lips met softly. The night turned to pure magic for Lexie. She snuggled into his embrace. The minute his lips touched hers, she felt as if she were going up in flames. He released her mouth, but crushed her to his chest and kissed her again, deeply. Lexie felt that her ribs were being crushed, but she didn't mind. She could feel the pounding of his heart equaling that of her own.

David felt that he couldn't get her close enough. When he released her the second time, both were trembling. He relaxed his hold on her, but didn't turn her loose. He kissed her again, gently this time.

Lexie felt as if she had the props knocked out from under her. She had been kissed before, but never like David had kissed her. She knew those kisses were special. No one else could affect her like David could. David looked almost as shaken as she did. She looked at him in awe, followed by the unpleasant thought *He probably thinks I'm a wanton or worse, but I simply couldn't help myself.*

Gently freeing herself, she raised her hand to cover her mouth. "Oh, why did you do that? What you must think of me!" she said breathlessly. Stepping back from him, her hand dropped to her chest, pushing against it to still her rapidly beating heart.

David quickly gained control of his emotions. He tweaked her nose, reverting back to his old friendliness and replied, "Got to get in practice. I'm an old engaged man now, you know. Besides, Carson may be watching, and we don't want to give him any reason for doubt, do we? And besides that, I need the practice."

"Please don't joke about it. What if someone finds out that our engagement is just make-believe? I'm sure Carson didn't believe us. We'll be the laughing stock of the train."

"Don't worry, honey. If they do, which is unlikely, we'll cross that bridge when we come to it. I'm not going to tell them, and if you don't, how will they find out? Just trust me. Besides, I'm over twenty-one, single, and in my right mind. Some people might even think it wouldn't be too intolerable to be married to me. Just don't deny we're engaged. You *can* tell your folks if you want. Better not tell them what a powerful wallop you pack though," he said cupping her face in his hands and placing a warm gentle kiss on her lips.

Lexie thought it better to ignore his last comment. "Please don't think I don't appreciate what you did. I do," she said when he released her face. "I just don't want to cause you embarrassment. Don't you feel you were trapped into this situation?"

"Not a bit. When you know me better, you'll find that I don't do anything that I don't want to do. If you don't believe me, ask my mother," he said grinning. "As for being embarrassed, believe me, we won't be. Engagements are broken all the time." He knew he was stretching the truth when he said that. "Now, I'd better be going. Good night, honey. Sleep tight. One more for the road," he said, pulling her back to him. He softly kissed her forehead.

"Good night, David. I hope you have a good night too." Suddenly in wild abandon, she did something she had never dreamed she would do. She stretched her arms up, put them around his neck, and pulled his head down until their lips met in a last lingering kiss. As she released him, she grinned enchantingly and said, "I need some practice myself."

David replied, "If that's what you do without practice, I shudder to think of what you could do to a man with practice. Goodnight, honey. I've got to go. You're too powerful for me to stay," he said, hugging her one last time.

She watched until David was out of sight, thinking how wonderful it would be if the engagement were the real thing, not a sham. She wished she could be as carefree as David seemed to be.

Lexie spent a restless night, vacillating between how wonderful David's kisses were and whether or not he would think her a wanton for initiating that last kiss they shared. *If only I could go to sleep. Much more of this worrying, and I'll be a nervous wreck*, she thought.

David was wrong about one thing. By noon the next day, people they didn't even know were congratulating him and Lexie. It was evident that Carson had not believed David's story, but was trying to arouse sympathy for himself and cause embarrassment to the couple. This just made Lexie more ill at ease.

Early that morning, before Lexie got up, David came to see Tom. "Tom, I need to talk to you. Could we go for a little walk?"

"Certainly," Tom replied, getting up from the campstool on which he was sitting.

The two men walked a short distance from the wagon. Tom asked, "Well, my boy, what's the trouble?"

David spoke in a low unhurried voice. "I've come to care a great deal about Lexie, and I'd like your permission to marry her."

Perplexed, Tom carefully studied David's tense face. He wondered why the secrecy. Surely David wasn't ashamed to tell him that he loved Lexie. Tom already liked David, and he thought he would be an excellent son-in-law. "How does Lexie feel about this?"

"I don't know. I haven't said anything to her about *really* wanting to marry her." With face deep-set in worry lines, David proceeded to tell Tom about the fake engagement. "She seemed so upset, I said the first thing that came into my head which was only what, truthfully, I wanted anyway."

"It's really too bad that Fullbrite fellow showed up," Tom said, looking into the distance, thinking about what David had said. Turning back to David, he said, "I'm grateful for your help. I think you know how much my family cares for you. Of course, you have my blessing to marry Lexie. I can't think of anyone who would be better for her," he said, patting David on the shoulder, "but she'll have to make the decision."

"Thank you sir. I'll take good care of her. I love her very much," David told him earnestly.

In the following days, David was very solicitous of Lexie, acting before others exactly as a newly engaged man should toward the woman he loved. He saw her every need and wish fulfilled.

Tom did not breathe a word of his conversation to Lexie or to Sarah. Since Lexie did not know of their conversation, she spent a lot of time wishing David's feelings were real instead of being play-acting.

One day stretched into another on the trail. While Lexie and Millicent were riding their horses one afternoon, Lexie noticed a young girl of about fourteen walking along the trail. The sole of her right shoe had come loose and was flopping as she walked along. It didn't fall flat, but kept turning back under her foot causing her to limp along the trail. A bloody footprint followed in her wake. "Hi," Lexie greeted her.

"Hi, I'm Becky Pratt." The girl was dressed in a faded cotton dress, but she looked immaculately clean. Her reddish brown hair was neatly braided and pinned around the top of her head.

"Lexie Fletcher, and this is Millicent Bond. Looks like you have shoe problems."

"Yes, and I don't have another pair. Guess I'll be extremely lopsided by the time we get to Oregon. It is very hard trying to walk right. Last night my foot had blood on it."

"It does today too. Listen, I've got more shoes than I can possibly wear. How about coming with me? I'll give you a pair of mine. Your foot looks about the size of mine."

"That would be great, but I don't know if my mother would let me accept them. We don't take charity."

"This isn't charity. It just makes sense to have good footwear. You will ruin your feet if you try to walk in those shoes. And you might get infection."

"Listen to her, Becky. You can't go all the way to Oregon like that," Millicent said.

Lexie and Millicent dismounted, and the three girls walked to the Fletcher wagon, Becky limping with every step. Lexie rummaged inside and came out carrying a pair of stout shoes. She gave them to Becky and told her to tell her mother that they were a necessity not a gift. "Tell her it is just Christian neighbor helping neighbor."

Becky thanked her profusely and sat down by the trail to put them on. When she had them on, she quickly jumped up and left in a hurry to catch up with her family, again calling her thanks over her shoulder. Her foot was so sore that she limped as she walked, even in the shoes Lexie had given her.

David had approached as Lexie and Becky were talking. When Becky was out of hearing, David said, "That was a very kind thing you did, Lexie. You make me proud to know you."

"That was nothing. Christians are supposed to share with one another."

"You're right, but too many people forget that." *I thought she was gorgeous in her blue dress the other night, but she looks just as good in this pink thing. Face it, man; she'd look good in a sack.*

"Hi, Millicent. You are looking extremely fit. Are you feeling okay now?" David asked.

"I'm feeling great. Just one thing could make me feel better. If Johnny would just come walking up, I'd be ecstatic," Millicent said, grinning widely. Lexie and David agreed laughingly that would be the thing. Both were thankful they could be together.

"Say, Lexie, are you doing anything this evening?"

"I'm not sure. David, are we doing anything this evening?"

"I've got to see some patients. If you want to do something with Millicent, I don't mind too much," David said with a hangdog expression and hands crossed over his heart. Lexie and Millicent laughed. "Seriously, I may be late getting back anyway," he said.

Lexie reached over and thumped him on the arm. "Silly man," she said turning to Millicent. "What did you have in mind, Milly?" Lexie asked.

"I'm making a quilt. I thought maybe you would come and keep me company while I work on it. I might even let you get started on one for yourself."

"Okay, I'll come as soon as I can after supper."

That night, as the extended family ate supper of fried ham, beans, and rice, the talk came around to what Lexie had done for Becky. "I'm sure there will be a lot more people like Becky," Sarah said. "I wish we had enough shoes to go around, but we don't. It's too bad we don't have a shoe salesman on the train."

"Maybe we could get some leather from hunting and make moccasins for people who need them. At least they would protect feet for a while. It makes me sad to think that I have money, and I'm unable to help them," David said.

"Get me the leather, and I'll make something. They may not look the best, but they'll be better than nothing," Lexie replied fixedly. "If only there were some Indian women around, they could show us what to do. Maybe we'll see some at the fort when we get there."

After the evening meal, Lexie walked to Millicent's wagon. Soon she and Millicent were deeply involved in sewing quilt blocks together.

"It's going to be a double wedding ring quilt. I'm going to use it on my and Johnny's bed. I want to have it finished before we get to Oregon."

"That's going to take a lot of sewing," Lexie replied.

"I know, but if you and Olivia will help me. I'll have it done." Millicent said excitedly, "I can hardly wait to see him. It seems ages since I saw him. I wish he'd have waited for us, but no, he had to go get everything ready for me. I know I should be appreciative, but I miss him so much."

Lexie thought it was time to interrupt her before she got maudlin. "Do you think you can count on Olivia? She's pretty taken up with John." Lexie stated hoping to divert her attention. Her ploy worked.

"She said that she would help one evening each week, and if we could ride in the wagon with them, she would help some most afternoons."

"That's great. I can help for awhile most afternoons."

"Oh, oh," Millicent said. "Here comes that Lenora Johnson. I don't like her at all."

"Neither do I," Lexie said softly. She watched Lenora approach.

When Lenora got even with the girls she stopped. "Well, how are you two little homemakers tonight?" she asked. Before giving them a chance to answer, she continued, "Have you seen David? I was supposed to meet him, but for the life of me, I can't remember where he said he would be." Lenora carefully watched Lexie's face as she said this. Of course it wasn't true. She kept her fingers crossed, hoping Lexie had too much pride to confront him with what she said.

"Sorry, I can't help you," Lexie replied airily. She carefully schooled her features so that none of her feelings showed. She didn't know whether to believe Lenora or not. She didn't believe David would pretend to be interested in her and then pursue Lenora. On the other hand, she really didn't have a claim on him and she hadn't known him long.

"Well, if you see him, tell him I'm lookin' for him. Toodle loo," she said and walked on.

"Toodle loo?" Lexie whispered, her eyebrows rose.

"Viper!" Millicent said and stabbed the quilt block she was working on viciously.

Lexie agreed whole-heartedly. She wanted to pull Lenora's red hair out, but at the same time, she was enveloped in black depression thinking that David might care for the other girl.

The two girls kept sewing until darkness covered the land, and they could no longer see to sew. They were just putting things away when David arrived to walk Lexie back home. Lexie wanted to hug him and at the same time, rant and rave at him. She opted for silence. Millicent was not so tame.

"Where have you been this evening, David? We haven't seen much of you lately," she said. Both she and Lexie knew that pioneer people treated themselves when they were ill. Unless it was an emergency they couldn't handle, they were unlikely to call a doctor.

"Oh, just here and there. You know how it is," he responded. He didn't tell them that Lenora's mother had suffered sunstroke that day, and that her frantic husband had called him to come, or that Lenora seemed more worried that she would have to do all the work than she was about her mother's health. He would save that information for Lexie and her family.

Mrs. Johnson was an underweight, overworked farm wife. Like Lenora, she had been a beauty in her day, but almost all of her flamboyant red hair had turned to gray. Although she was only forty, her face was deeply wrinkled from too many hours working in the sun. The years she had spent over-taxing her strength left her prey to the sun's fierce temperatures. The stroke had left her right arm and leg without much feeling. Her face on the right side twisted slightly to the side. David just hoped it would be normal again in a few days.

"Are you ready, honey?" He took Lexie's arm. Lexie stiffened, but allowed him to hold her arm. Perplexed, David looked down at her. "See you later, Milly," he said.

"Bye, Milly. I'll see you tomorrow." Lexie told her. She kept silent on the way home. She was upset because she felt David could have said where he had been if he didn't have anything to hide.

After they had walked for a few minutes, David asked, "Anything wrong, honey? You are awfully quiet tonight. Or are you just tired?"

"I'm fine," she said in a cold voice.

David pulled her to a stop. "What's wrong? Have I done something to upset you?"

"I'm sure I don't know what you are talking about. What could you possibly have done to upset me?" Lexie returned in a glacial voice.

"Brrr, it sure is cold out tonight. I think I need my heavy coat," David said. The temperature had seemed hotter that day than any other since the train left Independence.

Lexie ignored his remarks, turned away from him and walked on at a brisk pace. David usually had to pace his steps to match her shorter legs, but not tonight. "If I didn't know better, I'd think we were headed to a fire," David said.

Lexie sniffed and turned up her nose. She didn't reply, but just increased her pace.

For the next three days, Lexie kept David in a deep freeze. At supper the next night, she handed him his plate, turned her back on him without saying a word. Their usual nightly banter was totally missing. The others looked first at him then her. They wondered what was going on, too. She continued this silence throughout the evening. She was especially talkative to the other young men, but maintained her stony silence to David. David was so upset by her behavior that he didn't even think to mention Lenora's mother.

When they had finished eating, David said to Tom and Sarah. "Lexie and I are going for a short walk. We won't be gone long." Lexie stayed where she was standing. David walked over and took her arm. "Come on, this won't take but a minute." Rather than make more of a scene than she already had, Lexie let him lead her away.

"Now, tell me what is going on," David said. "What have I done or not done to put you in such a pelter?"

"You haven't done a thing that I *know* of. Why? Do you feel guilty about something?"

David let that pass. "Well, then, have you made up with Carson without telling me?"

Lexie sent him a look that would wither needles on an evergreen tree, turned, and walked back to the others. David was left standing with hands on hips, looking mystified.

This ritual continued for the next two nights. On the third night,

David didn't come to supper. Lexie was in torment. She could vision him with Lenora. *Maybe I treated him so awful that he won't have anything more to do with me.*

Things were made worse the next day when Lenora came by and thrust the dagger a little deeper. "Well, Lexie, you certainly are looking glum today. Things couldn't be better for me. I think I'm in love, and what's more I know he loves me too." She waggled a finger in Lexie's direction and continued. "I'm sure he'll tell you all about it soon."

With that she continued on her way, elated with the look she had created on Lexie's face. "Couldn't have done better if I'd tried. Carson, old buddy, things are looking up for both of us," she said softly. It didn't bother her at all that everything she had said had been untrue. She felt sure that she could capture David once Lexie was out of the picture. Lexie was left with feelings of rage mingled with despair.

That afternoon Millicent and Lexie were riding together. As usual, Olivia was riding with John Case. They were cantering along when over to the side of the Johnson's wagon stood Lenora and David. Lenora saw them coming. She quickly put her arms around David's neck and kissed him on the cheek. Lexie didn't notice how David quickly removed her arms from himself. She only saw Lenora. Lenora looked like she had just gotten a first glimpse of Heaven.

Lexie sucked in her breath sharply, and spurred her horse on toward the couple. David heard her coming and turned to see who it was. Lexie was amazed that he didn't look guilty. *Just the perversity of man*, she thought.

David turned to meet her. "Well, fancy seeing you here," he said. Lexie ignored him, cast a fulminating glance at Lenora, and rode past them. Millicent cast an unkind look at the two and followed Lexie.

"Oh, dear. David, I didn't mean to cause trouble between you and your girl," Lenora lied. "I was just trying to show my gratitude for your helping my mother."

"Forget it. I did only what any other doctor would do," David's hardened voice said. He shoved his hands into his pant's pockets. With head and shoulders drooping, he strode off. He didn't know what to do. He was terribly afraid he had lost Lexie.

If David thought before that Lexie had frozen him out, that night was like a blizzard. She was frigid to him, completely ignoring him during the meal. She didn't even serve him. She acted as if he weren't there. Sarah got his plate, filled it, and gave it to him. Handing him the plate, she shrugged her shoulders, letting him know she didn't know what was wrong with Lexie.

When they had eaten, David didn't say a word. He simply took Lexie by the arm and walked her away from the wagons. At first she resisted, then went willingly.

"Okay, let's have it. What's been eating you? I can't stand this any longer."

"I'd think you'd be more careful than to let a young girl kiss you in broad daylight. If you want her, just say so. I don't have any claim on you, but don't come honeying around me," Lexie spat out.

"What! You think I'm interested in her? Is that what's been eating at you," he asked, slapping his forehead with his open palm.

"Well, how do you explain it? Kissing one another in broad daylight?" Lexie said, keeping strict control to stop herself from shouting.

"Lexie, honey, now don't fly off the handle. I don't call anyone but you honey. Lenora's mother had sunstroke three days ago. If I had known that was what was bothering you, I could have explained days ago. And if you had looked at me instead of Lenora, you would have seen that she was doing all the kissing and embracing. I feel *nothing* for her."

Lexie wanted to believe him, but she was unsure of David. After Carson, it was hard for her to trust any man.

"Are you satisfied? Do you believe me? I can't stand this wall between us," David told her.

Lexie stood mutely as David lifted her head to look into her face. "Do you?" he asked. Silently, she shook her head yes. *With reservations*, she thought.

David let out a gusty sigh. He hauled her into his arms and lowered his lips to hers. Immediately both of them caught flame. David felt like he had just climbed the highest mountain and Lexie felt as if she had been dropped from a great precipice.

CHAPTER NINE

The following morning the train continued its journey westward. Each day the sun got hotter with no indication of rain in sight. At night, weary travelers circled their wagons with no wasted effort. They made quick work of the evening meal. Exhausted from the rigors of the day, the older people fell into bed. The young, who had more energy and were much more resilient, found nightly pursuits more to their liking.

David and Lexie never felt really sure of one another, but were under a watchful truce. Nothing more was said about an engagement. David was extremely hurt that Lexie didn't trust him, and Lexie, haunted by Lenora's lies, was wary. They gathered with other young people most evenings, each pretending to the other that everything was all right. Some nights they went dancing to the music of a fiddle, banjo, and guitar. Other nights they joined several others and played games of cards. Still other nights they gathered in groups for storytelling. On Wednesday evenings, they met with the older people for mid-week devotions.

Lexie told Olivia, "I feel as if the only time I see you is at devotions."

"Please don't begrudge me my time with John. I'm so happy. I've never been so happy. Just be happy for me." Lexie assured her that she was very happy for her.

The atmosphere in which the young people met was always one of conviviality. David and Lexie didn't want Millicent to be left out of the fun, so they invited her to go with them.

"You can't stay by yourself all the way to Oregon," Lexie argued. Millicent said she didn't want to be an unwelcome third, but David quickly reassured her that would not be the case.

On the third evening that they went to a dance, a young man named James Blackwell approached the three young people. "Hi, I'm James Blackwell. May I have this dance?" he asked Millicent. Millicent looked at Lexie as though asking permission.

"Of course," Lexie answered for her. "Millicent, dance with him. This is Millicent Bond. I'm Lexie Fletcher, and this is David Duvall."

"Glad to meet you," James told them. He was a perfect match for Millicent. He was tall, muscular, with rich auburn hair and green eyes. When Millicent didn't say no, he took her by the arm and led her to the other dancers. David and Lexie watched as Millicent came out of her shell. Soon she was laughing and having a good time.

"How come I've never seen you at one of these shindigs before, pretty lady," James asked.

"I've had a fever, and so I didn't get to go to the dance at the fort. But the real reason I haven't been to the activities is that I'm engaged to be married as soon as we reach Oregon."

"Who's the lucky man," James asked. "I take it he's not on the train?"

"No, he's already in Oregon waiting for me to come. I'm a very lucky girl. He is a wonderful man."

"Just my luck. When I meet the girl of my dreams, she's already spoken for."

Millicent wasn't sure if James was serious or not. He looked serious enough, but since she didn't know him, she decided he was joking. However, James was deadly serious. *We have time enough for me to give a whirl at changing her mind before we get there.* Although he felt bad about trying to take her away from her Johnny, he wasn't going to let that stop him.

James walked with them back to Millicent's wagon. The next day Lexie casually asked Millicent if she had told James that she was engaged.

"Of course I did. You don't think I'd keep it a secret, do you?"

That evening, Millicent and James drifted together again. Each night the same thing happened. Then the two started taking walks together.

Millicent stopped talking about Johnny. She didn't seem to care whether or not she got her quilt, which she had been so desperate to finish, quilted before she reached Oregon. Other young people quickly came to see them as a twosome. One afternoon after Lexie had seen the two embracing the previous night, Lexie asked Millicent what she intended doing about Johnny.

"Oh, Lexie, I'm so miserable. I thought I loved Johnny to distraction, but now I feel the same way about James. What am I to do? We didn't intend to fall in love. James says that he won't let me go, and I'm sure Johnny will say the same thing. It's getting so that I can't sleep at night."

It wasn't until Millicent said that, that Lexie noticed the dark circles under Millicent's eyes. "Milly, this is something you have to decide for yourself. You can't marry two men. You'll just have to make up your mind about which one you want to spend the rest of your life with. Just be careful to choose the right one, so that you won't be sorry later. I know that you know how serious marriage is and how long a lifetime with the wrong man would be. Have you prayed about it?" Lexie asked.

"Of course, I have, but I haven't gotten an answer."

"Well, the scripture says to wait on the Lord. I don't think anyone can help you with this." Lexie hated to see her friend so miserable, but she didn't know how to help her. "Are both James and Johnny Christians?"

"Both are baptized believers."

David and James had become fast friends since he and Millicent had come to know one another. David talked to James about his feelings for Millicent.

"David, she is the best thing that ever happened to me. I know what I'm doing is not very honorable, but I just can't walk away. Besides, she feels the same way about me. Would you like both of us to make the mistake of our lives, if I let her go? When she sees him again, she'll know which of us is right. I'm sure it will be me, at least, I'm praying it will be."

Day after day rolled by. Temperatures were extremely hot. Some of the animals dropped in their traces. Food was not a problem. Everyone still had ample provisions, but the water was getting short. On good days, the train might make twenty miles, but on bad days, it might travel only seven miles.

Each day seemed longer and more grueling to Lexie. No longer could she spend so much time helping Millicent or visiting with her and Olivia as she had been doing. She spent more of each day driving the wagon to relieve Sarah while Tom saw to the other wagons and livestock. Sarah was not standing the heat well at all.

Several times Lexie saw Becky wearing her shoes. She was thankful that she had them to give to Becky. She saw others not so fortunate.

The train reached Fort Kearny, but it stopped only long enough to replenish supplies. The wagon master said they must continue on if they had any hope of reaching Oregon before the snows started.

At the Platte River, the train stopped, so the women could do their much-needed family laundry and replenish water supplies. Although it was designated as a time to rest, there was very little rest for the women.

Lexie helped Sarah as she did at home. A combination of the lye soap and the cold water soon had Lexie's hands and arms red and covered with a prickly rash. The itching made it almost impossible not to scratch them. *Maybe I'll get a little attention from David now, since it's almost time for the men to come to eat.*

David was trying to keep his need for Lexie from being too noticeable to her because he didn't want to rush her. He had come to know that she was unsure of him. He had been attentive, but not lover-like toward her when they were alone; however, he never missed what Lexie was doing or how she looked. As he approached, he saw her rubbing her arms. He observed the rash, as soon as he came close. He came over to her and carefully lifted up one arm to examine it. "Lexie, what have you been doing to become so broken out with rash?"

"I just helped Mother with the laundry. I do it all the time at home. I guess it's the soap. We put more lye than usual into it when we made it. We thought it would help disinfect things. My arms are about to drive me crazy with itching," she said, her body shaking with discomfort. "I've put baking soda on them ever since they started itching, but it hasn't helped," she said, freeing her arm to rub it vigorously against her side.

"Lexie, darling, I told you not to scratch those arms. I can hear you all the way in here. It will only spread the rash. Isn't that right, David?" Sarah called from within the wagon where she was resting.

"It certainly will," David replied. He cupped Lexie's face in his hands, quickly pressed a feather-light kiss to her lips, and said, "Don't rub it, I'll be back in just a jiffy." True to his word, he was back in only minutes. Lexie was still rubbing her arm.

"I can't help it," she told him when he scolded her gently. He made soothing noises and sat her down on one of the campstools. Deftly he applied a cream to the backs of both hands and to her arms.

"Tender little baby skin," he said, placing a kiss on her wrist. "Why didn't you call me to come? Surely you must have known that I'd have something to make you more comfortable?"

"Oh, that feels so good. I've been miserable all afternoon," she said, smiling up into his face. Her heart had done a flip-flop when he kissed her wrist.

"I repeat, young lady, why didn't you call or come for me?"

Well, if you must know, I didn't want to bother you. You haven't been around much lately," she said, her uncertainty showing.

"I can always make time for you and your family. I'll try to do better in the future," he told her. *Honey, if you only knew, I've been neglecting you, but not because I want to.* "This heat is getting to people, especially the older ones. I've had three cases of people who became overheated since yesterday. Only this morning, old Mrs. McGruder had sunstroke. Things looked iffy for a while, but she rallied. I believe she'll be okay. In fact she may fare better than Mrs. Johnson."

Lexie watched David intently while he was speaking. *There he goes again. I don't know why I get my hopes up. Just when I think he cares for me, he turns cold on me, brings in my family, and becomes all doctor. He's probably missing some girl from home, if not Lenora. I don't mean a thing to him, except someone who needed help to get out of an unpleasant situation. Maybe that's why he hasn't been around lately. He's afraid I'll expect too much from him. Maybe he even knows how I feel about him.* Lexie's face became as white as ivory, and she felt sick. She could feel the heat creep up on her face and neck until they were suffused with color. She felt she would just die if he knew how much she cared for him when he didn't care for her.

Lexie quickly turned away from him to keep him from seeing her embarrassment. She began filling the plates for the men with sweet potatoes and salt-cured ham, passing them to Sarah, who had come out of the wagon to help Lexie with the meal. Sarah added beans and dried apricots to each plate. Sarah made a special effort to help with the evening meal and eat with the others. Lexie and Tom were very worried about her and tried to get her to rest more.

David wondered what he had said to cause Lexie to blush so. He thought she looked adorable when she blushed. He hoped her thoughts were about him.

The meal was eaten with the usual warm camaraderie, but David was quieter than usual. He seemed worried about something. As soon as everyone had finished, Lexie started to gather up the dishes, but Sarah forestalled her, "Lexie, I'll do dishes tonight. You shouldn't have your hands in water. Should she, doctor?" She only called David doctor when she wanted his professional opinion.

"No, she definitely should not."

"I'll do the dishes tonight," Tom said. "Mother, you sit down. I can have these done in a jiffy."

"All right, but I feel a fraud for not helping."

Tom led Sarah over to a rocking chair that he had unpacked for her when she became ill and seated her. He began to gather everything needed to wash the dishes. Abe, who had not left yet, quickly offered his help. Tom accepted with alacrity. He handed a dishtowel to Abe and picked up a kettle of water from the fire and poured the hot water into the gray granite dishpan. He added soap flakes and plunged his hands into the hot dishwater.

Turning to Lexie, David asked, "Lexie, are you very tired tonight?"

"No, not tonight, but tomorrow I may be. The days seem to get longer and each day harder. I don't understand how those women and children can walk all day and then do all the evening work too."

"All I can say is they are a sturdy lot. Since you are not too tired, let's go for a walk, if your parents don't mind. I want to talk to you."

Turning to Tom and Sarah, he asked, "Do you mind if Lexie goes for a stroll with me?"

Tom turned around, shook the hot soapy water from his hands, and answered for the both of them. "Don't mind at all. Just see that the Indians don't get her," he said, tongue in cheek. They had seen no signs of Indians, nor did Tom expect to see any. He was thankful that David and Lexie seemed on good terms again.

David and Lexie laughed, and Sarah smiled gently. David offered his hand to Lexie and asked, "Coming?"

"All right," Lexie said, smiling and took his hand. *All right is mild to what I feel. Wild horses wouldn't stop me.* "It looks like others have the same idea," she said as they passed several other couples walking. When David only nodded, she added, "You are awfully quiet tonight. Are you worried about something or someone?"

"Yes, I guess you could say that I am," David answered.

"Anything that you'd care to talk about?" Before he could answer, she blurted out, "Does it concern our fake engagement?"

"I'll tell you in just a few moments," he said, squeezing her hand.

As soon as they were far enough from the wagon so that they wouldn't be overheard, David stopped, turned Lexie to face himself and asked, "Lexie, just how important was Fullbrite to you?"

Surprised, not expecting such a question, Lexie answered, "We dated for several weeks. Why?"

"Is that all? Did you promise to marry him?"

"No, I didn't!" she replied, shaking her head no vigorously. "He asked me to marry him, but I told him no. He wasn't then, nor from all indication, is he now a Christian. And you know what the Bible says about being unequally yoked. He said some very unkind things. I guess you could say that he said brutal things to me, and I refused to see him again. I've discovered since then that I never could have married him.

I never loved him. I was certainly thankful that I hadn't agreed to marry him. It would have been much harder to break it off, if I had agreed to become his wife. Now you know the whole story," she said earnestly.

"Did anything unusual happen after that?"

"Well, I'm not sure I know what you mean, but I thought one thing was strange. I don't mean to sound like a braggart, but I always had a number of gentleman callers before Carson started coming to my house. After we broke up, no one came. Is that what you are talking about, something like that? Do you think *he's* the reason they stopped coming?"

"Exactly. Today, one of the men on the train, I don't even know his name, said to me, 'I hear you just broke up an engagement between Carson Fullbrite and that Fletcher girl. A man shouldn't try to steal another man's property.' He then proceeded to tell me that Carson was telling everyone that you were engaged to him, and that I came between you two. That's probably why no fellows came calling, for which *I'm* thankful. And that's not all. Have you noticed that Fullbrite is always around somewhere watching you?"

"No, you're joking, surely. What do you mean, he watches me?"

"I mean that he's always somewhere skulking around, scuttling out of sight when someone is coming, but he watches everything you do." Taking her by the shoulders, he said, "I want you to promise me that you'll never go anywhere alone or stay by yourself. Promise me?" he asked, cupping her face in his hands.

"Well, I guess so; at least I'll try. Do you really think he'd hurt me?" she asked unbelieving.

"I don't know, and I don't want to find out the hard way. Don't look now, but if you look closely, I'll bet you'll find he's following us now."

Lexie looked at the peaceful night. The stars hung low like a canopy over their heads. It was hard to believe that someone who had professed to love her would hurt her. Surely David was mistaken. They walked past a group of young people dancing. "Hi, you two. Come join us," Ted Jones, a lively, tow-headed young man, called.

"Thanks, but not tonight. Looks like fun though," David told him.

Lexie and David walked on past the dancers. "I'll look now," she said quietly. Lexie casually turned to look back as though she were watching the dancers. Really, she was scanning the area to see if she could see Carson. Sure enough, she spotted him flatten himself against a wagon when she turned around.

"I see him!" she whispered, clutching David's arm. "He's right back there, and when I turned around, he huddled against a wagon. I can't believe it. I still find it very hard to believe he would hurt me."

"Come on, I'll take you home. I'll have a talk with Tom about this."

"Oh, no, please don't trouble him unnecessarily," she begged. "He'll tell Mother, and she's a worrywart anyway. Besides you know she's not well. It might cause her to become worse if she knew. It might just be a coincidence that he was there."

"Too many times for coincidences," David said, shaking his head. "Tell you what, I'll pray about what you've said, and then I'll try to follow God's leading. Will you trust me to do that?" David didn't tell her that he'd already been praying about what he should do. He knew that some men went off the deep end when a woman thwarted them. A sense of urgency flooded his being. He felt sure that God was telling him to warn Tom of the suspected danger to Lexie. Despite what Lexie said, he planned to see Tom first thing in the morning.

CHAPTER TEN

The morning brought misty gray skies and a black horizon. By the time the wagons were ready to roll, it had begun to rain. Soon after, the sky opened up and torrents of rain came down. At noon, the rain was still pounding down on the wagons.

Some of the wagons were not waterproofed well enough to withstand the onslaught, and possessions, as well as people, were getting soaked. Others had wagon toppings oiled with linseed oil. Buffalo hides and tallow or tar waterproofed the sides of their wagons.

The train stopped at noon, but only leftovers from breakfast were eaten. No one tried to build a campfire.

The heavy rains soaked into the dry ground. The trail rapidly became a quagmire of mud. Still, the rain continued coming down in sheets. People who wore oilcloth coats were much more comfortable than those without them. The water rolled off the waterproofed coats and hats. Those without waterproofing covered up with cloth coats or blankets, which soon became saturated.

The rain was coming from the southwest. Since the train was traveling in that direction, drivers were constantly working to keep their teams headed into the rain. Those driving the stock had no less trouble, for cows, as well as horses and oxen, would try to bolt away from the herd going west.

When the wagons stopped for the night, the rain had not let up at all.

Supper for the Fletchers consisted of hardtack, beef jerky, which David had purchased at Fort Kearney, and dried fruit. Lexie and Sarah still had a few lemons, but they didn't even try to make lemonade. Everyone settled for cider. Though quarters were cramped, the rain would inundate the food, so drivers grabbed their plates and headed for the inside of their wagons. David squeezed inside the Fletchers' wagon to eat with them.

When they were finished, David said, "Well, there will be no night activities tonight. No dances, visiting, or walks in the moonlight." Before anyone could comment, he turned to Lexie and continued, "Lexie, you said you'd trust me, so I'm going to tell your folks about Carson Fullbrite. He ignored Lexie's look of alarm. "Tom, I meant to tell you this morning, but because of the rain, I was sure Lexie would be safe today."

"What do you mean, Lexie safe?" Sarah asked, concern coloring her voice. "Is Lexie in some kind of danger?"

Lexie sat twisting her hands, looking distressed as David informed them of what he had observed. She felt that he was making too much of it, but on the other hand, she *had* seen Carson shrink against that wagon.

"Who knows what he might do, maybe nothing, but I don't think any of us want to take that chance. It's doubtful that he'd do anything while your wagons are so near the front of the line. Too many people following could see what he was doing, but when your wagons go to the back of the line, there could be danger for her," David told them.

Lexie looked at her parents. Sarah had her hands clasped over her breast, her face full of horror. Tom's lips were drawn in a straight line, his teeth clenched. Tension was visible in every line of his body.

"You are really beginning to frighten me," Lexie said in a soft, timid voice, trying to make light of the situation. She looked from one to another but could see only deep concern on their faces. David took her hand in his and squeezed gently. Lexie thought his look was one of love and understanding. She hoped she wasn't mistaken. It almost made her cry.

"Sorry, honey, it's for your own protection," Tom said, patting her on the shoulder.

"Yes, we must take no chances. I never did like that Carson Fullbrite anyway," Sarah declared.

All agreed that Lexie would need careful watching for anything hurtful Carson might try.

After a wet, uncomfortable night for the travelers, the rain had not slackened at all. No fires cooked breakfast. Many people left without eating at all. Small children drank milk, if their families could provide it. Others nibbled on leftover biscuits or hardtack.

The temperature had dropped during the night so that the pelting rain seemed almost frigid after such hot temperatures of the previous days.

As the rain soaked the ground, mud grew deep. By noon it was ankle high on the men's boots, by afternoon, almost knee high. Most women and children took to the wagons.

The wagons slipped and skidded around in the deep mire. Frequently a wagon got stuck, and neighboring drivers were forced to push it out of the deep ruts made by earlier wagons on the trail or because it sank down in the ever thickening mud. Soon the wagons of the Smythe train started making their own ruts to challenge others that would be following.

Since the Fletchers' wagons were close to the front of the line, they didn't have as much trouble as those behind them. Tom and his drivers helped pull others from layers of mud to get back on track. Sarah and Lexie had a hard time controlling their team. Lexie fervently wished that the train would stop, but it continued on. David was unable to help. He was busy with a difficult birth, the first of ten on the train.

About two o'clock in the afternoon, the train came to what was normally a small stream. Usually crossing it would have been no problem, but today, because of all the rain, it was swollen, and the churning water was surging swiftly downstream. Many of the men left their wagons and gathered at the stream to consult with one another about the safety of crossing.

"I say we go now and not wait until it stops raining. Who knows how much longer it will be before it stops," young Caleb Taylor said.

"Are you willing to endanger your whole family just to get across a day sooner?" Henry Blakemore, a middle-aged farmer, asked.

Most of the men seemed to have forgotten that wagon master Smythe would make the final decision. "Why don't we ask Mr. Smythe?" David asked. "It's his business to know these things."

Mr. Smythe, usually very decisive, answered, "I'm not sure about what we should do. The creek is in a bad way, but those snows that we'll run into will be bad too. My best suggestion would be to wait, but I think we'll decide this democratically. Majority rules."

Shouts of "Yes, vote, majority rules" rang out, but some of the men just shook their heads, mumbling about how foolish it was to even think about crossing today. A show of hands showed more in favor of crossing. This time angry shouts filled the air, amid raised arms waving victory signs. The trail had been wide, and wagons traveled four abreast. It was decided to have them cross one at a time.

When it came time for the first wagon to enter the flooding stream, the driver balked. "I'll not enter that river. I value my family too much to put them into danger," Joshua Johnson, a middle aged, levelheaded man, declared. "Besides, I voted no!"

"I'll not force anyone to cross today. I think it's too risky to go today, too, and I'll not take the responsibility. Anybody crossing is responsible for his own actions," the wagon master said.

A young hothead, Caleb Price, who had been most vocal about crossing today, spoke up. "Well, I'm not afraid. Johnson, you sissy, get your wagon out of my way."

Wagon master Smythe spoke sternly. "Mr. Price, that remark was uncalled for. I just hope you don't rue your decision before the end of the day. Flooding is nothing to sneeze at. It is extremely dangerous because we can't judge depth. I think an apology is due Mr. Johnson."

Price swallowed a couple of times, extended his hand and said, "You're right. I was way out of line. My apologies, Mr. Johnson. Sometimes I let my fool tongue run away from me."

Joshua Johnson took Price's hand and shook it. "That's all right, friend. All of us want to get to Oregon before winter. Maybe I am a coward. I'll move my wagon back. You go right ahead."

The men returned to their wagons, and the Price wagon took the lead. Mrs. Price came from inside the wagon, holding her three-month-old baby, wrapped in a blanket and a piece of oilcloth. A wife of less than two years, she was still very deeply in love with her husband and trusted him completely. She sat down by her husband on the wagon seat and placed the baby in her lap.

A clicking of the reins, and the horses started forward. At the edge of the water, the horses balked. Their eyes rolled. They threw back their heads, and tried to turn away from the churning flood. Price flicked his whip on each horse's back, then a second time harder when they still shied and failed to move. When the whip cracked a third time on their backs, the horses surged forward into the water. The crowd on the bank shouted and cheered.

The Price wagon had reached a distance of almost halfway across the water without a hitch when a log, being swept along on the fast moving current, smashed into the side of the wagon. The wagon lurched drunkenly. Mrs. Price screamed, jumping upright to stand in the wagon, clutching the baby to her breast.

"Emmy, get down!" Price yelled.

A smaller log, on the heels of the first, hit the wagon, causing it to sway again. With a scream, Mrs. Price tumbled into the swirling water, still clasping the baby. The swirling current jerked the baby from the screaming woman's arms. Both she and the baby went under, came up, were whirled around and around, and went under again. The powerful current sped them downstream. They were totally helpless in the surge of flood.

An unnatural hush fell on the people watching. David yelled, "Men get ropes!" He and three other men quickly tied ropes around their waists. Four more men anchored those men to themselves. The first four men jumped into the water.

David prayed for help for the woman, baby, and for the rescuers as he dived into the foamy water. "Heavenly Father, please help all of us. Deliver all of us from harm, according to your will. In Jesus' name I pray, Amen."

Swimming as rapidly as possible, buffeted by the strong current,

David reached Mrs. Price first. Abe was right behind him. "Abe, you take her, I'll get the baby," he said breathlessly. David handed Mrs. Price's unconscious form to Abe, who was gasping for breath. She was limp and difficult to handle in the current. Samuel reached them as David handed Mrs. Price to Abe. The two men helped one another get her ashore.

David swam on downstream looking for the baby. He found the oilcloth and blanket. Farther downstream, he found the baby; face down in the water, caught in some brush at the side of the river. He hauled the baby out of the brush and held her above the water.

Men began towing him toward the bank. It was extremely difficult battling the current and holding the baby above the water. David was thankful for their help. By the time he reached the bank, Abe and Samuel already had Emmy Price out of the water. David had given up all hope of saving the baby, and he had serious misgivings about Mrs. Price surviving the ordeal.

The men had carefully laid Mrs. Price on the bank, and were attempting in vain to revive her when David reached them. Caleb Taylor was striving to pump the water out of her lungs. David handed the baby to one of the women, shaking his head negatively, and knelt to help with Mrs. Price. Women had gathered, watching silently, unable to check the tears that flowed freely.

Caleb Price stood on the opposite bank wringing his hands. Tears streamed down his face. "Oh, why was I such a fool. I knew it all. Oh, Emmy, why did you stand up? Emmy, what will I do without you, and my baby, my sweet little baby." He sank down onto the ground, consumed by his grief.

John Case and three other young men in the train immediately mounted their horses to swim across to comfort him. "We'll stay with him tonight. We're needed more there than here," John called back over his shoulder.

Olivia threw her arms around her mother and wept openly. "I'm so afraid for John and those other men. I'm afraid they will be swept away too. I didn't even get to say goodbye or tell John that I love him," she said, sobbing.

Mrs. Green held her daughter in her arms comforting her, a haggard expression on her face. "I pray to God you are wrong. I wish we were back home. Don't cry so. John knows you love him."

Lexie went over to Olivia to try to comfort her. She was very thankful that David was back safe and sound. "Livy, honey, don't cry so." Lexie always called Olivia Livy when they were especially close. "God will take good care of John. I just feel it in my bones. Remember that no matter what happens, God is in control," Lexie told her. She felt she couldn't tell even Olivia how scared she had been when David was in the water.

"I sure hope you are right." Olivia said tightly. "I don't think I could live without him. You don't have any idea what it's like to love someone to distraction," Olivia managed to get out between heart wrenching sobs. I know we're all in God's hands, but sometimes His decisions are hard to take."

Lexie thought, *Livy, if you only knew. You are not the only one who loves a man to distraction. At least you know yours loves you in return.*

The crowd stood watching with bated breath as one man's horse drifted downstream, but after a hard struggle in the rolling water, finally it recovered. With the rider still on its back, it reached the opposite side of the river.

David did his best to revive Emmy Price, but to no avail. Most of the women onlookers cried silently, tears streaming down their faces, mingling with the still pounding rain, but two women stood wailing.

"Look what's happened! I didn't want to leave my good home and go to a wilderness, but you had to have your own way. You didn't even care that I'm expecting, or that the baby will come before we get there. How would you like to have a baby on this miserable trail?" a short, very pregnant woman with red hair to match her temper ranted at her husband.

"Hush now Effie," her husband Clem Abbott, at least six feet tall, told her, patting her shoulder awkwardly. Effie jerked away from him, refusing to be comforted.

When the crowd saw that Mrs. Price was gone, men took off their hats, even though the rain pelted down on their heads, and all bowed their heads in prayer. Some even knelt in the mud. Since John Case was across the river, Tom Fletcher led the prayer for the Price family and for strength for all the people on the train.

The rain stopped that night. By morning, dark gray clouds had moved on, revealing patches of bright blue in the sky. Families were beginning to forage for something to eat for breakfast, since they still couldn't make a fire for cooking.

Sam had been on guard duty during the early watch last night. He told the Fletcher group that the rain had stopped about nine o'clock. While the extended family was eating, the sun pushed its first golden rays through the swiftly departing clouds.

"I'm so thankful to see that sun again. It seems ages since we saw it," Sarah said.

"Yes, maybe now we can get rid of that musty smell inside the wagon," Lexie replied.

Tom finished his breakfast and got up, set his plate on the table, and drained the last of his cider. "Well, *I*, for one, will be glad to have a cup of coffee again. That cider is good, and I'm thankful for it, but it doesn't come close to a cup of strong hot coffee in the morning." The others agreed.

"Guess I'll push off to take care of the animals." He gave Sarah a quick peck on the cheek and waved a hand in goodbye to Lexie. Turning to David he asked, "Are you coming, Dave?"

"Sure am," David answered, getting up, and handing his plate to Lexie. He looked at her intently, as though storing a picture of her, bent and placed a quick kiss on her cheek, and said, "I'll see you later." He said goodbye to Sarah and followed Tom toward the rear of the train.

The women cleaned up the breakfast dishes and began to plan what they were to have for supper. After that, they decided see what they could do to remove some of the mud from inside the wagon.

"Sarah said, "We have plenty of water, but it is too muddy to clean anything until the mud settles. We can't even do the laundry. We can, however, string a rope line from our wagon to our supply wagon and hang up some of the clothes that got wet," She picked up a saturated shirt of Tom's, holding it aloft.

"Good idea, Mother," Lexie said, squeezing water from a blouse. She handed the blouse to Sarah. "I'll find the rope." In a short time, the line was up and clothes were gently blowing in the breeze. Other women had the same idea, and before long, it looked like a regular Monday's washday. Lines were strung from tree to tree, wagon-to-wagon, and wagon to tree.

"Mother, I think I'm going to walk down to the crossing to see if the water has gone down any."

"Wait just a moment," Sarah replied. "I'm not going to let you go by yourself after what David said." She quickly climbed down onto the wagon wheel and jumped to the ground. "I guess I'm not too old to have a little jump left in me," she said laughing as she slithered in the mud. "Your old mother still has it," she said, trying to shake mud off her foot.

Lexie laughed and said, "Still spry as the proverbial spring chicken, and you are not old. Come on, let's go," she said. Taking Sarah by the arm they began sloshing through the deep mud, walking toward the water. Both of them were surprised when they reached the water.

A number of people stood looking at the ravages left by the flood while visiting with one another. The tragedy seemed to draw people together.

To everyone's surprise, the water had receded within its banks, so that the stream looked quite normal. Only the debris left on the bank gave indication of what had occurred.

"I believe we can cross today," one of the older men said.

"Not today," a younger man argued. "We need to wait for the mud to dry up."

Olivia's father spoke up. "If we wait for that mud to dry, we could be stuck here a week or more."

People began to argue the pros and cons of going on. About that time, wagon master Smythe walked up. He had heard their bickering. Taking the decision into his own hands, he said, "We leave tomorrow at the usual time. That's final, ladies and gentlemen."

The men who had spent the night with Caleb Price brought him back later that morning. Several of the older ladies in the train took him under their wings. They stayed with him during the short burial service

John Case held.

John told the people that Emmy Price was a good wife and mother. After a short eulogy, he read from the scripture Jesus' words, *I am the resurrection and the life. He that believeth in me, though he were dead, yet shall he live.* He also told them that Jesus said *I am the way, the truth, and the life. No man cometh to the Father but by me.* He followed by saying that Emmy had accepted that Way, that she and her baby were now resting in the arms of God. Hardly a dry eye could be found in the entire group.

Lexie stood, with head bowed, between her mother and David. David held her hand tightly. She said a prayer that Carson and the other people there who didn't know God would respond to John's words during the service.

Some of the men had worked all morning nailing a rough coffin together. Mother and child were wrapped in a blanket and buried together. As the coffin was lowered into the new grave, Caleb was overcome with grief and collapsed onto the ground. He had to be carried inside a wagon to lie down. He could be heard sobbing brokenly all afternoon. About dusk he fell into a fitful sleep.

Wagon master Smythe told some of the drivers at the end of the line to drive their wagons over the grave to keep wild animals and Indians from digging up the bodies. They made sure that Caleb Price was not told. David had given Caleb some laudanum, and he slept long after the train left the next morning.

Early the next morning the train started the trek across the water and on to the prairie. Some slipping and sliding occurred, but no further mishaps cropped up.

The temperature became hotter with each passing day. The sun beat down mercilessly on the weary travelers. The prairie grass, taller than a man standing, wilted and turned brown. The lovely purple, pink, and yellow wildflowers scattered on the landscape bowed their heads and died. After so much natural beauty, now all around the train was desolation. Since there was no wood to be found, grass became the fuel for the campfires. Children and adults alike gathered the long grass and twisted it into thick ropes to be used as firewood. Hands became hardened and calloused. The dry grass cut softer hands.

The livestock became skittish. Some of the men complained about the spooky, nightly guard duty. They had to be careful that no livestock wandered off or that none was stolen by Indians. So far, every day the count was right.

The tall grass gave way to barren places. Dust clouds from the wagons permeated the air. It rolled thick around the wagons. Men, women, and children alike covered their faces with bandannas to keep from breathing the choking swirls. After a few days of traveling in the unending dust, some families rebelled.

"Why should I be the one to catch all this dust?" Abe Turner, a large burly man complained to Mr. Smythe. "We've been eating this dust for days, now," he said, scratching his baldhead.

"Everyone takes a turn at being first and last and all the places in between. You agreed to the rules when you signed up. The only time you get out of line is if you are not ready to leave with the train, then you go to the back. If my rules are not to your satisfaction, you can always leave the train." After Mr. Smythe had adamantly given the same message to several families, complaints about the dust stopped. People voiced their dissatisfaction only within their families.

As the train progressed, people who had been too tired to visit at first became used to the grueling days. Women gathered in clusters to talk about home and the new life they expected to have. Children raced and played with one another to pass the long days. Each evening after dinner, people gathered together to play games, dance, and visit.

With each passing day, the land became more parched. People prayed for rain, but none came. Almost daily, someone collapsed on the trail and had to be treated for heat exhaustion. After a week of almost unbearable conditions, gray clouds gathered. Lightning flashed and crashed, streaking across the sky, followed by deafening rolls of thunder. The lightning was worse than most people had ever seen. Children began to cry, and refused to be comforted. Women hid their faces in their aprons. Some drivers had trouble controlling their teams and livestock.

Lexie and David were riding together on his wagon, giving Abe a break, when the lightning started. Suddenly the lightning crashed in a ball of fire into the ground right in front of David's wagon. The air crackled with its fury. The horses shied, and it took all David's strength to control the bucking team. The wagon swayed fearfully. Lexie leaned against the back of the wagon seat as hard as she could and braced her feet against the front of the wagon, her hands flattened on the seat, to support herself. When David had control of the team, he turned to Lexie. "You know, you are an exceptional young lady."

"What do you mean?" Lexie replied.

"With an almost runaway team, you never made a sound, and you never turned a hair. Most girls would have been screaming the house down."

"Oh, I was afraid, but I trust you." she said smiling sweetly. Her answer greatly pleased David. He gave her such a look of love that she felt her bones were melting.

"I'll do everything in my power to try to keep your trust," he told her softly.

Lexie was trying to think up a suitable reply when someone behind them yelled, "Fire!" People all over the train turned to look. One woman screamed, "We'll all be killed." As one, everyone walking ran and hopped onto the nearest wagon. Some climbed into the back, some in front. David and Lexie leaned over the sides of the wagon and could see a trail of smoke in the distance.

"It's a prairie fire! The lightning must have struck the prairie grass," David said. Everyone dreaded prairie fire. There was no sanctuary. People began whipping their teams in their efforts to outrun the fire. In the distance, Lexie could see a few rapidly licking flames spreading toward them. At break-neck speed, wagons began pulling out of line, driving six or eight abreast trying to escape the inferno coming toward them. Teams of horses swiftly outpaced the slower oxen driven wagons, leaving them behind.

"I see flames! What will we do?" Lexie asked anxiously.

"Hold on tight, dear. Don't be frightened. Mr. Smythe told me early this morning that we were only about six miles from the next stream. If we can reach it, and if it's deep and wide enough, we may have a

chance. Just trust in God, and we'll be okay, no matter what happens."
He whipped his team, and it lurched forward, increasing its pace.
"Lexie, honey, pray like you've never prayed before."

"I already am."

The smell of smoke became thicker. Black billowing clouds of
smoke came rolling toward the train. Pandemonium broke loose. Cries
of terror could be heard. Screams rent the air. Some drivers who
thought those in front of them were not going fast enough began
yelling, cursing, and swearing for the slower wagons to get out of the
way.

"You'd think instead of swearing, they'd be praying too," Lexie
said.

"Trouble brings out the worst in some people," David answered,
urging his team onward.

The wind began to rise, whipping the flames faster. It was becoming
difficult to breathe; the smoke was getting so thick. All along the trail,
animals were racing with the wagons, trying to outrun the fiery furnace.
A group of antelope trying to outrun the inferno raced past the wagon.
The wagons raced through the dark afternoon with no sign of water in
sight. Coughing, Lexie turned around to look at the wagons behind
them. Alarm covered every face. Children were crying, and mothers in
their terror were holding them in their arms, desperately trying to
comfort them.

While David drove, he prayed. *Father, I pray that you'll deliver all
of us from this fire. But if we don't make it, thank you for letting me
know of your love and salvation and for letting me know this wonderful
young woman. Please, let this ordeal be over quickly. In Jesus' name,
I pray. Amen.* "Lexie, honey, if we don't make it, I'm thankful to know
that we'll be together forever with our Lord."

"I know. I'm thankful too. I'd like to believe that everyone on this
train would make it to Heaven, but I know they probably won't."

Both Lexie and David turned to look behind them. They were
horror-struck to find the conflagration had advanced to just a few
hundred yards behind the last wagons.

"Please, Heavenly Father, please protect them and us." Lexie prayed aloud. "Please help us. In Jesus' name, I pray. Amen." She repeated the prayer over and over.

Suddenly a streak of lightning flashed alarmingly, followed by a terrifically loud blast of thunder. The windows of the sky opened and emptied a deluge of water onto the earth. The smoke grew thicker, but the flames began to disappear from sight.

"Thank you, God!" David shouted. "Thank you, Lord."

"I was never so grateful to see rain in my life," Lexie said. Forgetting herself, she grabbed David and hugged him. "I'm so glad we're okay." Black streaks from the rain and smoke ran down their faces.

David threw his arms around her, almost squeezing the life out of her. "Lexie, honey, the feeling is more than mutual."

Many people got down from the wagons and knelt in prayer of thankfulness. David and Lexie, with hands clasped, were two of the first to kneel in the rain. Two smoke covered scoffers came walking toward the front of the train. "Just look at them," one said. "Don't they realize it was just nature having her way when it began to rain? A few more minutes we would have made it to that river coming up." He was grossly overweight and wheezing as he spoke. It was evident that the smoke had not done his overtaxed lungs any good.

"I'm truly sorry for you," Lexie told them. "I'll pray for you." The two men had turned to look at her when she started to speak. They looked at each other, shook their heads, and continued walking.

"I'd better go find out if everyone is all right. All that smoke is very harmful to some of the people on the train, especially those with breathing problems," David said.

"I'll go with you as far as our wagons. I want to be sure Daddy and Mother are okay."

Soon everyone was back on their wagons and headed for the stream. Everyone drank to their fill, began washing away the grime on faces and hands, and cleaning up the smoke damage from the fire.

David was washing his face in the stream when a young man named Benny Matthews approached him. He was staggering along, coughing violently. He was a thin, cadaverous looking young man of twenty-five. His brown hair was lackluster. His cheeks had twin bright spots of red color. David knew without examining him that he was suffering from consumption.

"Doc," he said between bouts of coughing. "I think I got too much smoke today. I can't seem to quit coughing, and it's hard for me to breathe." He sank to the ground on his knees. "Could you give me something for it?"

Without needing to, David asked, "How long have you had this cough?"

"For about eight months. But it keeps getting worse all the time. Before coming out here, I worked as a miner back in Kentucky. My wife, Jane, and I thought that if we came west where the air was dry, I'd get shed of it. It hasn't happened that way. This morning I coughed up some blood. You got to help me, Doc. My wife is going to have a baby. If somethin' happens to me, who'll take care of them? You haven't met my Jane, have you, Doc?" When David shook his head no, Benny said, "She's a cute little thing. She has big blue eyes, and honey colored hair. She doesn't weigh more than a half a minute. Right now, she's like a little balloon with the baby. You'll like her. Everybody does."

"Benny, I'm sure that I will. Now, about that cough. I can give you some cough medicine. The only other thing I can tell you is to get as much fresh air and sunshine as possible. We are all in the hands of the Lord. He determines who lives and who dies." Knowing that Benny was not going to last long, David asked, "Do you know Jesus as your savior, Benny?"

"No, but I'd like to. My folks weren't much on preaching, so I don't know anything about the Lord. I believe in God though. I think we both know that since I coughed up blood this morning, I'm not going to get better. I been thinking that I should go to one of those prayer meetings. I sure would feel easier if I knew I was going to a better place."

"You go to the next prayer meeting. In the meantime, if you want to know the Lord, I can tell you how to get to know Him. You know that scripture tells us that all have sinned and come short of the glory of God. It tells us that the wages of sin is death. But God loved us so much that He was unwilling for any to perish, so He sent His only son Jesus to die for us to save us from our sin.

"All of us need salvation. Jesus paid for our sins by giving His life for us on a cross at Calvary. All we have to do is turn from our sins, believe that Jesus is God's son, believe that He died to save us from a devil's hell, believe that He rose from the grave on the third day, and believe that He lives in Heaven with the Father to give us eternal life. It's not what we do, but what He did. Would you like Him to come into your heart and save you?"

"Yes, more than anything."

"Then pray these words. Jesus, I believe you are God's only son, that you died for me, and that you arose from death the third day. I ask you to please forgive me for the sins I have committed and save me. I want to live for you, Lord. Thank you, Lord for saving me. Amen."

David listened to Benny say the words for eternal life, thankful that Benny had accepted Jesus before it was too late. When Benny had finished, tears were streaming down his face. "Thanks, Doc. You gave me the best medicine you could give me. I want Jane to know salvation's plan too. We definitely will be at the next prayer meeting."

David gave Benny a copy of a New Testament to take with him, telling him that he had underlined scriptures that helped him with his walk in the Lord.

When Benny had gone, David prayed for him and his wife Jane; that she too would come to know the Lord. He also gave thanks for the soul who had already come to know the Lord and for God's saving grace.

Word came early afternoon that there would be a special prayer service of thanksgiving that evening. When Lexie and her parents arrived at the prayer service, they didn't see David. In just a short while, he came. Lenora Johnson was with him. She was fairly leaping along to keep up with David's long strides. Furious, Lexie felt herself slip into the dark morass of jealousy. *Look at her. I could scratch out her eyes. And how dare he come with her after calling me honey and dear all this time!* David stopped, looked around, spied the Fletchers, and came toward them. Lenora walked beside him.

"Good evening," he said. "It looks like a big turnout. People truly are thankful for God's blessings. All of us could have perished easily."

Lenora, taking the bit into her own hands, interrupted. "Well, aren't you going to introduce me to these good people?" she said, smiling radiantly up at him. "It's always nice to meet new friends," she said gushingly.

Because she was looking at Lenora, Lexie didn't see the irritated look David cast at Lenora, but the good manners his mother had instilled in him triumphed. He introduced her first to Tom and Sarah, then to Lexie.

Lenora acknowledge the older Fletchers very nicely, but when David introduced her to Lexie, she merely replied, "Oh, I know Lexie," and then ignored her, turning to David. "Wasn't this afternoon just awful. I was never so frightened in my life," she said shuddering. David stood with a bland look on his face. Forgetting her phony southern accent, she continued talking animatedly to David and ignoring the other three.

Finally, Sarah, tiring of the one sided conversation and the bad manners, said grimly, "I'm going over where Robbie and his family are."

As she started away, Lexie said, "Wait for me. I'm going with you." Without a backward glance or even a short goodbye, she skipped away to catch up with her mother.

"Lexie, wait a minute," David called, only to be ignored. David turned an inquiring eye on Tom, who just shrugged his shoulders. With hands in pockets, he slowly ambled after his family.

Lenora, seeing that David was about to follow, slipped her arm through David's, picked up her accent again, and continued to tell him in lengthy detail how frightened she had been. David merely grunted and continued to follow Lexie broodingly with his eyes. His only thought of Lenora was that she reminded him of an albatross around his neck.

Determined to get away from her, David slipped his arm away from Lenora and stepped away from her to follow Lexie when John Case stepped up to the front of the crowd and began the service with a prayer of thanksgiving for their delivery that day. Not wanting to disturb the people who had gathered to hear the sermon, David stopped where he was.

The young minister's sermon compared how God had delivered Daniel from the lion's den and the fiery furnace with that of the travelers' deliverance today. The service continued with testimony time. Everyone who wanted to do so could talk about special blessings God had bestowed on them. Benny Matthews told the congregated people that God through Jesus had saved him and his wife Jane that day. The people responded jubilantly. The service ended with a rendition of 'Now Thank We All Our God' with the congregation seemingly trying to out-sing the others. A brief benediction followed. Many of the people there congregated around Benny and Jane to welcome them into the fellowship of the Lord.

After David had spoken to Benny and Jane, he turned to leave. Once more David walked in the direction of the Fletchers in hope of catching them. Lenora, a step behind him, suddenly sank to the ground, crying out, "Oh, my ankle." She clutched her ankle as if in dire pain.

David sighed resignedly and threw up his hands. He missed the knowing glances and giggles of Betty and Sally Clark watching him. "If she thinks those tricks will get him, I'll bet she's got another think coming," Betty said to Sally.

"No takers. Everyone knows he is besotted with Lexie Fletcher."

"Everyone but Lexie, I hear," Sally replied.

David walked back, and knelt on the ground beside Lenora and said, "Let's have a look at that ankle. He examined her foot and ankle gently. He could find nothing amiss. *Nothing is wrong with that ankle. I'd bet twenty dollars there isn't, if I were a betting man. She forced herself in here. I wonder what she'll try next.* "Let me help you to stand," he offered politely.

"I don't think I can walk," Lenora said pathetically. She started to sink back to the ground, but David hauled her upright.

I can't walk off and leave her on the ground, much as I'd like to, he thought.

She encircled David's waist with her arm and leaned heavily into him. Looking up at him adoringly, she said coquettishly. "How strong you are. I'll bet you could carry me easily."

David ignored her hints and started to lead her to her wagon.

The Fletchers had seen and heard the commotion. Tom said, "We'd better see if we can help David out of the mess he's in." The three of them approached David and Lenora. Tom offered to support one side of her, with David supporting the other. Together they would take her to her family's wagon.

"Oh, you don't need to bother. Doctor David will see me home," she said. "He's strong enough to manage little old me."

"Thank you, Tom," he said, ignoring Lenora. "I'd appreciate your help. Lexie, would you come too?" Given a choice, David wasn't about to go alone with Lenora. He had seen mantraps like her before, and he wanted to make clear his feelings for Lexie.

It was unfortunate that Lexie didn't know David's thoughts. It was all she could do to keep her nose out of the air. "No thank you. I'll go with Mother. I'm sure you'll feel *better* in the morning, with David taking such *good* care of you, Lenora," she said, her voice dripping icicles. Grabbing her mother's hand, she started in the direction of their wagon. *I'm sure this is not the way I should feel, but I hope she breaks her neck. David too.*

"Lexie, you weren't very sympathetic with Lenora. In fact you sounded down right shrewish," Sarah admonished her.

"I'm sorry, but I don't feel very kind. In fact, I'd like to smack her. Did you see how she blatantly threw herself at him? And he's no better. I think he enjoyed her fawning all over him."

"If ever I saw a man who was *not* enjoying himself, it was David," her mother replied shaking her head no. "I think he did all he could in the circumstances unless he announced to all and sundry that he wanted nothing to do with her. You were not very encouraging. I think you should apologize to him. Oh-oh, I think I dropped my favorite handkerchief back there somewhere. Do you think you'll be all right for just a few minutes alone?"

"Of course. I'll wait right here for you," Lexie said stopping to wait. "And I have nothing to apologize for."

Shaking her head resignedly, Sarah turned around and hurried back the way they had come. She hadn't gone far when Carson stepped out of the shadows. "Well, Miss high and mighty, how does it feel to lose out to another woman? I guess that brought you down a peg or two," he said, still smarting from her treatment at the dance.

"I'm sure I don't know what you are talking about," Lexie said haughtily, forgetting for the moment about the fake engagement.

A triumphant look spread over Carson's face. "I knew it. I knew you weren't engaged."

Trying to cover her slip, she said, "You think just because David took her home that he is interested in her? He is only being the good doctor that he is," she continued, as though she didn't believe his remarks for a second. She hoped she sounded convincing enough. She certainly wasn't convinced herself.

"Well, if you are engaged, and I'm a long way from being convinced, you should know how I feel. I don't like being a loser, and if you know what's good for you, you'll change your attitude, Miss High and Mighty."

"Carson, why do you persist in this? We were never engaged. I've told you there can be nothing between us. Do you really think I could forget the vile things you said to me? Besides, I just don't love you. I love David."

Carson jerked back his head as though he had been slapped. At that moment, Sarah came running back. Breathing hard, she said, "I'm sorry it took so long, honey. Good evening Carson," she said frigidly.

In acknowledgement of her greeting, without removing his hat, Carson dipped his head in her direction, and then ignored her. "I'll see you later, Lexie. Don't think for a moment I'll forget," he said he turned on his heel and went striding off into the night. As if they didn't exist, he walked past Tom and David coming back to the wagons.

Tom and David approached the two women. As soon as Lexie saw them, she said haughtily, "Please excuse me. I'm going to bed." She flounced over to the wagon and started to climb up.

"Just a minute, please, Lexie. I want to talk to you," David implored.

Stopping, she stepped down. "I can't imagine anything we have to say to one another." She turned back toward the wagon.

David looked at Tom in entreaty. Tom said, "Lexie, where are your manners?"

As she paused to reply, David, with a formidable look on his face, walked over to her. "If it were raining, you'd drown with your nose so high in the air."

Lexie shot him a look that would drop a lesser man in his tracks and turned to enter the wagon. His hand fastened firmly on to her arm. "I'm going to have a talk with you one way or another. If you persist in going to bed, I'll come right in with you," he said adamantly, meaning every word of it. He felt he had just about reached the end of his tether. He felt that he had tried to pry Lenora loose from himself all evening, and now Lexie's rejection of him tonight was simply too much.

He paid no attention to the raised eyebrows of Sarah as she and Tom exchanged glances. Tom waggled his eyebrows rakishly at Sarah. She couldn't hide a grin. Both of them knew their girl would be safe with David wherever she was. Both of them wanted whatever was the matter with Lexie taken care of. No more mooning around, they hoped.

"Ah, you wouldn't dare!" Lexie said, trying in vain to release her arm from his hold.

"Try me," he said quietly, a look of icy determination in his eyes she had not seen before. To her parents he said, "We'll be back in a little while. We have to get some misunderstandings cleared up." He marched her off into the moonlight.

He didn't hear Tom say to Sarah. "It's about time. She certainly has been leading him a dance."

"Can't you tell? She is in love with him. She has an acute attack of jealousy," Sarah told Tom.

"Well, deliver me from a love like that!" Tom returned.

"Tom Fletcher, you know that you've always had a love like that," Sarah said, putting her arms around him and kissing him roundly.

"Is that what I have? Then I wouldn't have any other kind," Tom answered, pulling her closer.

As David pulled Lexie along, she kept trying to free herself, but to no avail. "Let me alone!" she ordered. He paid not the slightest attention. She jerked away from him. Sprinting away from him, she tripped on a felled tree root that had been growing on the trail. In places roots and brush were beginning to stick up through the ground. She would have fallen, but David snaked an arm around her and set her back on her feet.

"You beast, let me go!" she shouted. Several people turned to see what the commotion was. David ignored them. Lexie was embarrassed to see that others could hear their quarrel.

"See what happens when you attempt to run from me?" he asked grimly, not turning her lose, but dragging her onward. Lexie battled him all the way, pulling and straining to escape from him.

Finally, he stopped and said menacingly, "Maybe this will control you." He took both her arms in his hands, jerked her to him and captured her lips. At first his kiss was savage but soon turned to one of passionate desire. Her ribs felt as if they were going to break, but she loved it. He kissed her until she felt she could hardly stand. Slowly she freed her arms to reach up to hold his lapels. She felt she needed something to help her stand. Gradually her arms moved up over his chest, and on to his shoulders. Her hands, of their own volition wrapped themselves tightly around his neck. She matched him kiss for kiss. When he released her mouth, she asked shakily, "Did you kiss Lenora that way too?" Her eyes were large pools of uncertainty.

"No, honey, I'm saving all those for you. I have no desire to kiss Lenora or any other woman," he said gently, pushing some stray hair back from her face. Both had forgotten that other people even existed.

Lexie's temper flared again. "Then how could you run to her as soon as she curled her finger at you? You even brought her with you to the prayer service. I was just beginning to believe you about the other time." Switching tactics, she declared, "But I'm sure it is no concern of mine what you do. I have no claim on you. Go to her and stay with her, for all I care," she said, her arms flailing like windmill blades.

David groaned audibly, "Listen, doll face," he said, cupping her face with both hands. "You've got to understand. I didn't bring her. I was coming from seeing Benny Matthews when she appeared out of nowhere. Benny is losing ground fast. His days are few, I fear. But getting back to Lenora, I swear I couldn't shake her. She hung on like a leech. Then to make matters worse, she acted as though I were her date. And you didn't help any. Why didn't you come with your dad and me to take her back to her wagon? You just abandoned me into her clutches. If it hadn't been for Tom, I could have been in deep trouble with her hanging on to me for everyone to see."

"I did no such thing!" Lexie said stomping her foot. Dust swirled around them. "If you didn't want her around, why didn't you just say so?"

"Did you ever hear of innate courtesy? Besides, I'm a doctor. I had to make sure she was all right, even though I was sure there was nothing wrong with her ankle."

David began to feel much better. Surely, such jealousy meant Lexie cared for him as he did for her. At the very least, she was not indifferent. "If I were interested in someone else, which I'm not, it sure wouldn't be her. I am not attracted to hefty women."

Lexie swallowed a gurgle of laughter. She could just imagine what Lenora would say if she knew David had called her hefty.

David didn't fail to notice the softening in Lexie's manner. He felt impelled to take advantage of that fact. "I like my women doll size with big blue eyes, black hair, and rosy cheeks," he said, taking in every contour of her face.

At the mention of rosy cheeks, Lexie's temper soared. She jerked her face free and stepped back as the satisfied look came over David's face.

Oh, no, you're not going get off this easily. You think just a little sweet talk, and I'm putty in your hands at best, or perhaps you're making fun of me, she thought. She whirled around starting marching back to the Fletcher wagon thinking that David was making sport of her. In three strides, David caught her, whirled her around and started her in the opposite direction.

Gone was the smug look; not even a vestige of friendliness appeared on his face. Lexie was shaken at the rage she saw on his face. "I haven't finished talking to you," he ground out savagely, hauling her along.

Lexie was almost overbalanced so that she stepped on the hem of her dress. She heard a loud rip, but David didn't seem to notice. He was dragging her along so fast that she had to run to keep up with him. "Stop it! You've made me tear my dress," she told him breathlessly.

Suddenly, he stopped so quickly that she bumped into him. He turned to face her. With squinting eyes he asked, "Just what do you mean, you have no claim on me? Have you forgotten our engagement?"

"No, I haven't, nor have I forgotten the reason for it. The whole thing was a mistake."

"No, m'am, that it certainly was not. The only mistake was pretending. Lexie, darling Lexie," he implored gently. "I've wanted to tell you for days that I love you to distraction. My life is nothing without you," he said enfolding her in his arms. "Look at me, love of my life," he told her when she wouldn't raise her eyes to his. He raised her chin and looked at her searchingly. "You are all I'll ever want or need."

Lexie slowly raised her eyes and looked at him wonderingly. "Say that again, please."

"What, that I love you with all my heart? It's true. I do, you know. I'd do anything in my power to make you happy. Please believe me," he begged desperately.

"Oh, darling, David. You don't know how I've longed to hear you say that, or how many nights I've cried myself to sleep thinking you didn't care for me," she said, throwing caution to the wind. He said he loved her, and she believed him.

"Not care? I'm almost ill with caring. I'm getting to where I can't eat or sleep for caring. All I can think about is you. I'm worse than a callow lovesick boy."

Lexie opened her mouth to reply when David fiercely caught her to himself and said, "Don't say anything," he pleaded. "Just let me kiss you."

Lexie threw her arms around David's neck. "Oh, David, if you don't, I think I'll perish," she said and surrendered to his kisses.

CHAPTER ELEVEN

Each day the wagons traveled onward. The weather turned hotter than ever. Some of the horses began to suffer from pulling such heavy loads in the extreme heat. A few of the animals died on the trail, causing delays while they were moved aside and other stock hitched to the wagons. The train began to pass discarded items that people had left for one reason or another, usually because of too heavy loads, or sometimes when wagons had broken down and everything except the most essential items had to be left behind. Now and then they would see a grave with a wooden marker beside the trail. No attempt had been made to hide these graves. A few markers had messages from other trains nailed to them. Some of the messages were about how much better it would be for the pioneers if they went to California instead of Oregon.

One sultry, afternoon, Benny Matthews came looking for David.

"Janie is about to have our baby. I need Doctor David."

"I don't know where he is, but I'll try to find him," Lexie told him.

When Lexie arrived with David, several women were already there. Mrs. Blair, Mrs. Johnson, Mrs. Anderson, and Sarah were jammed inside the wagon to offer advice, comfort and assistance. Jane's labor lasted all afternoon. The train stopped for the evening and still it continued. Lexie prepared a meal for Benny, Jane, and the women before she left to get the evening meal ready for her father and the drivers.

After a long, protracted labor a small baby girl was born. Benny thought the little red-faced bundle was beautiful. "Looks just like her mom," he said proudly. Suddenly, he was having a bout of coughing so bad that Sarah had to take the baby from him. He sat down on the ground, struggling to get his breath.

"At least I got to see my baby before the Lord calls me home," he said when the coughing had ceased.

By the end of the week, Benny had taken to his bed, just as Janie was able to be up. Lexie went for a while each day to help take care of the three of them. Janie would sometimes talk to Lexie about her fears for the future. "I don't know what will happen to us when Benny's gone. I don't know how we'll get by, and I don't know how I'll live without him," she said in anguish more than once.

Lexie's heart went out to the young family, but nothing could mar her own happiness. Not even Lenora bothered her. The world took on a rosy tint. She couldn't even bother about Millicent and James who were getting more serious every day. Delays no longer bothered her. During every free moment they had, she and David had their heads together making plans for their future. They only disagreed on one thing. David wanted to get married immediately, but Lexie had always dreamed of a big church wedding, a white dress, and Olivia as her maid of honor.

One night when David was extremely persistent Lexie said, "Please, darling, it's only three more months, and we're together every day," she begged. They were walking along the trail after supper.

"Yes, we see each other every day, but we're not really together. I want you for my wife," he said stopping. "Don't you understand, honey. It seems as if I've already waited a lifetime for you. I want you to be totally mine, but I'll abide by your decision." He took her in his arms. "I want you to be happy. It's just that I need you so. I never dreamed one little pint-sized girl could be my whole life, the center of all my thoughts," he said, flicking her nose. He continued trying to persuade her. "If we got married at Fort Laramie, like John and Olivia are going to, we could be together by the end of week after next. We'll probably be there for the fourth of July. Besides the fourth, we could celebrate two special occasions, their wedding and ours. Don't you think a double wedding would be nice?" he pleaded. "At least think about it, okay?" Hurt, he added, "Maybe you just don't love me as much as I love you."

Lexie had been listening wonderingly to everything David said. She hated to deny him anything. "I do love you, with all my heart. Never in my wildest dreams, did I imagine you cared so much for me. I promise, I'll give it a lot of thought. Maybe it's being selfish of me, but do you really want to start our life together in a wagon train, without any privacy? I've always dreamed of going on a honeymoon with my new husband."

"I guess getting married is not as important to you as it is to me," David told her dejectedly. "I want you anywhere and any time. I'll take you home."

"David, don't you know that you're my knight in shining armor?"

"It seems to me that running around in armor would be most unsatisfactory when you wanted to hug your girl, rather like wanting to get married and being unable."

Lexie made no reply as they walked back to the Fletcher wagon. She said a strained goodnight to him. Tonight there were no lingering kisses, not even a hug.

Neither David nor Lexie saw Carson Fullbrite following from a distance. He seemed extremely happy to see the tiff between the two young people, clasping his hands over his head and mouthing a silent *Yes!*

The next day, Lexie went to look for Olivia. She found her and John Case together riding on his wagon. She climbed aboard when invited and asked about their marriage. The couple told her that someone would be at the fort to perform the ceremony. If no army chaplain happened to be available, they would get a Justice of the Peace to marry them. Then when a minister was available, they would renew their vows.

"Are you really satisfied with those arrangements?" Lexie asked Olivia.

"I'll be satisfied with anything, just so long as John and I can be together, and we're husband and wife in the eyes of God," Olivia replied.

"Yes," John said, taking Olivia's hand and smiling at her. "We want to be together as soon as possible. After all, not everybody is blessed by God as we have been. Some people are meant to walk alone. Others wait almost a lifetime looking for the right person. Even when people are blessed like we are, no one knows how much time they have to be together. Think of Benny and Jane. He hasn't much time left. With us, every moment counts."

"Funny, Millicent said much the same thing. She told me the other day that she didn't think she would wait until she got to Oregon. She wants to marry James now."

After Lexie left the young couple, she went to find Millicent. She walked rapidly so that she caught up with Milly in a short time.

"Milly, I want to ask you something. Do you still think that I am foolish for wanting to wait until we reach Oregon to get married?"

"I certainly do. I told you before, nothing will keep me from marrying James as soon as we reach Fort Hall. Brother John wants us to wait, and so do my folks. They told me that I couldn't get married to James until I see Johnny. They think I'm fickle, that I don't know my own mind. But I do! I didn't know what my true feelings were before I met James. I just mistook friendship for love. I'm giving myself until Fort Hall to persuade them. If I can't, I'll get married without their blessings." Looking at Lexie intently she said, "Do you want to lose David?"

"Of course not. If he loves me, he'll wait for me."

"Lexie, you're wrong. Do you know how many girls on this train would give their right arm to catch David? I've been told that men are easy to catch on the rebound. Just remember Lenora. She is more than willing to step into your shoes."

Dejected, Lexie walked along beside Milly, head down, looking only occasionally at her. *Could I be this wrong?*

"Guess I'll go ride with my folks for a while." She stopped walking and waited for her folks' wagon to catch up. She climbed aboard and sat down to think about what her three friends had said. John and Millie's words kept echoing in her mind. They were certainly food for thought. She wondered if perhaps she didn't love David enough. She soon discarded that idea, knowing he was the love of her life, and that she loved him to distraction. She couldn't bear thinking that one of them might be called to their final home before she had become his wife. She bowed her head and prayed for guidance in her decision. So many changes had occurred in her life in such a short time that she was confused. The answer was a short time coming. She could hardly wait for evening to tell David and her folks.

During the afternoon, some of the men spotted a herd of antelope. As soon as the news spread, the train, which was following the river, stopped. Men grabbed their guns and scurried off to hunt the antelope with which to replenish the meat supplies. People were hungry for fresh meat. Gunfire could be heard sporadically all afternoon.

The women in the train thought this would be a good time to do the family's laundry and most of them headed for the river. The Fletchers had not seen Carson for several days and had begun to forget that he was a threat. Sarah started for the river ahead of Lexie who was looking through the food stores to decide what to fix for the evening meal. She was busy rummaging through the flour and cornmeal bins for the eggs that were stored in them. Without warning, Carson appeared at the back of the wagon.

"Lexie," he said, "have you decided to forget that doctor fellow? I notice no announcement has been made about a wedding." Lexie jumped, whirled around, letting the lid on the cornmeal box, slam shut. Carson hoisted a foot onto the back of the wagon and pushed himself up to climb inside the wagon.

Lexie put out a hand to forestall him. "No!" she said, "You can't come in here!"

As her hand touched his chest to push him away, he grabbed her arm. "Well, if I'm not welcome inside, you can just come out here with me!" he exclaimed, dragging her toward the opening. "There will be no wedding for you two," he threatened ominously.

"Carson, what are you doing? Are you insane? Turn me loose! If you don't, I'll scream," she told him, grabbing hold of one of the metal bars holding up the canvas top, resisting with all her might. His next words frightened her badly.

"Go ahead, scream. No one will hear you. No one is around. I made sure of that." He smiled wolfishly, grabbed her around the waist, and jerked her outside onto the ground. Lexie felt as if her arm had been wrenched from the socket. As soon as her feet touched the ground, he began to drag her along with him. Lexie dug her feet into the ground, her legs stiff, and resisted with all her might trying to stop him, but her strength was so unequal to his, she could not keep him from pulling her along.

"Help! Somebody help me!" Lexie screamed, only to have a hand quickly thrust over her mouth, effectively stopping her screams. With icy hot determination, he dragged her farther away from the wagon. Lexie tried to fight him. She kicked his legs and scratched his arms. She tried to scratch his face, but he grabbed her arms, holding her so that she couldn't reach it. Her efforts to free herself inflamed him. He just picked her up off the ground, hoisted her up under one arm, her head hanging down, her legs dangling behind them, kicking ineffectually in the air. With his other hand still covering her mouth, he began carrying her away. Lexie struggled desperately trying to get away. His hold was too tight. She thought her back would break if her neck didn't break first.

"Just a minute my fine feathered friend! Put her down! *Now!*" David bellowed as he rushed up to them. Seeing Lexie helplessly held filled him with an overpowering rage that overcame all feelings of restraint.

A rough hand grabbed Carson and spun him around. Carson dropped his hold on Lexie, letting her fall to her hands and knees on the ground. He assumed a fighter's stance, and spat out, "You, I might have known it would be you! You've been nothing but a thorn in my flesh ever since the first time I saw you." He took a wild swing at David who, with the grace of an athlete, easily parried the thrust.

"If you think that, you haven't seen anything yet," David spat as his temper soared. Usually pacifying, David could only remember one other time when he was so filled with rage. It was the only time he ever fought someone.

When he was fifteen, the school bully, a large heavyset boy, had been picking on a much smaller, underweight boy. The bully, Billy Travers, had broken Bobby Brown's nose and knocked out his two front teeth. David came upon them just as Billy knocked Bobby down. Bobby couldn't get up. Billy drew back his foot to kick Bobby in the stomach when David grabbed him. He let the full extent of his fury be felt. Although David weighed considerably less than Billy, he was athletic and graceful. Billy was overweight and awkward. He gave Billy the threshing of his life. When he was finished, Billy had cut lips, a bloody nose, and one eye swollen shut. Bruises covered his face. David, too, carried bruises and a split lip for several weeks, but he never regretted the fight. He could never stand to see someone or something mistreated.

No comparison of the feelings he had for Billy's treatment of Bobby could be made with Carson's mistreatment of Lexie. What Carson intended doing to her was unthinkable. David had never wanted to kill before. He made a right swing, catching Carson square on the chin. Carson's head flew backward, and he staggered drunkenly before regaining his balance.

"I told you before that Lexie is mine and for you to stay away from her. I don't intend to have to keep repeating myself, and I will not tolerate you even touching her," David said through clenched teeth, jabbing punches to Carson's face and stomach while deftly ducking those Carson aimed at him.

He connected a right to Carson's chest. He felt sure one of Carson's ribs cracked, but the man kept coming at David. For the first time in his life, he felt no pity for another human being. He continued to rain blows on the injured man.

Lexie heaved herself off the ground, cowering against the wagon. Every time Carson swung at David, she flinched. Once Carson connected with David's stomach, drawing a loud grunt from him. Lexie screamed. Immediately, she slapped her hand over her mouth. She didn't want to distract David. "Oh, Father, don't let Carson hurt him," she prayed audibly.

The two pounded away at each other until both were covered with blood. With a right uppercut, David knocked Carson to the ground. He lay there too exhausted to move. David stood over him with fists doubled. "Now get up and get out of here before I kill you! If I see you hanging around again, I'm going to have you thrown off this train even if it's in the back of nowhere, and you have no food or water," David hoarsely told him. David had never been so furious in his life. He wanted to pulverize Carson. Although he was exhausted, he was so furious, he almost wanted Carson to get up and start fighting again.

Carson thought he could see murder in David's eyes. He now knew that he was no match for the other man. He pulled himself to a sitting position, extended his hands, palm forward in a placating manner. Breathing hard, he said, "Okay, okay. I wasn't going to hurt her." He unsteadily pulled himself to his feet. "Just wanted to scare her a little." David knew Carson was lying. What Carson intended no woman should have to experience, especially not his Lexie. Although Carson could see the rage still in David's eyes, he defiantly ambled off.

Lexie ran and hurled herself at David, snuggling into his chest. She was unmindful of the blood that covered her hands and dress. His arms came around her tightly. "David, I thank God you came. I couldn't get away from him. He nearly frightened me to death." Looking up at him she said, "Oh, honey, your poor face. There is blood all over it," she said cupping his face in her hands. "Are you all right?"

"Sweetheart, are you all right? He didn't hurt you?" David asked her, still holding her tightly. He took her by the arms and moved her back a fraction and said, "Here, let me look at you." When Lexie nodded yes, he asked again, "You're sure?"

"I'm sure. Are you? Did he hurt you much?" she asked, closely examining his face.

"No, he never got in a lick that really counted. I'm fine. I'll just use some ointment."

She pulled him to the side of the wagon and got down the wash pan. "Let's get you cleaned up." She poured water into it and with a soft cloth began gently to bathe his face and hands. He had a cut on his left cheek and a bruise above his right eye.

"I'll be fine," he said, taking her hand that held the washcloth. He held it away from his face. "It's you we have to worry about. Honey, that man is dangerous. It's not safe for you to be alone at any time."

"I believe you. I wasn't alone for more than a few minutes. I was just about to go to the river. That's where Mother went. I told her to go on, that I would catch up with her. Maybe I took longer than I thought. I was just looking to see if we had enough eggs to make scrambled eggs for supper tonight."

"It's a good thing I got back when I did. It seemed to take a lifetime to reach you after I heard you scream. Are you *sure* you're all right?" he inquired, moving back a step searching her face carefully.

When Lexie told him again that she was fine, he said, "If you're sure you're all right, and you don't need me to stay with you, I need to go back to get my antelope. I dropped it on the trail when I heard you scream. I don't want it to go to waste. Meat is too scarce. I'll take you down to your mother and then go get it, if you think you'll be okay. We'll have fresh meat tonight," he said as Lexie dumped out the water she had used to wash his injuries.

"You go get it. I'll be fine with Mother. Many people can use the meat. I'm sure there will be uses for the hides too. If we could find an Indian woman, she could show us how to make moccasins for those whose shoes are wearing out. And I've already seen several people who need them. My shoes won't fit because they are too small," she said, hanging up the wash pan.

"Every thing about you is small, darling, except your heart. It's as big as the outdoors."

Late afternoon, men came bearing their trophies from the hunt. They began to skin the animals, and wives sliced off portions to cook. They were careful to preserve the rest. Life in the train was lively that night.

While they were eating, Lexie laid down her plate, walked over to David and held out her hand to him. Looking up at her, he smiled tenderly, and clasped her hand. She smiled and said, "I've got an announcement to make, that is if David hasn't changed his mind because of my selfishness." Immediately, joy radiated from his face. He almost threw his plate onto the ground, jumped up, and grabbed

Lexie in a tight embrace. He kissed her lingeringly. He didn't care who might be watching.

Ending the kiss at last he asked, "No, my darling girl, does that convince you that I haven't?" Releasing Lexie from his tight embrace, he kept his arm around her shoulder.

Color suffused Lexie's face as she turned to her parents. She was surprised that they didn't look upset to see a man kissing her so passionately. Holding tightly to David's hand, she said, "Mother, Daddy, we are going to get married."

Tom said dryly, "Now I wonder why isn't that a surprise to us?"

"Now, don't tease them," Sarah said. "How soon? Not before we get to Oregon? I don't think I can cope with a wedding on the trail."

"Yes," both David and Lexie said in unison. They erupted into happy laughter.

"We'll get married at Fort Laramie," David told them, looking to Lexie for confirmation. Lexie nodded yes.

Best wishes came from the three young drivers and her parents. Then everyone dug into the dried apple pie that Lexie had made. For the rest of the meal, the couple and Lexie's parents happily discussed wedding plans. The drivers sat listening silently with wide smiles on their faces.

When the meal was finished, Tom and David slipped away while Sarah and Lexie were doing the nightly cleanup and repacking the gear. The men didn't tell the women where they were going. They went to call on wagon master Smythe. They told him what had transpired that afternoon. Tom also announced the engagement of the young couple.

"We'll keep a close eye on her, but if you could have a talk with Carson Fullbrite, it might solve the problem," Tom told him.

"I most assuredly will. There's no reason for anyone on this train to be scared out of her wits, not to mention a few far worse things, nor is there any excuse for Fullbrite's behavior. That young man may find himself alone out here. It's a big country to be alone in."

Tom and David were somewhat reassured by Mr. Smythe's remarks, but they still didn't intend to let down their guard.

Mr. Smythe congratulated David on his engagement, and the two

WAGONS HO!

men returned to the Fletcher wagon. David said he had to see a patient, a little girl running a fever so high it had brought on convulsions. Her mother had been unable to get the fever down. He said goodbye to Lexie and her parents and left.

"I'll see you in the morning," he told them.

Before everyone had gone to bed that evening, Mr. Smythe searched until he found Carson Fullbrite. "Mr. Fullbrite, I got some very disturbing news this evening," he said.

"Oh, what might that be?" Carson replied.

"I hear you have been disturbing a young lady that you knew before coming on this trip. And I'm here to tell you that it had better not happen again, or you will be removed from the train, forcibly if necessary."

"Just what am I supposed to have done? I can't imagine what you are talking about," Carson answered innocently. He had made sure that no one would see the scratches on his arms. Despite the hot weather, he wore a long sleeved shirt. He planned to say that his horse shied and that he had been thrown to explain away the bruises and cuts on his face.

Mr. Smythe calmly related the story as told him by the two men. "Is that true? Did you pull her from the wagon?" Smythe was certain that Tom and David had been truthful, and he knew Lexie for a levelheaded girl, not given to fantasy.

"Well, certainly not as you make it sound. I asked her to go walking with me," Carson denied, looking as innocent as a baby, inwardly seething. "I certainly didn't hear her object. Before I knew what was happening, that Duvall fellow jumped me. I thought he was supposed to be a healer, not a butcher."

"Well, that's the story as I got it, and I'm giving you fair warning, don't let it happen again because if it does, your days on this train are history. Understood?" Mr. Smythe stated sternly. Without waiting for an answer, he turned on his heel and walked away leaving Carson frowning darkly behind him.

"I don't see how I can be held responsible for the ranting of a silly girl," Carson called to Smyth's back. *If he thinks his threats scare me, he'd better think again. I'll do what I please with Lexie. That girl belongs to me, no one else. The sooner she learns it, the better it will be for her.*

Lexie didn't sleep well that night. She alternated between thinking about how wonderful it would be to be married to David and worrying about what Carson might do next. The weather didn't help either. It was very hot inside the wagon. It seemed as if no breath of fresh air could get in. She was beginning to feel the results of Carson's rough treatment. She turned onto her side, but it was bruised and hurting. Her arm had a bruise and ached badly. She finally drifted off into an uneasy sleep, only to be awakened by the rifle fire announcing a new day.

Everyone noticed the dark circles under Lexie's eyes, but no one commented on them. Sarah looked as bad as Lexie. She had spent the night worrying about what Carson might try next.

On July third, a shout went up. Fort Laramie had been sighted. When the train pulled into Fort Laramie, preparations were underway for a big Fourth of July celebration. People on the train were eager to contribute to the celebration. Flags were already displayed everywhere, and a festive atmosphere prevailed. A flurry of families getting out their Sunday best clothes, and women hastening to get extra food prepared could be seen all through the train.

Lexie saw a number of Sioux Indians milling around the fort. Soon she spied an Indian squaw, an extremely overweight woman with coal black braids hanging down her back. She wore a buckskin dress with lots of fringe on it. She was working with a buffalo hide. Lexie told Sarah, "I'm going over to talk to that Indian woman about making moccasins, *if* she can speak English."

Aunt Leona, who was with Sarah and Lexie, looked at Sarah. The two said at the same time that they wanted to go with her, so the three walked over to the woman. Lexie was able to converse enough to be understood with the Indian in sign language and English. The woman spoke some broken English. "Me show how," she said proudly. She was delighted to be able to show the white women how to make the soft shoes. It wasn't often that white people asked an Indian for help. By suppertime, each woman had made a pair of the soft leather shoes. Each had made a different size, so that anyone who needed a pair would have a better chance of getting a reasonable fit.

A tearful Millicent sought out Lexie. "Now aren't you glad that you decided not to wait to get married?"

"Gosh yes, I can hardly wait. Have you been crying?"

"Yes, and you would too if you were me. My folks have forbidden me to marry James until I can see Johnny and get him to release me from our engagement. I can't convince them otherwise. Since I'm underage, I'll have to obey them. I wish I could run off with him and get married."

"Milly!" Lexie cried. "You wouldn't elope! Besides, there is no place for you to go."

"I know, I know," Millicent wailed.

"What does James say?"

"James isn't happy, but he agreed. I just keep thinking of Benny and Jane. They love one another so much. Now Jane is going to lose him, and poor Benny will never see his little girl grow up."

"Oh, Milly, I'm so sorry. I know how badly you two want to start your life together, but you're young. You have plenty of time." Lexie was thankful that there were no such complications in her life. She and David would get married and live happily ever after, but a niggling doubt kept creeping into her mind. Suppose the same thing happened to her and David that was happening to Benny and Jane. She didn't think she could stand it. She wasn't even going to consider Carson.

On the morning of the Fourth, the military held a parade. The commander of the fort, a gray-haired man, very much on his dignity, spoke to the gathered crowd about westward expansion. After the parade, games followed, mostly cards, foot races, and horse races. At noon everyone stopped the frivolity to eat. Tables were loaded with a variety of foods. It was a feast indeed for the travelers.

The weddings were scheduled for early evening. David had been kept away from Lexie all that day because it was considered bad luck for the groom to see the bride before the ceremony. Late afternoon Lexie began to feel ill. She tried to pass it off, but Sarah noticed that she was ill. A little while later, Lexie began to vomit and run a fever. Chills followed. Sarah put her to bed and called for David to come. She told him that Lexie was in no condition to be married that evening.

When he saw how ill Lexie was, he swallowed his disappointment and agreed that she was too ill for the ceremony to take place that day. Lexie objected strenuously. "I am going to get married today. I've waited long enough. Maybe God is punishing me for wanting to wait until we get to Oregon." No sooner than the words were out of her mouth, she was violently sick again.

David held her head over the basin and concern overshadowed his disappointment. He told her they could be married later. "A few more days won't matter. I'm not going to change *my* mind, and I'm sure not going to let you change yours. And God doesn't punish one for things like that. Marriage is a serious commitment and not to be entered into lightly. You only needed time to make up your mind."

Lexie didn't know when she had ever felt so ill. She knew she really had no choice. They would have to wait because she felt too ill to stand; however, she couldn't keep the tears from sliding down her face. David tenderly wiped them away and gave her a concoction to ease the vomiting and bring down the fever. Lexie was fast asleep when Olivia and John said their vows before the army chaplain, nor did she awake for the celebration afterwards. David didn't leave her side even though she was asleep.

Just after the ceremony was finished, a reception was held. Olivia's mother had made a huge wedding cake from supplies she had gotten at the fort, and apple cider was served along with tea and coffee.

Just as Olivia and John were preparing to sneak off from the reception, some of the young women of the train, called to Olivia. "I'll be right back, darling," she told John and went over to see what they wanted. The women quickly surrounded her and pulled her away from the train.

"We're kidnapping you," Millicent told her gleefully.

"Milly, how could you be so cruel?" Olivia wailed. Amid much giggling, the girls pulled her along.

"John, help me," she cried.

"Hey, bring back my woman," he called and started to pursue them.

Immediately, he was surrounded by a group of young men.

"Goin' somewhere, Preacher?" Ben asked with a big grin on his face.

"Come on, fellas. A man only has one wedding night. One day your turn will come, and I'll remember this."

Without speaking, only laughing boisterously, the men hustled John onto a horse, and they rode him away from camp.

Mrs. Irene Blair, a small rotund woman, wearing a navy blue dress and a white apron, pushed her gray bun on the top of her head to a more stable position, and said indignantly, "Whatever, next, treating the preacher in such a fashion."

"It's just good fun. It's commonplace where we come from for the women to kidnap the bride and the men run the groom out of town. This is the closest to a town we'll see for a long while," Millicent's mother replied. It was hours later when the newlyweds finally were reunited. Both accepted the fun in the spirit it was intended.

David sat with Lexie, and so he didn't see the wedding, nor was he a party to the events following, but he heard about what happened from several people. He was determined that the same thing wouldn't happen to him and Lexie.

He thought that Lexie had a reaction from an insect bite that she had on her arm. It seemed logical because the insects were in great supply on the trail. It was almost three days before the fever broke. Lexie was left with no more strength than that of a baby calf. She felt as if she were all legs and too weak to use them. By the time the fever was gone, the train had been moving for two days.

When David told Lexie about the events of Olivia's wedding, she was amused but felt awful about missing her own wedding. In her depression, she began to doubt that she would ever marry David. He patiently reassured her time and again that they would be married as soon as she recovered. He reminded her of the Bible verse that said, '*I have called thee by name; thou art mine. When thou passes through the waters, I will be with thee and through the rivers, they shall not overflow thee.*' "That's the way God feels about his children, and that's the way I feel about you. I will do my utmost to protect and love you forever."

By the morning of the fourth day, although she was weak and still looked wan, she felt much better. And she was in a much better frame of mind. She even rode on David's wagon with him and Abe for a good part of the day.

That evening when the train stopped, Lexie and David went for a walk. Since they had ridden most of the day, David felt the exercise would do both of them good. Walking along, they heard groups of people singing camp songs and hymns.

One group had a storyteller. He was telling a story about a big brown bear that got into a settler's cabin and made an awful mess. Several children squealed fearfully when they heard that a big brown bear came into the cabin where the mother and two girls were in bed; then clapping their hands with delight when hearing that the bear didn't harm them. Another group of children uproariously sat on the ground guessing riddles, while still another group played hide and seek, darting in and out from between wagons, squealing gleefully.

Several groups of women sat making moccasins or doing mending for their families. Men gathered here and there playing cards or practicing archery. The train had become a close-knit community. Tom and Sarah were enjoying the company of Robbie and Leona and Mr. and Mrs. Blair.

Holding hands, David and Lexie talked about the life they would have together. David told her they would have to live in a log cabin that his friend had rented for him until they could get a house built.

"Will there be enough money for a house? A real house? I still have some of my salary. In fact, I have most of it."

"Money is one thing you'll never have to worry about, sweetheart."

"I didn't know that doctors, especially country doctors, made a lot of money."

"I inherited a lot of money from my grandmother. She was probably the richest woman in America, and I was her sole beneficiary. Someday I will have a large estate from my folks, which I hope is a very long time coming."

"I've been wanting to ask. Don't you miss your folks?"

"Of course I do. Dad and I are praying that he can persuade Mother to come out here to live at the end of this year when he retires."

They continued talking about their families, about how they would furnish their home, and about their dreams of the future. I want to see a church built as soon as we get there, if there is not already one. I also want to build a clinic, one that accepts all patients, regardless of means of payment. My money can see to that. I'm a firm believer that money should be used to help others. Every town needs a school. I'd like to build one unless one already exists. You might even get to teach until the children start coming."

Lexie forgot how badly she had wanted to teach. Her mind fastened on the word children. "Just how many children did you have in mind, sir?" Lexie asked.

"Well, at least two, that is if it is God's will, a girl who looks just like her beautiful mother and a rapscallion like his father," David said, hugging her to his side.

"Oh, David, how can you? Comparing yourself to a ne'er to do well," Lexie said with a shudder. David just laughed.

As they continued walking through the star-studded night, Lexie wanted to know when they would get married. She thought it was well and good to know about their future life, but first, they had to get married. "Before we start having children, don't you think it would be a good idea to get married? Are we going to get married on the trail or wait until we get to Fort Hall?"

"I'm going to let you decide. You know how well you feel. I'm going to have a lot of loving stored up for you, and I want you to feel good and strong. I think I was too insistent and rushed you too much before."

Lexie's mind became a muddle. Did he think she got sick on purpose? Didn't he want to marry her now? "Have you had second thoughts about getting married?" she asked him.

David stopped abruptly and hauled her into his arms. "No, sweetheart, never doubt my love for you. I just want you well and happy." Lexie had her face turned into David's chest, so he missed her grimace of pain.

Lexie reassured, looked up at him dreamily and sighed. "I just want you anyway I can get you." Her answer couldn't have pleased David more.

"There are two women who are about ready to deliver their babies. I really would like for that to be over before we get married. So many women die in childbirth, that I don't want to take any chances with them. I don't want any interruptions of our wedding this time. No more postponements for us," David said feelingly.

"Then maybe we'd better wait for Fort Hall," Lexie said, trying not to feel so disappointed.

"Fort Hall it is then. I hate to wait that long, but I want you all to myself when we do get married, as much as is possible on a wagon train. We can always trade spots with the last wagon. That would give us privacy for at least one day. We just might have to drive a little faster to catch the train," he said, tongue in cheek.

Lexie turned a bright crimson. She didn't know what to say to David.

"Me and my big mouth. I'm sorry, honey. I didn't mean to embarrass you. It just that you already seem a part of me because I love you so much. Forgive me?" he asked penitently.

"Of course I do. Maybe we'd better turn back. I'm feeling pretty tired."

Had they not been so engrossed in one another, they would have seen Carson not too far behind, darting in and out from the side of the wagons. Just a few people were on the same side as he. Since no one was paying attention to him, it was easy for him to stay hidden.

CHAPTER TWELVE

Lexie rolled over onto her left side and was immediately awakened by the pain she felt in her side. She rolled over onto her back and wondered how much longer until morning. Even with both front and back flaps open to get fresh air, from where she lay in the wagon, it was impossible to see anything but darkness. She had been awake only a few minutes when the air was pierced with the reverberation of gunshot. Lexie groaned and pulled herself out of bed. She wondered how much longer her side would hurt this badly. Her arm was very painful and covered with a dark purple bruise.

Sounds of the encampment waking were soon heard throughout the area. Lexie and her mother prepared oatmeal for breakfast. Before it had finished cooking, the men came tramping in for the meal. David walked over to Lexie. He took her in his arms. As soon as he tightened his embrace, Lexie sucked in her breath in pain.

"What's wrong, honey? Are you feeling sick again?" David asked worriedly. Lexie had not told him about her side.

"Nothing, really."

"Nothing my foot. I know pain when I see it. Give me a little credit."

"I just have a bruise on my side."

David squinted his eyes. "How did it get there? Carson no doubt." When Lexie nodded yes, he said, "Honey, I'm sorry. Sorry that he hurt you, and that I did too. You know the old saying, I'd rather it be me?

Well, it's true. I'd much rather it be me hurting instead of you." Coming from anyone else what he said would sound phony, but Lexie knew David didn't have an untruthful bone in his body.

"Hey, you two lovebirds, come and eat, or we'll be at the back of the line," Sarah told them.

With a dazzling smile, Lexie took David's hand and led him over to the food. This morning Abe asked the blessing on the food. A quiet man, he was not bashful when it came to prayer. The meal was eaten in silence, and everyone hurried to finish chores to be ready to roll when the call 'Wagons ho' came.

Before the call came, Mr. Smythe came by. "Folks, it looks like we may be in for trouble. Last night three head of cattle disappeared. It must have been Indians."

"Didn't the guards see anything?" Tom asked.

"No, they didn't. That's not very surprising, especially if the thieves were Sioux. They can steal anything right from under your nose and not be detected. We're going to have to double the guards each night. I'm going to start with unmarried men first."

"I'll do tonight," Ben offered.

"So will I," Abe said.

"Do you need one more, I'll help," Sam said.

"Good, I can use all three of you. What about you, Tom?"

"I'll help tomorrow night. I think someone needs to stay with the women."

"You're probably right. Thanks, fellows, felt sure I could count on you."

"Captain, remember I'm more than willing to help any time too," David said.

"I appreciate your offer, doctor, but we've been through all that before," Mr. Smythe said with a smile. With a wave of his hand, he started on down the line.

When the men had finished breakfast, they left to tend the stock and hitch up the wagons. Lexie and her mother quickly repacked the wagon.

David didn't appear for lunch at noon. Lexie wondered where he was. Abe said that he didn't know. Just as the train was about to pull out after the noon break, she saw him running toward them. Lexie felt that her heart was overflowing with love, and she dropped what she was doing and ran to meet him. They embraced and Lexie asked him, "Where have you been. I've saved you some lunch, but you'll have to eat it on the way."

"Thanks, honey. I'll have to eat later. You know I said last night that the little Appleby girl was running a high fever? At first, I thought that she had what you came down with, but then I was told that this morning she complained of a sore throat. Shortly after that, she had another convulsion. Last night she started vomiting too. This morning, she was broken out in a red rash. It even makes her face red. I'm afraid it's scarlet fever. If it is, more people are likely to get it. I think we're in for a bad time."

"What can I do to help?" Lexie wanted to know.

"You know, you're going to make a wonderful doctor's wife," he said, quickly embracing her. "I can handle everything for a while, but if this turns out to be as bad as I think, I'll need you to be another set of hands for me. But only if you are able. I don't want you getting sick again."

"I want to help. I'm sure I'll be all right."

"If you are sure that you feel well enough, come ride with me for awhile, and we'll decide what needs to be done first." By noon, three more cases had been diagnosed.

Sarah had taken to lying down inside the wagon for a large part of each day because she wasn't feeling well. She had been feeling exhausted, but she insisted that she wanted to help. She told Lexie to go on and help David. She said that she and Tom would look after everything concerning the stock and wagons. She would see to the cooking. When David and Lexie expressed their concern for her health, she insisted, "I'll manage. Don't worry. I'll be all right. I'll probably feel better if I'm up doing something." With that, they had to be content. Sarah could be very adamant when she chose.

David asked Lexie to accompany him to the Appleby wagon. As they were getting ready to leave, David took hold of Lexie's bruised arm. Lexie drew a quick breath and flinched. David immediately demanded to know what was wrong.

"Oh, it's just that bruise. It's really nothing." She didn't want David to get upset again. She pulled her sleeve down as far as possible, but he still saw the livid bruise.

"Darling, why didn't you tell me that it was so bad? I should have looked at it when you first told me. Is your side that bad?" She was neither able to lie to David nor to keep the tears from gathering in her eyes. She blinked the tears away rapidly and nodded. She wasn't about to tell him that her side looked a lot worse than her arm. "I feel like grinding Carson into the ground!" he said smacking his fist into his palm.

"Honey, I think you've already done that. I bruise easily. It doesn't take much pressure for me to bruise. So you'll have to be careful when you beat me," she said, trying to put him into a better frame of mind.

"I ought to beat you for saying that," he replied, planting quick kiss on her nose.

David treated her like precious glass for the rest of the afternoon and tried to make her change her mind, but she insisted that he let her help. Like Sarah, she too had a strong will, and upon occasion would not be thwarted. Throwing up his hands in defeat, he decided that she probably was able to help.

Olivia and John quickly volunteered to help. Millicent volunteered to do what she could. David asked her to take care of children from families who had ill parents, Anxious mothers wanted to help nurse their children. The good women of the train volunteered to help Sarah prepare extra food to take to the families who were ill, but fear ran rampant. Most people wouldn't come near the sick.

Mrs. Irene Blair became a regular fixture around the Fletchers' wagons, helping prepare the food. Sarah felt she was a Godsend. Several of the hardier young men were to deliver food to the families who needed it. Some people thought those young men could ward off the fever. Constant prayer vigils were begun. An atmosphere of dread settled over the train.

Robbie came and told Sarah that he didn't know when he could get back to visit. His boys were down with the fever. "That's why we haven't been here to help you. Leona and I are worried sick."

"You and your family will be in our prayers constantly. Don't worry about helping. We're making it fine. Just take care of those boys, and be sure to let us know if we can help in any way," Sarah told him.

That day began two of the hardest weeks Lexie had ever known. She went from patient to patient sponge-bathing faces, hands, and arms in an effort to keep the fever down. Bedding and nightwear needed numerous changes because of the sweating associated with the high fevers.

Clothing and bedding had to be collected and boiled or burned in the hope that would stop the infection. Men carried the water and made the fires, but the women were left with the hot job of standing over the boiling water in the searing heat, stirring the clothing to make sure every inch was boiled.

Holding basins and cleaning up after frequent bouts of vomiting were other ways Lexie helped tend the ill. She spent hours rocking two very small babies with the fever while their mothers tended their older children who were sick with fever. She fed children whose mothers were too ill to care for them.

David was run off his feet. He got virtually no sleep. He was called out both day and night. Fevers ran so high; it was almost impossible to bring them down. David prayed almost without stopping. He thanked God that they were near the river, for the need for water was great.

David and Lexie had no time for each other. The only time they saw one another was when he gave her instructions about tending the ill. Both he and Lexie hardly stopped to eat, and then they went right back to tend the sick. Worry and fatigue lines appeared around David's eyes and mouth. Lexie developed dark circles under her eyes and her cheeks lost their rosy color. Both of them lost weight. Lexie worried that David would catch the fever, and David worried that Lexie would.

The intense heat and the smell of vomit and sweaty bodies were overpowering. At times, Lexie became so nauseated that she felt she would be sick, but she was determined to stay, to help in any way or anywhere she might be needed.

Sarah and Tom offered to help, but David told them they would be more help if they continued to oversee the food preparation and take care of the animals of those who were down with the fever.

Many of the children contracted the disease, and quite a number of adults caught it too. No one could understand how some came down with it, and others were immune. The source of the disease remained unknown. For the first forty-eight hours, both Lexie and David got no sleep. After that, they slept in snatches, trying to keep up with the heavy workload.

Lexie wondered if Olivia and Millicent were as tired as she was. She hadn't even seen them since the illness started. She had seen John, but when she asked him about Olivia, all he said was that she was 'holding her own.' Lexie wasn't sure what that meant.

As Lexie's pallor increased, David begged her to rest, but she refused. She hardly took time to eat. Usually, she just bolted down whatever was placed before her. Several times David found her leaning against a wagon, tears running down her face. "I feel so helpless, and the children are so sick."

"I know. I feel the same way. I'm supposed to be a doctor and know how to heal people," he said, hugging her, "but both of us have to remember, that we are doing all we can. Only God decides who lives and who doesn't."

"I know. I know. But it is just so very hard to see the children, as well as the older people, so frightfully sick."

After the first three days of trying to battle the fever while traveling, the wagons pulled into a circle and stopped. Three people, one little eight-year-old boy and two little girls, ages six and ten, died that night and were buried the next day. Two days later, an old man, John Jamison, died.

Most people didn't attend the funerals for fear of catching the scarlet fever. Those that did attend tried to comfort grieving parents and Mrs. Jamison.

John Hawkins, a burly man employed by Mr. Smythe, carved names with a hot iron on wooden boards to use as grave markers. They didn't bury these dead as they had Mrs. Price. Instead, they piled stones on top of the graves to keep animals from digging them up. They did this because some people had complained that the other way was too uncivilized. Caleb Price was especially vocal about the way his wife and child had been buried.

"It's a disgrace," he complained loudly. "To think that my wife and child were treated so. You'd never done it, if I'd been awake. They must have been mashed flat. I tell you, it's inhuman. It's bad enough for a man to lose his family without having nightmares about how they were buried." And so, the way people were buried was changed.

One afternoon, after an almost sleepless week, Lexie was climbing down from the wagon where three members of a family of four were ill. Without warning, the world started to tilt, darkness rose up to meet her, and she collapsed in a heap on the ground.

David just happened to be coming to check on the family, and he saw her fall. He sprinted over to her, lifted her up in his arms, just as she was regaining consciousness. She looked up at him through dazed eyes. Every vestige of color had drained from her face. David looked as if he had lost his most precious possession. His face was as white as Lexie's.

"Oh, David, where did you come from?" she asked, weakly. She struggled feebly to free herself. "You must put me down and go back to the sick. They need you so much. I'm fine. I just got dizzy for a moment. I should go back too." Her voice was a mere thread. She knew that David wouldn't allow her to go back while she appeared so weak, but she was unable to help herself. All her strength had just disappeared.

Cradling her tightly against his chest, he said, "Oh, yes, you're fine all right. You beautiful, wonderful, doll," he added, nearly beside himself. He was disgusted with himself because he had allowed her to work so hard and so long. "What are you trying to do, kill yourself? I want a live bride that I can hold in my arms, not to be mourning a corpse when we reach Fort Hall. If you don't stop working so hard and get some real rest, you'll be my next patient. I should never have allowed you to work so hard. It's a miracle that you haven't caught the fever."

"I don't think you could stop me," she said putting her arm around his neck. It was an effort just to hold up her arm. "I just want to do my share. I'm not working nearly as hard as you are," she said, summoning up a smile, dimpling adoringly. "Where are you taking me? Put me down. I can walk. I'm perfectly all right." A more hollow-eyed girl David had yet to see.

"You are going to your folks' wagon to lie down. I absolutely won't take no for an answer. Do you want us to have to postpone our wedding again?"

"You know I don't. I'm too heavy to be carried." Lexie protested.

David ignored her plea and carried her all the way. "There, fair maiden," he said, kissing her and helping her onto the wagon. Lexie was surprised. She was almost too weak to return his kiss. Her legs had turned to jelly. She couldn't stop their trembling. "I want you to sleep for the rest of the day and all night. We haven't had any new cases today. Everyone seems to be improving except the little twin Smith girls. I don't think they are going to make it. The fever is terrible for three-year-olds. I've done all I know to do for them. They truly are in the hands of the Lord."

When Lexie protested that she would feel better after a nap, he said, "I can handle things without you tonight. Olivia and John have been absolute rocks. I'll have them to help me. Tomorrow we'll make Olivia rest. Abe is always willing to help. He's quite good with patients, and Milly has done her share, too."

Although she felt guilty, Lexie climbed onto her bed, thankful for the respite. Once she closed her eyes, she fell asleep immediately. The evening meal came and went, and she slept on. She awakened the next morning to the smell of coffee. She hadn't even heard her parents get up. She felt refreshed, as she hadn't in days, although she still felt weak. She got up and put on clean clothes. Even without washing, she felt much better once she had changed clothing, for she hadn't bothered to undress the previous day. Soon she was ready for breakfast.

As soon as David arrived, he made his way over to Lexie. "How are you feeling, sweetheart?" His eyes examined her face closely.

"I'm fine. What about you? Did you get any sleep at all?" she questioned him, taking in the lines around his eyes and mouth.

"I got about four hours. I feel like a new man. The Lord heard our prayers. The Smith girls are better. Thank God that we won't have another distraught mother to comfort. We haven't had any more come down with the fever. Praise God. I really think we're out of the woods. I talked with Mr. Smythe, and we will be leaving first thing in the morning."

"That's wonderful!" Lexie exclaimed. "You need to get some sleep. May I watch your patients for you?"

"Abe and John are taking watch for now. I'm going to bed as soon as I eat breakfast," he said, yawning hugely. "I think I could sleep for a week." He put his arms around Lexie and his lips met hers. Her lips, soft and warm, felt so good to him. "Goodnight love," he said.

He slept for the rest of the day, and then after a quick meal, went back to check on his patients. Everyone seemed to be better. That night many prayers of thanksgiving were offered to the Lord. A spirit of rejoicing abounded in camp.

Early the next morning, the train pulled out at the familiar call 'Wagons ho!' About noon, Sarah began to feel sick. "I don't think I've got the scarlet fever, but I feel so strange, and I do have a fever, I think." By early afternoon, she was chilling and vomiting, but no rash appeared.

"Won't there ever be an end to this fever business? I believe this wagon train should be called the Tragedy Train of 1843 instead of Oregon train," Lexie bitterly told Tom.

"It will have to end sooner or later, I guess," Tom replied despondently.

Mrs. Blair was instantly on the spot to see how she could help. Most others were afraid of catching the fever and stayed away. Leona was still tending her sick boys and couldn't help.

"I'm never sick. I'm healthy as a horse," the little round lady told the Fletchers. "I'm not afraid. I know that Lexie and Sarah would be the first to come to my aid, if I needed help." And she set to work cooking and cleaning up after the meals.

Sarah was not improved the next day or the day following. She just seemed to get weaker, and the fever continued. In the afternoons, it seemed to soar. During the night of the third day, she was only semiconscious. Lexie never left her side. She bathed her and tried to get liquids down her. Sarah just seemed to slip farther away.

Tom was beside himself. He spent every moment the train stopped at her side. He left the care of the animals to Ben and Sam. That night Sarah was totally unresponsive. She had slipped into a deep coma early that morning. Lexie was outside fighting tears and repacking the supper dishes.

David was tending to his stock. The drivers and David had cleaned up after the meal and gone to help with the stock.

Mrs. Blair had gone back to her wagon, complaining of a bad headache. "That's what I get for bragging that I'm never sick," she said. Lexie prayed that she wasn't becoming ill too.

Tom was inside with Sarah. He picked up the unresponsive hand and held it to his cheek. Holding her hand, he bowed his head and sent yet another prayer to Heaven begging for the Father's intervention and the healing of his love. In his grief he began to beg aloud. Suddenly he was overcome with emotion and broke into loud heartbreaking sobs. "Father, I beg you, please spare my Sarah. Please don't take her. Whatever will I do without her? Oh, Father, you know I need her so." His arms enfolded her. His head dropped to rest on Sarah's chest. With tears falling, he spoke to her. "Darling, Sarah, please don't leave me. I simply can't go on without you. I need you, Sarah. Please get well." He placed a kiss in the palm of her hand.

Outside, Lexie could hear him sob. She had never heard her father cry before. It completely unnerved her. She too, broke into uncontrollable sobbing, dropping her head into her hands. She had prayed all day for Sarah's healing, and had just about given up hope. Too clearly, she remembered the faces of the two little girls, the little boy, and Mr. Jamison cold in death from scarlet fever. Suddenly, she heard her father call, "Sarah," and then loudly, "Sarah!"

Lexie's heart dropped into her shoes. "No!" she cried. Running to the front of the wagon, she practically jumped inside. "She's dead, isn't she?" Lexie cried wildly.

"Lexie, calm down," her father told her, smiling wobbly. "She squeezed my hand. She's going to be all right. God heard and answered my prayer." He leaned over and kissed Sarah's cheek. "Sarah Fletcher, I love you with all my heart."

Lexie squeezed in beside her Father, took Sarah's hand, and said, "Mother, I love you too."

Both were surprised to hear a thread of a whisper, "I love both of you. I heard you calling me, Tom. I think I'll sleep now. Please don't worry."

Both Lexie and Tom dropped to their knees fervently thanking God for the gift of Sarah's life.

CHAPTER THIRTEEN

The stifling heat cast a pall of lethargy over the train. Overworked women began to show the strain of the trip. It became commonplace for more than one woman to suffer from heat exhaustion in a day's time. The trail became steep as the train moved toward the mountains, taxing the strength of women and children to the limit of their endurance. Tempers became frayed. Arguments broke out about placement in the line and because some thought others were getting preferential treatment regarding the best grazing space.

The alkali dust, still present, dried out the skin, and lips cracked open. The grass dried up so that it was hard for the stock to forage for food. Children suffered as much as the women. They became cranky, and some didn't want to eat.

Temperatures soared so that it didn't cool off at night. People had trouble sleeping in the wagons because of the unbearable heat. Many that had not done so before began to sleep under their wagons, attempting to get relief. To add to the misery, no rain fell. Mr. Smythe called a council and told everyone to ration water. Each person was limited to one cup a day.

"If we're careful, we can make it to the next stream," he told them.

People began to grumble among themselves. They blamed Mr. Smythe for all their troubles. Caleb Price was most vocal. "We hired you to lead us to Oregon, not bring us out here to die of thirst. A cup of water a day is not enough in this heat." Others nodded agreement and some expressed their displeasure with Mr. Smyth's leadership.

Tom Fletcher raised his hands and voice, "Listen to me, people I don't think Mr. Smythe ever claimed to be God. He no more controls this drought than you do. If you think a cup of water a day isn't enough drink more, drink all you can hold, but when you run out, don't come begging or trying to steal water from the rest of us."

David spoke up, "He's right you know. We owe Mr. Smythe an apology." He looked straight at Caleb Price as he said this.

Caleb Price was not a bad man. He just let his tongue control him at times. He looked ashamed and then sheepish. Then he said, "Mr. Smythe, I'm sorry. I let my fool tongue run away from me as usual."

"Mr. Price, all of us do that at times. Let's just pull together, and we can beat this drought." Others began to agree, and soon the crowd dispersed.

At last the train reached the stream where Mr. Smythe had told them they would be able to replenish water supplies. To their dismay, it had completely dried up. All they could do was trudge onward. They expected to reach the next water source within the next week. Their only worry was that it was not a really stream, but more like a water hole, spring fed.

They traveled for seven more days, with more people running out of water each day. It was not uncommon to see people begging for water from neighbors. Mothers gave much of their cup of water to their children causing themselves to become dehydrated and weakened. Many took to their beds, too weak to walk.

Mothers became more fearful because now and again a human skull or complete skeleton could be seen lying along the trail. They were afraid the same thing might happen to them and their families. To make matters worse, food that could be cooked without water was becoming scarce. Some people went to bed fighting hunger pangs.

Teams of horses dropped in their tracks causing delays. Because of the scarlet fever, they were already behind schedule. Indians raided the stock more often.

Each night the guards were especially careful keeping watch, but they were unable to catch them. Finally, on Friday night, Clem Abbott spotted an Indian in red and yellow war paint cutting loose four head of cattle. The Indian was young, barely out of his teens. His body glistened with sweat and oil in the moonlight. He was dressed in a loincloth only. He was leading the cattle off when Clem yelled, "Stop, you thieving varmint."

The Indian whacked the lead cow on the rump, and shouted an Indian war cry. Immediately three more Indians in full war paint appeared. Each grabbed a cow by the ear and sprinted off into the night, pulling the cattle with them. With the cries of the Indians, the shouts of the guards, and the noise of the bawling cows, pandemonium reigned.

Caleb Price, who was also on guard took aim and fired. One of the Indians fell to the ground. No sound issued from his mouth, but he lay writhing in pain. The bawling cow took off after the others.

The guards ran over to capture the Indian. The Indian staggered to his feet, waving a knife at the guards. Blood covered and ran down his side. His greasy body glistened in the moonlight. His headdress, a wide leather band with a white feather stuck into it, held long stringy, black shoulder-length hair.

He took a swipe at Caleb who whacked the Indian on the wrist with his gun. The knife fell to the ground. Hatred spewed from the red man's eyes and mouth.

Caleb Price had no love for Indians. An Indian had scalped his grandmother when she was quite young. His grandmother Price was a feisty lady. She wasn't going to let an Indian get the best of her. An arrow had entered her shoulder. She pulled it out, blood soaking her chest. When she saw others around her being killed in the attack on their tiny settlement, she lay very still and pretended to be dead even when the brave jerked her head backward. She was not killed when the Indian pulled back her hair and separated her scalp from her head with a sharp knife. "It was all I could do, not to scream or move, but I was not going to let him know that I was still alive. His smell was worse than the pain." Caleb was never sure about that.

She always said that she was thankful the Indian didn't have a tomahawk. She would laugh and say, "I wouldn't have been a living legend then." She carried a wide scar and a big bald spot, which she kept covered with a mobcap, but she liked to show it off. She took pleasure in showing people. Caleb always wondered why she wore the cap, for she would jerk it off at every opportunity and show everyone the scar.

Caleb could remember the first time she removed her cap to show him. He had felt physically ill, gagging until he vomited. His grandmother had told him, "Caleb, act like a man. Many things that happen to a person are worse than this."

"Shut your filthy mouth!" Caleb yelled at the Indian, ramming his gun into the Indian's stomach. The Indian groaned and fell back to the ground.

"Here, no cause to act like that. He's already hurt bad," Clem admonished Caleb. Caleb ignored Clem and sank to his knees beside the Indian. He quickly bound the Indian's hands. Clem helped the Indian stagger to his feet. "We'll need to get David to dress his wound," he said. "We can't just let him bleed to death."

"You're going to help that heathen? He would have killed you if he could have. I won't lift a finger to help him." Caleb's whole attitude spoke of anger.

"I was taught to treat others as I would like to be treated," Clem returned.

Suddenly, the sound of many horses' hoofs rang out on the hard ground. Indian war cries sounded loud and close by. Screams of the women resounded throughout the camp. Children awakened from sleep began to cry. Men bolted out of wagons and from other sleeping places, some only half dressed, guns loaded, ready to defend their families. Braves pulled their horses to a stop and dismounted. They sat cross-legged on the ground while a few formed a circle and began a war dance.

"I didn't think Indians attacked at night," Clem said. "This must be one important Indian we have."

"They aren't going to attack, at least, not now," Caleb answered him. "This is just a show of strength. If they had been going to attack, they would have circled the wagons by now and be shooting."

Mr. Smythe, John Hawkins and several other men came running back to the stock enclosure. "What do they intend to do? Attack?" Clem, who hadn't believed Caleb, asked. "We caught this one stealing cattle. Three others got away with three head of our best cows."

Mr. Smythe and the other men walked outside the enclosure. All had their guns ready, showing the Indians they meant business. The Indians frantically danced one more time around their circle, stopped, and sat down waiting expectantly.

A tall, bronzed warrior wearing fringed tan leather breeches and a tan leather vest fastened with small bones and leather loops stepped forward. He wore a full-feathered white war bonnet. In his left hand, he carried a long spear. A long eagle feather dangled from the end of it. He raised his hand in salute. After Mr. Smythe returned the salute, he said, "White man got son, Give back. No trouble."

"Your son and three other braves steal cattle. White man punish," Mr. Smythe returned, gesturing with his free hand. His right hand never wavered; he held his gun steady.

"Tribe hungry. Not take much. Indians starve." As the Indian spoke, he continually moved his head from side to side.

"If you take our cattle, white people starve," Mr. Smythe told him.

"Give son back, or we have war in morning. No want war, but will be war if not give son back," he said, shaking a finger in warning to the white men.

"Boys, bring that young fella over here," Mr. Smythe ordered. Caleb and Clem half dragged and half carried the semiconscious young man over to where his father could easily see him. A murmur came from the Indians. The chief stiffened when he saw his son.

"Your son is hurt. White doctor try to fix. If war comes, he'll die," Mr. Smythe told him. He walked over and cut the ropes on the young man's hands to free him.

The chief looked from his son to Mr. Smythe. "Why you do this? Help Indian?" the tall Indian chief asked suspiciously.

"It's just our way. We don't want trouble with your people. We just want to pass through to other land and to be left alone."

"You fix son, and we give four horses for cows. If no fix, war."

Mr. Smythe stood with head bowed thinking. "Can we have your word that you won't take more of our cattle?"

"Fix son, and we take no more cattle. But if he die, wipe out train," he declared his hands moving in a wide sweeping arc.

"Boys, take him to Doc Duvall's wagon. We'll do our best to make him well," Mr. Smythe said.

"Chief come too." Men could see the determination in his face. He turned to his warriors and said, "Go back to camp. Come back in morning," Silently, the Indians mounted and walked their horses off into the night.

The white men admired the chief for his bravery. He didn't know that he could trust the white men. They thought it took a lot of courage for him to send his warriors back to their camp.

Clem and Caleb pulled the Indian youth's arms up over their shoulders to support him. They knew that he couldn't make it by himself to David's wagon.

Just as they were about to leave, David arrived. He took one look at the Indian brave and said, "Bring him quickly." He ran on ahead and placed a comforter, clean sheets, and a feather pillow for a bed on the ground next to the wagon for the young brave. "Put him down here," he said. The two men lowered the brave onto the pallet bed that David had fixed.

David lost no time in kneeling to attend the wounded man. He was not an Indian to David, only a human being who needed his help. He checked the wound and turned the young man over. The bullet had gone all the way through. Blood ran out his back and onto the sheets. "Thank goodness I don't have to remove a bullet under these conditions. I've got to stop the bleeding." He began cleaning the wound, front and back, applying pressure, and packing the wound.

Other men and a few women had come to see what was transpiring. "Folks, you need to go on back to bed and let Doctor Duvall do his job," Mr. Smythe told them. The onlookers began to disperse.

Lenora Johnson, who had been one of the first to come to watch said cajolingly, "Oh, you don't mean that. Why can't we stay?" she asked in a sugary voice, which had no effect at all on Mr. Smythe. The other men ignored her.

"Because you got no business here," Mr. Smythe told her in stern voice. "Why aren't you with your parents? You should have been in bed hours ago. I'll bet your parents don't even know where you are. Young girls like you just ask for trouble. Now git!" he said, shooing her away with his hands.

Lenora's face turned bright red, but she didn't say a word. She merely turned on her heel and ran off. Mr. Smythe had seen Lenora's antics before. "That girl needs a good 'hidin.' If she were my daughter, she'd get one too," Mr. Smythe, nodding his head up and down, said to no one in particular. Several of the departing men chuckled.

"I believe I've got the bleeding stopped," David said, as he completed dressing the wound. Turning from Mr. Smythe to the chief, he said, "If your son doesn't get an infection, he should be all right."

"You strong medicine? You make well?"

"I'll do my best. It all depends on our Heavenly Father," David replied. Standing, he offered his hand to the chief who took it reluctantly. He had heard of the white man's God, but didn't know if he believed there could be a god other than his Great Spirit.

For the next three days, the two Indians were treated with kindness and respect. The chief said his name was Running Fox, and his son was named Bear Claw. Even Caleb Price seemed to unbend a little. At least he treated them in a civil manner.

On the morning of fourth day, Running fox announced, "Bear Claw better. We go now. Send horses for cows today. Running Fox shook hands with Mr. Smythe and turned to David. "You good man; you be my friend from now on. If need help, you call. Your God is good God. We go now." The chief went to his horse and mounted. He extended his hand to his son, who took it and with his father's help mounted behind him. The two slowly rode off.

CHAPTER FOURTEEN

That night clouds gathered, and a slow rain started. The rain gradually gathered strength until it was a downpour. People who had been sleeping in the open grabbed bedding and rushed to get inside. Men put out containers to catch as much rainwater as possible. Soon the water kegs on the wagons were filled to overflowing, and enough extra was caught to bathe and shampoo hair. In the morning, the talk was of how thankful they were that the drought was broken. The grumbling stopped. People became friendly to others again, and happy gossip once more was heard in camp. Prayer services became swelled with people. With the arrival of the rain, came much lower temperatures. The searing heat spell had also been broken.

Each day the train wended its way into the mountains. Grass became green again and more trees appeared. The trail became more rugged. The alkali dust disappeared.

David was returning to the Fletchers' wagons for the evening meal when he passed the Johnson's wagon. Mrs. Irene Blair and Mrs. Bertha Johnson, Lenora's mother, were talking.

Bertha Johnson was in size much like Lenora, but there the likeness stopped. Once she had been a beautiful girl like her daughter, but Mrs. Johnson had lost her good looks. Years of overwork and disappointment in life had changed her. Now she was plain of face, wrinkled and angular.

She dressed neatly in cotton dresses and big billowing aprons. She wore her gray and red streaked hair pulled stringently back and put in a bun on the nape of her neck.

She was not self-centered like her daughter, but she thought she was never wrong about anything. She rode roughshod over her husband, but could not conquer Lenora's fiery temper. Lenora's personality was too much like her own. She continually looked for wrong in people so that she could criticize them. She never felt better than when she was 'cutting some uppity girl down to size.' She was unaware that others knew how she felt.

As David drew near, Mrs. Blair called to David, "Doctor David, please come here. I think you should hear this," she said frowning.

"Hush, Irene," Bertha said quietly but with emphasis, waving her white apron to catch Mrs. Blair's attention.

"Tell him what you said, or I will," Mrs. Blair told her unwaveringly. "I don't believe in gossiping behind a person's back."

"Oh, very well, I'll tell him, but you know I'm right." Bertha said with a sniff. "Sir, some people think it is disgraceful the way you and that Lexie girl behave in public." The 'so there' was in her voice, if not in her words.

"Excuse me. I'm going home." Mrs. Blair turned and walked away.

"Just what do you mean?" David said austerely.

"I mean the way you two are always kissing and hugging where anyone can see you," she said self-righteously. Lenora says it's disgraceful."

"I believe even the scriptures say 'Greet one another with a kiss." David answered.

"Yes, well, I think it says with a brotherly kiss, doesn't it?

"Perhaps it does."

"Well, you ain't her brother," Bertha returned ungrammatically, waggling a finger under his nose.

"Well, I'm certainly her brother in Christ, and I'm the man who loves her and will love and protect her as long as I have breath in my body. That includes protecting her from busybodies. Neither Lexie nor I have done anything wrong.

"While we are talking about shameful behavior, maybe you should do more looking at Lenora's behavior. Just how does she know what we have been doing?" Not waiting for an answer he continued, "She has made a pest of herself ever since I met her, always taking hold of my arm, brushing up against me in a most embarrassing way. I'm not the only one she has behaved badly with. She's tried to annex nearly every single man on this train. I'm sorry, I shouldn't have said anything, but when somebody criticizes my Lexie, a good, God-fearing woman, I see red. Good evening to you, Mrs. Johnson." With a stiff bow, David walked off.

Mrs. Johnson, who had been turning red from holding her breath squawked, "Well, I never! Insulting me right at my own home. Homer, Homer! Just wait till I tell you." It didn't occur to her that she had been insulting.

David heard Homer say resignedly, "What is it now, Berthie? Who ruffled your feathers this time?"

David felt ashamed that he had let his temper get away from him. *I really should apologize,* he thought, but he continued on his way. He couldn't bring himself to go back. He had almost reached the Fletcher's wagon when he met Lenora coming toward him. *Oh, no, not her, not now.*

As Lenora approached him, she cooed, "Oh, Doctor David, I haven't thanked you yet for helping me when I turned my ankle." Gone was the phony southern accent. She had dropped that when she heard two girls mocking her. She walked up to him, bold as brass, put her arms around his neck, and kissed him on the mouth.

Lexie who had been watching for David saw the whole thing. Lenora knew that Lexie was watching, although she pretended she didn't. She just wanted to make Lexie jealous and drive a wedge between her and David. She wouldn't have been bold enough to kiss David like that otherwise.

Jealousy reared her ugly head. Lexie felt rage rip through her. She stomped toward them. She was going to have this out with them.

She didn't see David pull Lenora's arms from around him, but she hadn't taken three steps when she saw him jerk his head away, place his hands on his hips, and say angrily and loudly enough for anyone to hear, "Lenora, leave me alone. I am not interested in you or any other woman besides Lexie. Lexie is the only woman I'll ever love. Go bother someone else who is interested for a change, although I don't know if you can find one. You are getting to be a joke around the camp." *I've never talked so unkind to a woman and now I have to two in the same day.*

Lenora gasped, drew back her hand, and slapped David across the face. The smack resounded in the air. A deep red handprint was left on David's face. "You'll be sorry you said that," she ground out between clenched teeth. "I'll get even. See if I don't." She whirled around, skirts billowing, and bolted up the trail toward her folk's wagon.

She began to feel sorry for herself. First, Mr. Smith's scolding before all those men and now David. She felt she had never been so insulted. She wondered how many people had seen and heard David. If what David said was true, everyone must be laughing at her behind her back.

She took no responsibility for her past actions. Blaming everyone else, she began to sniff and blink her eyes hard to keep the tears at bay. But they escaped, and ran down her face. "They'll be sorry they treated me this way. I'll make them all sorry," she cried. She reached her folk's wagon just as her mother was climbing down. She was so wrapped up in herself that she didn't notice that her mother was swollen up like a peacock.

"Young lady, I want to talk to you this minute," her mother told her, pointing her finger at Lenora.

"Oh, Mother, not now," Lenora returned. "You don't know how mortified I've been."

"I've been a little mortified myself after what that doctor said about you."

Without compunction, Lenora replied, "I'm sure whatever he said was a lie." Lenora was afraid of what her mother would say next. "I'm so angry I can't see straight. I'm going for a walk to calm down," she added. She knew that to avoid the lecture that was sure to come was just to walk away.

"Oh, no you're not! You stay right here. I have a few things to say to you, young lady."

Lenora paid no more attention to her than she ever did. She simply walked away from the wagon train, crying as she went. "They'll be sorry they ever treated me so mean. When I don't come back, they'll wish they'd treated me differently." She walked deeper into the woods until the train was no longer in sight.

When she could no longer hear the sounds of the nightly camp, she sat down under a huge pine tree. She thought about all the dire things she would like to do to Lexie: choking the life out of her, boiling her in oil, holding her head under water. Oh, how she longed to see her suffer. *David needs his just desserts, too. I hope Carson takes her away from David. But first, he'll have to plan better than he did the last time,* she thought disdainfully.

From there her thoughts turned to how bad everyone would feel if she never returned to the train. She could envision the tears shed at her funeral. Never once did she accept the fact that she was the one in the wrong.

Suddenly, she realized that it was getting dark. In the deepening dusk, she saw a gray wolf run through the forest just a few yards from her. Two young Indian braves, running silently through the forest, followed the wolf. They were so busy concentrating on the wolf that they didn't notice her. One drew his bow, fixed an arrow and let it fly. The wolf screamed in death and fell to the ground.

Lenora slapped her hand over her mouth to keep from screaming herself. She quickly realized that she was alone in a huge forest. Anything might happen to her. Gone was her petty desire for revenge. She sat very still until the Indians had dragged the wolf out of sight. She got up from under the tree to start back.

Realization dawned upon her that she didn't have the faintest idea which way to go. She could see no path that would guide her home. Panic rose in waves in her. She began to shake. Again, she wanted to scream, but she was afraid that she would attract an unwanted animal or worse the Indians. She had heard stories of what Indians did to white women. She sank back down under the tree, her body quivering.

Lenora was not a praying girl, but she desperately felt the need to pray now. "Heavenly Father," she prayed aloud, "please let my daddy find me."

She had never respected her father. She thought he was weak to let her mother run all over him, but now she realized how wrong she had been. It took a strong man to put up with her mother. She realized that despite the treatment he received from her mother, he still loved her. Right on the heels of that thought came the unpleasant one that she had not treated him any better than her mother had. "Maybe he won't even want to come find me. I've been such an ungrateful daughter," she wailed out loud. The tears fell faster.

Suddenly like lightning striking, she realized how badly she had acted. It was as if a list appeared in her mind, enumerating the things she had done wrong. She realized that she needed to repent before it was too late. She might never get another chance. Lenora had never accepted the gift of salvation from Jesus, the Son of God. She had always thought she had plenty of time. She would deal with it later. Now she wanted that salvation more than anything in the world.

She knew that to receive salvation, she had to make a change and ask Jesus to forgive her sins. She must trust him to do it. Then she had to make Jesus the Lord of her life. Lenora's folks had always taken her to church, but she had let the *Word* flow over her head. Now she was eager to learn about spiritual things.

"Jesus, please forgive me for sinning. I believe that you died for me. I ask you to save me. I want to make you Lord of my life.

"Heavenly Father, if you'll just let them find me before something dreadful happens to me, I promise I'll be good. Please forgive me for the things I've done and for the awful thoughts I've had about Lexie. In Jesus' name I pray," she prayed aloud, hiccoughing and sobbing.

When she had finished praying, she placed her hands in her lap and sat very still. She felt that a great weight had dropped from her. Strange noises came from every direction. She heard the cry of what she thought was a wolf. She wondered if it would find her and make her his next meal. She leaned her head against the tree and closed her eyes. She couldn't understand it. With every sound, she thought she should be more frightened. She wasn't. She just felt at peace.

Lexie walked to meet David. He put his arm around her and said, "Sorry you had to hear that, but she is the living end. I'm sure my mother would not approve of her son today if she could have heard me. I was always taught to be polite to women."

"She's never had to put up with Lenora. Let's forget all about her. Food's ready and the others are there. Olivia and John have invited us to stop and visit with them tonight. Olivia said they have some good news to tell us.

"I hope Milly and James are there too. She feels that everyone is against them because of Johnny. I think it would be much worse if she married Johnny when she loves James. Then all of them would be unhappy."

"I agree, but this is something they will have to work out themselves. All we can do is remain good friends. Come on, beautiful. I'm suddenly starving." Taking her hand, they walked at a fast pace, arms swinging, to the Fletchers' wagons.

The Fletchers were just about ready to retire for the night when Homer Johnson came up to the wagon. "Sure hate to bother you folks, but has anybody here seen Lenora? She didn't come home for supper, and she still hasn't come. She's never done that before."

All looked at one another, then Tom said, "Sorry, Homer, but none of us has seen her. Would you like me to help you look?"

"I'd sure appreciate it. She left in a bad humor this afternoon. She's such a headstrong girl. I'm afraid she might be hurt somewhere," he said, with a catch in his voice, "or worse. I'm just about at my wits end, and her mother is half out of her mind with worry."

Sarah said, "I'll go sit with Mrs. Johnson until you get back."

"I'll come too," Lexie said, getting up to follow.

"I sure appreciate you folks helping us," Mr. Johnson said.

"I'll help you look for her too," David offered. Ben, Sam, and Abe got up from the kegs on which they were sitting and said they would also go.

Mr. Johnson told them where he'd already been and each went in a different direction to search for Lenora. They were to meet back at the

Johnson's wagon in half an hour. Back at the Johnson's wagon, the men told the Johnsons that no one had seen Lenora since mid-afternoon.

Little Tommy Howard said that he had seen her walk into the woods, but that he had never seen her come back. He said she could have come back without being seen because he had left to play with some friends soon after she left. "I called to her, but she didn't answer me. She seemed in an awful hurry, too," he told them.

Mr. Smythe had joined the men in the search. He spoke now. "I think we'd better assume she is still out there in those woods. Henry Blakemore has two dogs that he has done some tracking with. I'm sure he would help us look for Lenora and would lend us his dogs to track her." Mr. Johnson agreed that it might be a good idea.

"Men, get your lanterns. We'll need them. Doc, bring whatever you think she might need. She may be hurt. We'll meet back here in twenty minutes. Mr. Johnson, you'd better bring a shawl or blanket. This night air is getting brisk. Oh, and bring something Lenora has recently worn, so the dogs can get her scent," Mr. Smythe continued. The men hurried off to get the lanterns and the dogs.

Within fifteen minutes, all the men had returned. In the group was a young man, Richard Ryan. When the train had first left Missouri, he had tried to get acquainted with Lenora, but she was on the trail of David and paid no attention to him. Later, when she was having no luck with David, she thought perhaps she had been too hasty, but Richard, a shy man, wasn't taking any chances at being rebuffed again.

Richard, a ruggedly handsome man, stood head and shoulders above the other men. He had curly sandy hair and green eyes. No matter how hard he combed or slicked down his hair, two curls would escape and droop down over his forehead. His muscular build was the envy of many men. Richard was twenty-five, and he thought it was time to look for a suitable wife for himself.

He had come west with his father and mother. His father was a carpenter. He employed three men in Richmond, Virginia, and when he decided to pull up stakes and come west, his employees did too. Richard was a carpenter like his father, but he was also a fine furniture maker. Many of his tables and chairs and bedroom pieces adorned the finest homes in Virginia.

He didn't know why he had come to look for Lenora, that flighty piece, always walking around with her nose in the air, but something led him on.

Before they started, the men bowed their heads in prayer. Mr. and Mrs. Johnson thanked the men profusely for coming to help search. Mrs. Johnson gave one of Lenora's dresses to Henry Blakemore for the dogs to smell.

"Here is the dress she wore yesterday," she told Mr. Blakemore. The dog's sniffed Lenora's dress, got her scent, and began pulling at their leashes in a hurry to be off.

"Spread out as much as you can, men. We'll start to look where the little Howard boy saw her leave," Mr. Smythe told them.

Amid much barking of the dogs and straining at their leashes, the search began. Once the dogs seemed to lose the scent and ran in circles, but soon they were on the trail again. The men called to Lenora every few minutes, but no answer came.

The hour had grown late, and the men were tired, but they never wavered in their purpose. Lights from the lanterns bobbed up and down like gigantic fireflies in the dark forest. Occasionally, someone would stumble on the rough terrain, and once Henry Blakemore, being pulled along by the dogs, stumbled on a tree root and fell. Henry managed to hang on to the dogs. The men helped him up, dusted him down, and the search continued. It seemed that they walked for miles.

Finally, when they were about to give up in despair, one of the men called, "Here she is, beneath that large tree," he said pointing toward a huge tree. Lenora sat huddled on the ground, resting against the bark of the tree, sound asleep. She had cried until she had worn herself out. Now, she sat not ten feet away from the man who found her. The searchers rushed toward the sound, all-talking at once. Lenora awoke with a jerk and raised her tear-stained face to look at the men who stood peering down at her. She had smudges of dirt on both cheeks where she had rubbed them with dirty hands to wipe away the tears.

"Thank God we found you," Mr. Johnson said and knelt beside her, grabbing her in a bear hug. "Are you all right? You're not hurt?"

She struggled to her feet. "I'm fine, now that you're here. Daddy, I've been such a fool, but I told God that if you found me, I'd change and be good. And you found me, and I will," she said, hugging her father. "The most important thing that ever happened to me is that I also asked Jesus to save me, and He did."

She looked at David and said, "David, I'm sorry for the way I've acted toward you and Lexie. Please forgive me." David nodded yes, and Lenora continued, "Do you think Lexie will? I've been really mean about her."

At first David was skeptical about Lenora's salvation, but then the thought came to him that God works miracles every day. He replied, "Let's just forget everything that's happened in the past. If I know my Lexie, and I do, she'll welcome you back with open arms. When we found out you were gone, she and Mrs. Fletcher went to keep your mother company. Now, right now, we need to get you home."

Mr. Johnson wrapped the heavy wool shawl around her shoulders. "Oh, that feels good. I was getting really cold," Lenora told him, shivering. With his arm around her, they started back to the wagons.

Lenora was thankful that she didn't get a scolding from her father, but then she thought she shouldn't be surprised, he was such a gentle, forgiving man. She couldn't understand why she hadn't realized that before. She had always thought she was so smart. Now she knew she had a lot to learn.

The emotional strain was beginning to tell on Lenora. Walking along, she began to lean heavily on her father.

Richard was engulfed with compassion for the young girl. He moved quickly to her side and spoke to Mr. Johnson. "Sir, this little lady is just about tuckered out. Would you object if I carried her back?"

"You mustn't do that. I'm too heavy for you to carry," Lenora said, tiredly.

Mr. Johnson looked over Lenora's head and said, "I don't mind at all. I was just wishing there was some way of getting her back, so that she wouldn't have to walk all that way."

Without another word, Richard scooped up Lenora just as if she were a baby and cuddled her to his chest. She felt good in his arms.

Lenora had always dreamed of a man strong enough to carry her, but as she was such a large girl, she towered over most men and never thought finding one strong enough was possible. As they walked along, he would look down at her pretty face. Always he found her looking at him as if in wonder.

"I didn't think any man could carry me like this. I'm so big."

"I've carried things much bigger than you."

By the time the search party reached the wagons, the first pink rays of the new dawn were creeping over the eastern horizon. Richard carried Lenora to the wagons. He set her feet on the ground. "Here you are, safe and sound," told her.

"I can't thank you enough. I don't know if I could have walked all that way or not," Lenora said. "I have a lot to be thankful for and a lot of things that I've done to make up for."

"Right now, you need some rest. Miss Johnson, could I come calling on you some evening?" Richard didn't know why he asked that. He thought she would probably just laugh at him. To his surprise she answered him sincerely and with a smile.

"Of course, you may, anytime."

Richard couldn't remember when he had felt so elated. "Great! Could I come tonight?" he asked eagerly. "That is if you are rested enough for company."

"I'll be fine by tonight. You've done all the work."

Lenora watched him walk away. She was seeing him for the first time. *I wonder why I never really saw him before. He's so strong. He wasn't even breathing hard. His muscles rippled. They felt like strong bands around me. He's good looking, too.* Lenora hugged herself, wishing it were evening.

Tom and David went with Mr. Johnson and Lenora to the Johnson's' wagon. The three women were sitting quietly. Mrs. Johnson's face looked ravaged. When she saw Lenora, she jumped to her feet and ran to hug her. "Oh, honey, I'm so glad you're back. Are you hurt? Please don't ever scare us like this again."

While Lenora explained to her mother everything that had happened to her, the Fletchers' and David said goodnight to Mr. Johnson. They shrugged away his thanks and slipped away while Mrs. Johnson was listening to Lenora.

"I wonder what Olivia and John's good news is. Guess we'll find out tomorrow," Lexie said.

"Yes, and let's hope tomorrow, or rather today, is a much better one than yesterday," David said.

"Amen to that," Tom added.

Early the next morning, a highly agitated Lenora came to the Fletchers' wagon. Lenora's color was high. "Lexie, could I please talk to you?" she asked.

"Of course, you may," Lexie returned. "Come let's walk for awhile." The two girls walked a little way from the wagons. "Is this private enough?" Lexie asked, hoping to ease the other girl's discomfort.

"Yes, this will do fine. Lexie, I accepted Jesus as my Savior last night when I was in the woods. I'm going to try to get forgiveness from everyone that I have treated badly. I've treated you shamefully. Not only did I try to take David away from you, I've said plenty of mean things about you. I want you to know that I'm sorry. I really would like to be your friend," she finished with a sob.

Lexie reached up and put her arms around Lenora, her eyes full of tears. "Of course I forgive you. I'm happy to be your friend now. I thought some pretty mean things about you when you were trying to take David. I'd better ask your pardon also."

The girls hugged one another, smiling mistily through their tears. "Let's just pretend that nothing bad ever happened," Lexie said.

Lenora shook her head and said, "Yes, let's do. Lexie, there is something else I have to tell you. It's about Carson Fullbrite. You've got to stay away from him. He has not given up on you. He still intends to get you away from David. He said the other day, he would have you one way or another, and that if he couldn't have you, no other man could. God forgive me, but before last night, I was willing to help him. He's obsessed with you. All he talks about is how he's going to get you back. I would be scared silly if I were you."

"I *am* afraid of him." Lexie told Lenora about the failed kidnapping plot. "I don't know what to do. I think the only reason he wants me is simply that he knows I don't want him. My family, David, Sam, Ben, and Abe scarcely let me out of their sight. What else can I do?"

"I don't know. I truly don't. I guess that I could try to reason with him. I don't think it would do any good, but if you want me to, I'll try."

"No, that would probably just infuriate him more. He might even try to harm you too," Lexie, said, unable to control a shiver.

"I thought about that. When he finds out we're friends, he may turn on me anyway. I'm just going to let God take care of me," Lenora decided. "I need to get back to help Mother. I'm trying to make up to her for all the bad things I've done. She told me that she promised God that if I came back safe and sound, she would turn over a new leaf. She said she told him she would be nicer to Daddy and not be so critical of others.

"Do you think Olivia and Millicent will be my friends when they see how much I've changed?"

"I'm sure of it. I know Olivia and Milly pretty well, and I know they don't hold grudges," Lexie told her new friend.

"I can't wait for everyone to see how changed I am. I've got to run. Bye," she said, waving until finally, she reached the Johnson wagon.

CHAPTER FIFTEEN

When David came to breakfast he looked weary and sad. "What's wrong, David?" Lexie asked. "Didn't you get any sleep at all?"

"No, afraid not. Got some bad news. Benny Matthews was called home last night. We had hardly gotten back when James sent for me."

"Oh, no," Lexie cried. "Poor Jane. Is she alone?"

"No, several women are with her. The funeral will be later this morning before we leave."

"I must go see if I can help with anything," Lexie said. Lexie had continued to help Jane each day since the baby had come, and now she was filled with sadness and compassion for the young woman left alone.

"I'll go with you," Sarah said. "David, you eat and go get a nap. Someone will wake you for the funeral."

The train seemed extra quiet that morning. Many had already been told that Benny was gone. As the two women approached the Matthews' wagon, several women were milling around Jane. Jane's face was puffy and red, but she had herself under control. John, Olivia, Millicent, and James were there to give her comfort. Millicent sat, holding her hand.

Lexie approached Jane and wrapped her arms around her. "I'm so sorry, Janie," she said. Jane dropped her head onto Lexie's shoulders and broke into heart wrenching sobs.

Before noon, Benny had been laid to rest, and the train continued on its journey. James had been driving the Anderson wagon since shortly after Mr. Anderson had the amputation, but Mr. and Mrs. Anderson told him they could manage by themselves.

"Mrs. Matthews needs your help much more than we do. Just know that we have appreciated your help, much more than you'll ever know."

Jane was thankful to have someone to take over the driving. She had worried about how she was to take care of a new baby and drive too. She knew she had to put her trust in God to take care of herself and the baby. She was sure that James had been sent from Him to help her.

She wondered what she would do if James and Millicent married before they got to Oregon. She knew that they would want to get their own wagon at Fort Hall. She was also concerned how she would make a living for herself and the baby. She pushed unwelcome thoughts away. If God was taking care of her, and she believed He was, He could handle these problems too.

She was grieving deeply that she had to leave Benny in such a forlorn place, and she could not understand why God took Benny away when he was so young, when she needed him so much. She was unable to express a coherent thought to James as they rode together. She sat on the seat by James, wrapped the baby more securely in her blanket, cuddled her to her chest and prayed for understanding.

James had admired Jane's courage ever since he met her. Glancing at her, a feeling of pity for the young woman left so alone swamped him. He knew that she had no family except Benny and the baby. He had no trouble understanding what that was like. He had been orphaned at ten. His thoughts wandered to how she would make a living when she reached Oregon. Looking at her and the baby, he smiled. He just hoped that he and Millicent would be able to help her through the oncoming difficult days. He determined that he would do his best to aid her and the tiny blue eyed Sara Jane.

James had left Missouri with a horse and two pack mules. He had planned to help with the cattle or to help some family with the driving. He had been lucky to have three families need him to drive temporarily, and now Jane and the baby needed him. He wanted to get a farm when he reached Oregon. He had carefully hoarded the money he had made working as a hired hand on a farm in Missouri doing without things he really needed so that he could buy a good sized acreage in Oregon. He knew at first that he and Millicent wouldn't have much, but he intended to see that Jane and Sara Jane wouldn't go hungry, and that they would have a roof over their heads.

A few days later the train stopped at three o'clock in the afternoon. Although the train was traveling over the lower passes of the mountains, a steep pass loomed in front of them. On both sides of the trail ahead of them, tops of much taller evergreen trees on snow-covered peaks flirted with and seemed to disappear into the clouds. Strewn over the ground, huge rock formations littered the landscape.

Lexie thought the scenery was beautiful. She thought about little boys piling up rocks to make miniature mountains. She wondered if God in all His splendor had sat down and done the same thing making the mountains. It was September now, and Lexie missed the brilliant colors of the tree leaves with which the Master Painter soon would color the landscape at home.

Mr. Smythe said they would stop early and rest. He told them to plan to get an early start in the morning because he felt sure some people would have severe trouble getting over the steep pass.

The train pulled out at daybreak, six wagons abreast. Soon the six dwindled down to one at a time. As the morning wore on, the trail rose higher and higher. It became much harder for the teams of six oxen or horses to pull the wagons until finally, with the animals straining to the limit of their endurance, the men fastened ropes to the wagons and helped push and pull wagons to the top. The hard part wasn't over when they reached the top of the pass. Going across the top wasn't too bad, but then the men had to plant their feet into the ground and exert all the strength they possessed pulling back to slow the wagons to keep them from breaking loose and plummeting downward in their descent. To make things worse, dark snow clouds were forming on the horizon. By noon it had begun to snow.

"We can't stop now," Mr. Smythe told them. "If we don't get over now, there's no telling when we'll be able to. We don't want to get stranded here. It's not unusual to have snow in the higher elevations this time of year, but I just hope this isn't going to be a bad freaky storm."

One by one the wagons rumbled up and over. It was a struggle. Not only did people suffer from the snowy, cold weather, but from the loss of valued possessions. They began throwing away possessions that were not necessities to lighten their loads. The chimes of a grandfather clock rattled loudly as it struck the ground. A crate of china followed with a splintering crash.

The Fletchers' turn to ascend the steep incline came. They were near the end of the line. With the oxen slipping and sliding in the newly fallen snow, they started up. The wagon with the publishing equipment was to go first, since it was the heaviest. Men were lined up on both sides and behind the wagon, helping to move it. Only Carson Fullbrite stood alone. Since he had no wagon, he didn't bother with helping anyone else. He watched while other men, with freezing hands, struggled.

Suddenly the lead oxen of the Fletcher wagon slipped and began sliding backward. The other oxen were pushed backward, and the wagon lurched drunkenly against a rough outcropping of rock. The right wheel ran over the rocks. Shouts of the men permeated the air. A sickening crunch followed, and the wheel snapped. Spokes of the wheel flew into pieces. Equipment began turning over. Men on the right side of the wagon quickly strained to hoist it up so that it wouldn't turn over while Tom and Ben pulled off the wheel. With the men straining every muscle to hold the wagon up, a new wheel was pushed into place and fastened. Tom, Ben, and Sam crawled inside the wagon and turned the fallen equipment upright and secured it more firmly. Once more the wagon started up the mountain.

Suddenly down the line, shouts could be heard. Lexie turned to look. She saw a wagon careening back down the trail. With every turn of the wheel, the wagon picked up speed. Shouts of 'Jump!' filled the air. She couldn't tell who the family was. Lexie saw a woman toss a small child out of the wagon, and she followed close on the heels of the little boy. A man jumped out on the other side. All three went rolling down the grade. Swearing men and screaming women rushed to their aid.

The wagon gained momentum until it was swaying right and left, its top almost touching the ground. It ran over a small outcropping of rock, and with one last lurch, it landed with a splintering crash on its side.

Lexie saw the man roll to his feet. She recognized him to be Clem Abbott. He stood swaying for a moment, and then he ran to Effie, his pregnant wife, and knelt beside her. He raised her to her feet. Effie assured Clem she and the unborn baby were all right, and the two of them raced to the little boy, Lemuel, who lay so quietly on the ground. The mother fell down beside the child. "He's not breathing!" she screamed. Lexie held her breath.

Putting her head over his heart Effie cried, "His heart is beating!" She raised him up and blew hard into his face. When nothing happened she opened his mouth and blew inside. With a jerk and a loud cry, the little fellow regained consciousness. Both mother and father wrapped arms around each other and their son thanking God for a safe delivery from harm. Only after prayer of thanksgiving did they go to inspect the wagon.

Almost everything was ruined. "What will we do?" Effie wailed. "We have nothing now. She dropped her head into her hands and cried bitterly. Clem stood silent, head hanging. He was too upset to even try to comfort Effie. Little Lemuel stood tugging on his mother's skirt for attention.

"Now don't you fret none," Mrs. Irene Blair said, walking up to Effie and putting her arms around her. "I know people will help you get a fresh start."

Mrs. Clarence Anderson had reached the two women and spoke quietly. "Your family can come in with us. We'll make do. We have to pull together."

Several other families offered to help replace what was lost when Simon Walker spoke up. "I'll loan you a wagon. One of mine is almost empty. "I'm sure we can repack my things and fit them into my other wagons."

"I don't know what to say," Clem told them. One tear followed another until he had a stream of tears coursing down his face. Effie, too, was crying.

"Thank you all," she said.

The men lost no time in moving the Abbotts' things into the borrowed wagon, and once again started up the side of the mountain.

The rest of the journey was made in safety. By nightfall when the last wagon was safely at the top, six inches of snow lay on the ground, and it was still snowing.

Everyone slept inside that night. A cold breakfast was eaten, and the journey was resumed. Mr. Smythe warned them that it would be too dangerous to stop. "Sometimes the snow gets to be thirty inches or more." Tom and David measured the snow when the train stopped at noon. It was twelve inches deep.

People and animals alike had great difficulty trudging through the thick white carpet. Lexie wondered if she would ever get warm again. She hoped mothers had enough warm clothing for their families. She and Sarah had dug out more blankets for the young drivers. She consoled herself with the knowledge that in five more days, they would be at Fort Hall and she would become Mrs. David Duvall.

Two days later a break in the weather came. The snow had stopped, and the sun came out warming the land. Snow melted, leaving a muddy mess, but everyone was so thankful for the warmer weather, they didn't complain about the mud.

Along the way, signs were beginning to appear declaring that California was much better territory in which to settle than Oregon. Some signs were even nailed over grave markers. The climate was much nicer and the ground much richer, so said the signs. California was portrayed as truly a land of milk and honey. After the snow, some people desired a warmer climate than that of Oregon. Some families openly stated their desire to go to California.

Three days later, a shout rang out, "Fort Hall! Fort Hall!" Men and women alike sent shouts of glee to the skies; however, before the first wagon had reached the fort, two riders galloped out to meet them.

"Don't come any closer!" a blue-coated soldier shouted. "Stop!" he commanded, pulling his gun. The wagons kept rolling toward the fort. "We got cholera! We've got cholera! We are quarantined. Almost half our people are sick," he cried desperately.

With no time wasted, the disheartened families in the wagons turned and began to travel on.

Fort Hall was the last place that people could turn to go to California. One trail split off to go to California and the other went to Oregon.

Mr. Smythe called a council meeting that evening. "Folks, we may have a hard time until we reach Fort Boise. We can hunt plenty of game, but some of you may be low on staples. If you are, see if you can barter with your neighbors for supplies. Some of you have milk, eggs, and butter. You might have livestock you can spare to get what you need. Some of you ladies have handwork you might trade. If we act as good neighbors, we'll make it."

The next morning, twenty families met with Mr. Smythe. "We are going to go to California instead of Oregon. We want the warmer climate," Caleb Price, who had been chosen leader, told him. Mr. Smythe tried to reason with him, to no avail. By noon the cutoff had been reached, and the twenty families turned southward. Several of the unmarried men went with them. A total of sixty people left the train. Lexie and David could hardly hold in their disappointment. They hated to see the train separated.

Since they couldn't stop at Fort Hall, it meant another delay of their wedding. Both walked around with sad faces. "Let's get married on the trail," Lexie told David.

"Honey, I'd like nothing better, but I know you want a church wedding with all the trimmings. I think you'll always regret not having one if we go ahead now. I don't think Mr. Smythe will want to stop for a wedding celebration. He wants to get through the Blue Mountains as quickly as possible. Let's wait a few days before we decide." Lexie agreed halfheartedly.

The morning dawned bright and fair. The weather had been cooperating nicely. The temperature had been unseasonably warm, and the snow had melted. However, it was still a brisk, chilly morning.

When the train was on its way, Lexie, Olivia, and Millicent planned to go help Jane as they had done each morning. All of them knew that Jane didn't really need help caring for Sarah Jane. Most mornings they did nothing except visit with her and hold the baby. Sarah Jane was a good baby, a placid baby, and she hardly ever cried.

This morning the girls had just started their walk. They hadn't walked half a mile when Olivia said, "John and I never did tell you our good news. Too many things happened so that we put it on the back burner. It didn't seem right for us to be so happy when others were so sad and upset. *But*, I can't wait any longer. John and I are going to have a baby!" she said, jumping up and down.

"Olivia, you don't mean it!" squealed Millicent.

"Livy, that's wonderful!" Lexie said. "When is the happy arrival?"

"Well, we're not sure, but we think in August."

"Do you want a boy or a girl?" Millicent asked.

"I'd love to have a little girl. John says he'd like to have a boy, but both of us will be happy if we just have a healthy baby like Sara Jane. Isn't she gorgeous?"

"She's adorable," Lexie agreed. "She seems so tiny, yet so healthy."

"I can't wait for James and me to have a baby. James says we can have a whole houseful if I want them. I want a big family. Being an only child is a lonesome life, I can tell you. Lexie agrees with me, I'll bet."

"Of course, I do. I used to wish and wish that I had a little sister."

"I can't wait to get to Oregon so that we can get things settled. Then James and I can get on with our lives," Millicent said.

"I wonder if I'll ever get married, forget having children. It seems that everything is against David and me. I get so upset I could just cry. When I think that I tried to persuade him to wait until we get to Oregon, I could sit down and howl," Lexie said. "Now, I want to get married, but David knows how much I wanted a church wedding, so he wants us to have a church wedding. I know he just wants to make me happy, but I'd be happier if we didn't wait now.

"Mother is just as bad. She's holding out for Oregon too. I think Daddy is on my side, but he won't say anything."

The girls walked along, silently. Lexie scuffed her feet along, now and then kicking a rock to relieve her frustration. Olivia and Millicent traded wry smiles. Millicent was walking between the two girls. She reached into her pocket and pulled out a white lace-trimmed handkerchief and wiped her forehead.

"Gosh, it sure is hot this morning. I thought in late October, it was supposed to be cold in the mountains," Millicent said.

Lexie and Olivia turned to look at her. "It's not hot, Milly," Lexie said.

"Well, *I'm* hot!"

The girls walked a little farther. Suddenly without warning, Millicent grabbed her chest. In a thready voice she cried urgently, "James," and crumpled to the ground.

Lexie and Olivia fell to their knees beside the silent girl. Lexie lifted Millicent's head and placed it in her lap. Olivia grabbed her hand and began patting it gently. "Livy, get David!" Lexie screamed. Olivia jumped to her feet and started running. "Help, we need Doctor Duvall! David!" she screamed.

"Millie, Millie, Millie, answer me," Lexie coaxed urgently, picking up Millicent's hand and rubbing it. Tears streamed down her face. "Oh, Milly, you can't die. Please don't die," she begged. "Where is David? Why doesn't he come?"

Others from the surrounding wagons came running to see what the commotion was.

"Someone get James, and Millie's folks," Lexie said, taking charge.

Shouts and people running brought the train to a halt. In just a few minutes James came running to Millicent, closely followed by Jane carrying Sara Jane. James dropped to the ground and tenderly lifted Millicent from Lexie's lap onto his own.

"Milly," he cooed. "Milly, don't leave me," he begged. Unmindful of people milling around, he raised her head and kissed her. He continued, "Milly, I've been alone most of my life. I can't let you go."

David came hurrying up. He knelt and placed his hand on the pulse in Millicent's neck. He looked up at James and nodded his head negatively. "I'm sorry, James, she's gone."

James' face crumpled and tears rolled down his cheeks. "Why?" he asked.

"She never hurt anyone. Why?"

David was at a loss for an answer. Jane handed Sara Jane to Lexie and knelt beside James. She put a comforting hand on his shoulder. "I know how you feel, James. I felt the same thing myself. We just have to trust God's will. He knows what's best. Come with me."

"No!" James cried, holding Millicent closer to him.

"James, there is nothing more you can do for Milly," David told him. "Let the women make final preparations for her." He attempted to lift Millicent from James' arms.

"No! I told you no!" James shouted. He held Millicent tighter, refusing to budge as David, Tom Fletcher and John Case pleaded with him.

"Folks, please go back to your wagons. We'll stop here until tomorrow morning. We'll have funeral services this afternoon."

"No! You aren't going to stick my Milly into any hole in the ground. Just try it," he said threateningly.

Mr. and Mrs. Bond came running, Mr. Bond limping with every step. Out of breath, Millicent's mother cried, "Oh, not my baby, not my little Millicent." She got down on her knees and gently loosened the hold James had on Millicent.

James released Millicent into her mother's arms, but didn't move. He sat with head bowed, hands hanging loosely in his lap, tears running down his cheeks.

Cradling her daughter in her arms, she began softly to hum a lullaby. Mr. Bond sat on the ground by his wife, looking lost and dazed. Hardened men got handkerchiefs and wiped tears from their eyes. Women cried openly. Not a dry eye could be seen.

Tom and Sarah walked over to where Lexie sat on the ground sobbing. One on each side of her, they lifted her up. "I hate this tragedy train," Lexie cried. They tried to comfort her as best they could, but she was inconsolable. Olivia had found her parents who were trying to comfort her. John and David had managed to get James off the ground and were talking earnestly to him.

"I know how hard this must be for you, James, but we have to go on."

"What for? Everything I've ever wanted has been taken away from me. Just tell me why should I go on?"

"Well, I don't know why God did what He did. Some day we'll find out, but I do know that He still has a purpose for you, or you wouldn't still be on this earth," John told him.

Hands doubled stiffly at his sides, James didn't respond, but he didn't argue.

"Think you'll be all right now?" When James jerkily shook his head yes, John continued, "Come, go home with Olivia and me for today and stay for as long as you'd like. We'll love having you."

"Thanks, maybe later. I've got to go help Millie's folks. They feel as bad as I do."

James walked back over to where the Bonds still sat holding Millicent. "Mom and Dad Bond, we can't do anything more for Milly." James caught his breath in a sob. "Let's let the women get her ready. Oh, she looks so beautiful," he sobbed. He bent and kissed her unresponsive lips. Mr. Smythe and John Hawkins tenderly lifted up Millicent and bore her away. James helped both parents to their feet.

Jane came over to the Bonds. "Mr. and Mrs. Bond, please come and have the noon meal with James and me. I know what you are going through. It hasn't been long since I lost my husband, and I know you need to be around people. I also know that you won't feel like cooking, Mrs. Bond."

Clem Abbott spoke up. "I'll see that your stock is watered and taken care of today."

Brokenly Mr. Bond told them, "You are good friends and neighbors."

CHAPTER SIXTEEN

"Sweetheart, what's wrong?" David asked Lexie as they walked on their nightly after-dinner stroll.

They went walking every night whether they were bone-tired or not. It was their time to be alone, or it had been until other couples decided they needed time alone too. Lenora and Richard were one of the other couples that had gotten together since leaving Independence. Lexie and David had talked about how many new families would be started upon reaching Oregon if not before.

"Nothing. I'm just tired." Lexie said, not looking at David.

David stopped, gently turned her to face himself. "Come on, tell papa what the trouble is. Is it Milly?"

Lexie kept her eyes on the ground. David put his hand under her chin, raising her face to his. Lexie looked at him and said, "No, but I miss Milly very much. I guess I always will."

"Well, tell me. I know something is troubling you."

"I feel silly, but I can't help it. I'm frightened."

"Of what? Has Carson been bothering you again?" he asked antagonistically.

"That's just it. I haven't seen him at all," she began. She told him what Lenora had told her. "I'm afraid he might do something to hurt you too," she said.

"You quit worrying and let me take care of Mr. Fullbrite," David told her.

The very next afternoon, Lexie was walking beside their wagon. She had fallen behind a little, so that she could not be seen from the driver's seat. Out of nowhere, Carson appeared.

"Lexie, I want to talk to you," he said belligerently.

"Get away from me. I don't have anything to say to you, and I don't want to hear anything you might have to say to me. Just leave me alone," she told him, shaking.

"That's too bad, but you are going to listen," Carson said, grabbing her arm.

Suddenly David and Richard stepped from behind the wagon. "Let her go, Fullbrite and get out of here," David said with authority.

Carson dropped Lexie's arm as if it were a hot iron at the sound of David's voice. He thought about tackling David, but when he saw Richard too, he said, "Okay, I'm going. I'll see *you* later, Lexie," he threw over his shoulder as he brazenly walked away.

"I think we'd better not let Lexie out of our sight. He's not going to leave her alone," David said.

"Couldn't we go to Mr. Smythe about this?" Richard asked.

"And tell him what? Carson hasn't done anything yet," David said.

From that time on, Lexie was never left alone. Samuel, Ben, Richard, or Abe managed to keep her in sight, as well as David, Tom, and Sarah.

James flicked the reins of the team, and the wagon rolled on. Sarah Jane was sleeping inside the wagon. Usually, James and Jane talked freely and seemed content in each other's company. This morning Jane waited for James to begin a conversation. They had expressed their hopes of the future to each other. They had shared their grief over their loss of Benny and Millicent. This morning James was reticent. From time to time Jane would look at him, wondering why he didn't speak. James kept his eyes straight ahead.

"What is wrong, James? You've hardly spoken this morning."

James turned his eyes on Jane, shook his head and replied. "Nothing." Jane didn't miss the frown drawing his eyebrows almost together.

"Something is wrong. Won't you please tell me? I'd like to help."

James let out his breath in a deep sigh. "All right. I'm sure most people don't feel this way, but that old crone, Mrs. Henderson, is gossiping about us."

"I don't understand. What about us?"

"She is saying that something is going on between us because we're together so much." Jane sucked in her breath, looking disturbed. She sat for a while, wringing her hands.

Finally, she turned fully to look at him and spoke. "What do you suggest? I guess I can drive myself."

"No! I'll not have that. Janie, look, I know that I'm not much to look at, and I know you are still in love with Benny, but you need a man to take care of you and little Sarah Jane. No, don't say anything. Just let me finish," he said as Jane opened her mouth to speak. "I wanted to die when I lost Milly. I'm sure you felt the same way about Benny, but life goes on. I have come to care for you deeply, and I love Sarah Jane as if she were my own. Since I've been driving for you, we seem like a family, a family I never had. It's just no good being alone. I was thinking we could get married, and maybe some day you could learn to love me," he finished earnestly.

"James, no one else could have been a better friend. I don't know how Sarah Jane and I could have gotten along without you. I saw you suffering as much as I, but you never said one word. I'd be proud to be your wife. I care for you too."

"Yippee yea!" James shouted. "Let's talk to John Case tonight. We can get him to marry us tonight. That ought to silence the old biddy."

"James, you're not just marrying me to keep people from talking? Won't people talk about us getting married so soon?" Jane asked, concern showing in every inch of her body.

"No, and no. I really want to marry you, for me. People who count will understand that you need a husband and father for little Sarah Jane. I certainly need someone to take care of me. Just look at me." Jane couldn't help laughing at the hangdog expression James pulled onto his face. She believed what he said because she wanted to believe what he said was true.

As soon as Wednesday devotions were concluded, James, carrying Sarah Jane, took Jane's hand, and together they walked up to John Case.

"Brother John, could we talk to you?" James asked.

John extended his hand to both and asked, "What can I do for you?"

"You can marry us tonight," James said. He laughed at the shocked expression that spread over John's face.

"We know that it's very soon, but Janie and Sara Jane need a man to look after them. I need someone in my life, too. Millie's folks understood."

"Congratulations, my friend. I couldn't be happier for you. I think you and Jane are making a wise decision."

Word spread fast and within thirty minutes John had the congregation back, and James and Jane were made husband and wife. People rushed to the newlyweds to congratulate them.

Richard, who hardly let Lenora out of his sight, stood with her, Lexie, and David during the ceremony. "This kind of thing could be contagious," he said, smiling at Lenora.

People began to drift away, leaving only John and Olivia, Richard and Lenora, Lexie and David, and the newlyweds. "You're lucky," Olivia told the bride and groom. "You caught everyone by surprise. No one had time to prepare a wedding night trip for you as they did for John and me."

Everyone laughed and James said, "We're always one step ahead of them. Besides who would look after the baby if they did that. Seriously, I feel lucky to have Jane and Sarah Jane," he said squeezing Jane's hand.

After a few minutes more of lively conversation, the couples said goodnight and separated. Lexie said to David, "Do you think when we get out of these mountains, things will be easier on the trail?"

"No, from what I hear from Mr. Smythe, the Columbia River will be the worst thing we encounter."

"Why?"

"The Columbia River is full of rapids and white water. It will be the boat ride of a lifetime." David noticed the look of fear that passed over Lexie's face.

"Darling, don't fret. I'll take good care of you," he said, hugging her close to his side

"I'm sorry. I wish I were not such a coward," she told him.

"Never mind. I think I'll keep you."

They watched Richard and Lenora walking a short distance ahead of them. They were intently involved in conversation.

"Looks like there may be several more couples who are going to get married before we reach Oregon," Richard told Lenora.

"Really, who?" Lenora said.

"Ben and Samuel Bradford are marrying sisters. I think their names are Betty and Sally something or other."

"You must mean Betty and Sally Clark."

"Yes, that's it. Lenora," he said earnestly. "I've watched the change in you. You have become a wonderful person. Anyone would be glad to have you for a friend. How do you feel about me?" Richard stopped at turned Lenora to face him.

Lenora, wary of giving away too much of the feeling she had for Richard, said cautiously, "Why, I like you very much."

Richard took Lenora by the arms and gave her a shake *"Like!* What a milk and water term! Is that all you feel? Like?" Anger was starting to take hold of him.

Lenora didn't have red hair for nothing. Her temper matched the fire of her hair. "Stop it! What do you want me to say? I haven't heard you say of any undying devotion to me. Just how do you feel about me?" she spat, jerking away from him.

With a groan, Richard hauled her into his arms. "I'm sorry, honey. I thought you knew how I feel."

"Well, I don't. You'll have to spell it out for me."

"Everyone in this whole camp knows that I'm crazy about you," he told her. "I love you. Now, you wild woman, tell me what you really feel. Do you really just like me?"

"To repeat what you just said, everyone in this whole camp knows that I'm crazy about you," she mimicked him. With love filling her eyes, she hugged him back.

Richard held her tighter and lowered his face to hers. Their lips met in a long satisfying kiss. David and Lexie were getting close to the couple now. Richard released Lenora and turned to the other couple.

"Guess what? This beautiful woman loves me. Me. Isn't that great?" He was so excited that David and Lexie expected him to kick up his heels and do a jig.

"That's no surprise to us. Everyone knows how you two feel. What took you so long to grasp it?" David asked them dryly.

The excited couple stood looking at each other grinning happily.

"Congratulations, you two," Lexie broke into the conversation. "I hope you'll be very happy. Are we going to be invited to the wedding when we reach Oregon, or are you tying the knot before then?" Lexie asked.

"Oregon," Lenora said.

"Before," Richard said simultaneously. As soon as the other spoke, they turned to look at one another. Lenora and Lexie began to giggle. David tried unsuccessfully to hide a smile. Richard only looked dazed.

"Where have we heard this story before?" Lexie asked David.

"I think you two had better have a talk before you try to answer any questions." David said. "It might save frayed nerves if you do."

Before Lexie and David talked with Richard and Lenora again, word came from John Case at Sunday night service that the Bradford brothers and the Clark sisters would be married in a double wedding on Wednesday evening.

At once, busy housewives began to sort through possessions to see what they could give the couples for wedding presents. Since the Fletchers' drivers would have wives, Tom and Sarah began to make provision for the sleeping arrangements for the two couples.

Richard and Lenora announced that they would marry the following Wednesday night. Lexie heard the news with sadness. She was happy for each couple, but she desperately wished that she and David were to be one of the couples.

The men and women planned for the enforced wedding trip the night of the wedding, but Ben and Betty had made their own plans. They were able to sneak away right after the ceremony without being caught. Amid much laughter and teasing, Samuel and Sally were caught, and the trip away from camp for Samuel began.

The two young couples were still basking in their happiness when

Richard and Lenora's turn came. Lenora and her mother had worked frantically to plan Lenora's wedding. She and her mother had made a light blue dress, trimmed in white lace. The couple had asked David and Lexie to stand up with them. Lexie wore a midnight blue dress with full sleeves and a square neckline. The weather was so warm that they had taken off their coats for the ceremony so their pretty dresses would show.

A reception with cake and cider followed the service. All during the ceremony and the reception, while people were enjoying themselves, Lexie sank deeper into what she called her black glooms. Every time she looked at David, she wondered if she would ever become his wife.

David knew something was bothering her, but he couldn't figure out what it was. When he asked, she had replied, "Nothing. Won't it be great to have so many friends when we get to Oregon?" David followed her lead and didn't question her more.

After the wedding cake was all gone, the crowd began dispersing. Lexie and David wished the couple much happiness and left. David kept glancing at Lexie, trying to understand her silence. Finally, he could stand it no longer. He stopped, turned Lexie to face him and said, "Okay, let's have it. Don't tell me nothing is wrong. I know better. Honey, don't you know you can tell me anything?"

"All right, but don't you dare laugh at me. I wonder if we'll ever get married. I can see me now, a skinny, old maid."

David let out a bellow of laughter, slapping his thigh.

"Don't you dare laugh at me," Lexie cried, thumping him on the chest. "I told you not to laugh."

"Simmer down." David said, taking her in his arms and hugging her. You'll never know how funny it is to think of you as a skinny, old maid. There must be a million men who would see to it that you never become that," he said tenderly.

Lexie submitted to his embrace, but tears welled up in her eyes. "It just seems that we are never going to get out of these mountains and to Oregon. Life's so short. Why do we have to wait? You said when I wanted to wait that maybe I didn't love you enough, well, maybe you don't love me enough," she said and flounced off.

In an instant, David caught her. "You don't really believe that. I will happily marry you tonight if that's what you really want. I have only been trying to make you happy, sweetheart."

"David, do you really mean it? We don't have to wait?"

"I mean it with all my heart. I can hardly wait to make you mine."

"Let's go tell Mother and Daddy. What about John Case? When do we tell him?"

"Just as soon as we talk to your mother and dad."

"Every mother dreams of her daughter's wedding almost as much as her daughter does," Sarah said. "If you *are* going to get married before we get to Oregon, please give me at least three weeks to prepare. Lexie, I have that white piece of wool material. I can make you a coat to match my wedding dress. You do want to be married in my dress, don't you?"

And so the wedding plans began. Sarah made the white coat. She had brought her dress because she had kept it for years for Lexie to wear, and she wasn't about to leave it behind. She took a piece of white satin and made a cover for one of Lexie's Bibles.

David wanted Lexie to have a bridal bouquet. Since no flowers were available for them, he asked the ladies he met if they knew how to make silk flowers. Finally, after a week of searching, he found that Effie Abbott made them. He employed her to make three soft pink roses with green satin leaves and stems. Sarah attached these to the Bible Lexie was to carry.

The next two weeks brought the train out of the mountains. The weather was much warmer than it had been while they were descending the mountains. Lexie doubted that she would even need the coat her mother had so lovingly made for her. Sarah and Lexie carefully washed and ironed the white wedding dress.

When Lexie tried on the lace-trimmed dress which had a heart shaped neckline, fitted bodice, and long tight sleeves, she looked a vision. Sarah refused to let David see her, but she called Tom to come look. He thought Lexie was the most beautiful girl he had ever seen, except for his Sarah.

The day of the wedding dawned, just like any other day on the trail. The wedding cake was ready, and cider and coffee were to be served with it at the reception. In the excitement, everyone had forgotten about Carson except Lexie. She thought that since this was her wedding day, and he had made no unwanted advances, she should forget about him. Since all eyes were set on wedding festivities, no one saw him leave the train mid-afternoon and ride into the forest.

At four o'clock the call "Wagons circle" came, and the train settled down for the night. Dinner was a hurried affair at the Fletcher wagons with the two recent brides, Betty and Sally teasing Lexie about married life. With dinner over, all hurried with the dinner clean up and to get into their wedding finery.

Tom and Sarah were dressed and waiting for Lexie to get out of the wagon. Lexie came to the opening, and Tom helped her down. Just as her foot touched the ground, David came. He caught his breath when he saw how beautiful Lexie looked. He walked over to her and took her in his arms. Sarah groaned and said, "David, don't you dare muss her dress."

"I'll be careful, but what's a little mussing between friends?" he asked without looking at Sarah. With his eyes on Lexie, he continued, "You are exquisite, the most beautiful thing I have ever seen."

"And you are the most handsome man in the world," she returned.

"If you two are ready, we'd better go. It's almost time to start the ceremony," Tom said. "Everyone else has already gone." The ceremony was to be held at the front of the train where the two lead wagons met in the circle.

David turned Lexie loose, and she stepped away. In that split second, the crack of a rifle rang out in the air. Without a sound, Lexie dropped to the ground like a rock. Sarah screamed.

Tom didn't know what had happened and ran to Sarah thinking she was hurt. David dropped to his knees, crying out, "Lexie, darling." Blood ran down her chest. "Quick, get some cloths and hot water! We've got to stop this bleeding."

Horrified, Sarah stood with her hand over her mouth, unable to move. Tom bolted inside the wagon and returned carrying a sheet. "Here, use this," he said.

Blood poured down the front of Lexie's dress and began to pool at her side. David applied pressure to the wound. Others hearing the uproar came running to see what had happened. Several men mounted their horses and rushed into the wood to find the shooter.

Before they had gotten out of sight, Carson came galloping up to camp. His eyes looked like those of a wild man. His chin and his hands were trembling. He flung himself off his horse and onto the ground beside Lexie.

"Lexie, I'm sorry. Please don't die. I swear I didn't know what I was doing. I must have been crazy," he said looking at the others. "Please forgive me. I'd rather be shot myself than have her hurt. I just couldn't stand the thought of her marrying someone else," he said, taking one of Lexie's hands in his.

David looked murderous. He jerked Lexie's hand away from Carson. "Do you mean *you* shot her?" he ground out.

Carson hung his head and shook it yes, his whole frame shaking.

Without stopping his treatment of Lexie, David told him in an icy voice, "I ought to kill you. If she dies, you *will* pay and pay dearly," he said.

Rough hands reached down as Mr. Smythe and John Hawkins dragged Carson to his feet. Weeping, his face crumpled. "I'm sorry, Lexie, I'm truly sorry," he said as they began to drag him away. A crowd of men circled around Carson to make sure he didn't escape.

"Wait," came a thread of a whisper. "David, please make them wait." The men stopped at David's command, and her faint voice came again. "Don't hurt him. If Jesus can forgive me for all the bad things I've done, we can forgive Carson." Lexie was unable to say more. She felt a great weakness come over her, and she sank into stygian blackness.

Looking shocked, the men released Carson's arms when Lexie asked them not to hurt him. He dropped his head into his hands and cried. "I'm so ashamed," he said.

"That's enough of that," John Hawkins said gruffly. He and Mr. Smythe each took Carson by the arms again and led him over to Zeke Williams.

"Zeke, come stand guard over Fullbrite, will you?" Mr. Smythe said. "Hawk, you stay with them and see that Fullbrite doesn't get away. We'll decide what to do with him later." The two men led Carson away.

"Let's get Lexie inside. We've got to get that bullet out." David said. Sarah, who had been standing like a statue, came alive with a jerk. She quickly climbed into the wagon and made Lexie's bed ready. David picked up Lexie and carried her to the wagon. He handed her to Tom until he climbed inside, then took her and laid her carefully onto her bed.

Sarah cried as she carefully cut Lexie's dress to get to the wound. She prayed aloud, "Father, please don't take my Lexie. Please don't. I beg you in the name of Jesus." Sarah was thankful that Lexie was unconscious and didn't feel the pain.

David was voicing his own prayer silently as he worked over Lexie. He poured ether onto a cloth and held it over Lexie's face so she wouldn't feel the pain when he extracted the bullet.

"I don't know if I can do this or not," David said as he started to remove the bullet. His hands were shaking badly.

"If you don't, she'll die," Sarah moaned. "Don't let my baby die, please!"

David pulled himself together and set to work. He knew Sarah spoke the truth. An hour later, the bullet was out, and the bleeding had slowed to a trickle. "If she doesn't get infection, she should make it," David told them as he rose from the bedside. He sank back down by Lexie, shaking.

Tom patted him on the shoulder. "Son, you did a fine job. She's in the hands of the Lord now." The Fletchers and David sat up through the night ministering to Lexie.

It was a subdued train that broke camp the next morning. The train traveled an extra hour each day in order to find the warmer temperatures for Lexie's benefit.

Lexie tried to climb out of the fiery, darkness. She felt as if her body were on fire. In her delirium, she cried, "David, help me. Where are you? I need you!"

"I'm right here, darling," David told her, brushing her hair away from her forehead in a caress.

Although the wound was a clean one, Lexie developed a fever.

"She has an infection," David said. "I feel so helpless. I'm doing everything I know to do," David told the Fletchers.

Sarah and David took turns bathing Lexie's body to bring down the fever. "I'm so hot, so very hot," she said as she tossed and turned, trying to dislodge the covers that Sarah and David kept over her. They made sure she stayed under the covers, trying to keep her from developing pneumonia.

"Here, Lexie, drink this," David said as he attempted to keep the fever, as well as the pain, under control. He raised her head, and Lexie swallowed the concoction.

She tried to fight her way back to the light, but every time she sank back down to layers of darkness. Sarah and David had their hands full trying to get nourishment down her.

The fire that consumed her disappeared, but in no time an icy world greeted her. "Cold, cold, I'm freezing, Mamma, come get me. Mamma?" she moaned, her body shaking.

"Here, baby, Mamma's here." It took the strength of both Sarah and David to keep her in some measure of comfort. Whether David was treating her or just holding her hand, he frequently told her, "I'm here, darling, I'm right here." It seemed to soothe her for a while. The periods of fever and chills lasted for days.

Carson was kept under constant guard. Mr. Smythe hadn't decided what to do with him. If Lexie died, he planned to hang him, but if she lived, he thought he would save him for a court in Oregon.

Carson had nothing to do but stare into space and think. He could hardly believe that someone he had shot could forgive him. Maybe there was something to this Christianity stuff after all. He wished he had a Bible. Finally, after several days, he asked Zeke if he could get one for him. Zeke didn't believe he was sincere, but he had one for him by that evening. Carson wasted no time in reading it.

The next morning, he asked Zeke how Lexie was. "She is still very sick. She's unconscious most of the time and talks out of her head."

"Do you think I could see her when she is better? I just want to tell her that I'm now a born again believer. I accepted Jesus as my savior last night. I'm not just saying that to keep from being punished. I know I deserve to be punished. I really am a changed man."

Zeke, who was a Christian, said, "I'll take your word for it until you prove differently."

The word soon spread through the train that Carson had become a Christian. As one day dragged into another, he could hardly eat. He lost weight. Most of his waking hours were spent reading his Bible. At least once a day, he and Zeke traveled to the Fletcher wagon so that he could see how Lexie was faring. He always asked them to pray for him and to forgive him. Together, they prayed for Lexie's recovery. Others began to see that the Lord had changed him. Many felt sorrow that he was suffering, too.

The train reached the Columbia River. Men cut logs to make rafts to take the wagons across the treacherous river. Wagons were anchored to the rafts, and the first raft was released into the water. Before crossing, ropes were tied to trees, and the long coils were put on the rafts to tie to trees on the other side to keep the rafts on course. Six men had long poles to help guide each raft. All was well until the raft was nearly across the river. Suddenly it seemed as if the raft hit a whirlpool. Taylor Moore was standing at the back of the raft. His pole snapped as if a puny matchstick, catapulting him into the frenzied water. His head disappeared from sight. Screams and shouts rent the air. Men and boys began running along the bank, trying to see where Taylor was. Women covered their faces with their aprons and prayed.

"There he is!" Robbie Whitfield yelled. Taylor's head broke above the water. The raft had been flung downstream close to Taylor. Taylor was a strong, robust man, but it took every ounce of effort for him to swim the few strokes to the raft and grab it. The current was so bad that he couldn't pull himself aboard. The other men on the raft had their hands full keeping it from breaking apart and could not help him. After what seemed an eternity, the men got the raft under control, and Taylor climbed aboard.

John Hawkins, on his mighty horse, swam the frothing cauldron. As he reached the other shore, a loud cheer rose from the opposite bank.

He tied the ropes to sturdy trees upstream from the whirlpool so that the rafts wouldn't be caught again. Once the raft had cleared the whirlpool, it took no time to land, and the next rafts entered the water. Each family crossed without incident.

This crossing was different from the last one for Carson. This time he helped every wagon cross.

David thought that one good thing came from Lexie's injury. Since the Columbia was such a violent river, she didn't experience the fear she had with the other crossings. She didn't know when the wagons crossed.

Oregon!" shouted John Hawkins. "We are in Oregon!" The shout was taken up, and people everywhere stopped wagons, running to friends and loved ones hugging and crying, "We made it. We're really here. It's a beautiful place."

"What's all that racket?" Lexie asked tiredly. Opening her eyes for the first time in weeks, she looked around her. "What happened? What am I doing here?" she asked weakly.

David looked into lucid blue eyes. "Hallelujah! Her fever has broken," David, feeling her forehead, called to Sarah. "She's going to be all right. My darling, how do you feel?" he asked her tenderly.

"Weak, but I'm hungry. Oh, my shoulder hurts awful." Suddenly her face became a picture of disappointment. "We didn't get married, did we?" Tears welled up in her eyes.

"No, but we will, just as soon as you are able. We are in Oregon now. Just two more days and we should see Stringtown. Oh, sweetheart, you don't know how wonderful it is to see you better. All of us have been so worried," David told her, gently wiping away a tear that slipped down her face.

Sarah stuck her head inside the wagon. "Did I hear Lexie talking?" she asked eagerly. Crawling inside, she embraced Lexie and then David. Tears ran down her face as she looked down on her beloved daughter.

Lexie held her mother and said, "Don't cry, momma, please don't cry. I'm all right."

The three of them sent a prayer of thanksgiving to the Heavenly

Father for saving Lexie's life.

"What happened to Carson?" Lexie asked later.

"Nothing yet. He's going to be turned over to a court here in Oregon. It will go easy with him because he is now a born again believer," David told her. "He's been put on his honor. He's been coming to see how you are every day. He truly is a changed man."

"Can't we do something to help him?" Lexie asked.

David and Tom promised to see if they could. They came back with the news that if Lexie was satisfied, he wouldn't be punished.

Carson came to see Lexie to ask her forgiveness and to thank her. "I'm so sorry, Lexie. I wish I could do something to redeem myself."

"Oh, Carson, I forgive you, and I believe the Lord's redeemed you," Lexie told him.

It was only a short distance to Stringtown now. By tomorrow afternoon the train should reach its destination, Mr. Smythe told everyone.

A thanksgiving prayer meeting was called for that evening. The train turned out in full force. Carson was the first to attend. "I want everyone to see that I'm different now. I want them to see what a change Jesus has made in my life." John and Zeke walked with him.

Lexie wanted to attend too. She was still weak, but determined. David and the Fletchers hesitated and then gave their approval. Carson came to her, knelt down at her feet and begged her forgiveness for the second time.

"Get up, Carson. I told you that I forgive you. Jesus forgave me. I'm sorry it took something like this to make you see Jesus, but I'm awfully glad you did."

Lexie and her family had already asked that Carson not be punished. They thought he had suffered enough because of remorse. Mr. Smythe came to them. "Tom," he said, "Do you still feel that Carson should go unpunished?" He placed his hand on Carson's shoulder.

"Lexie, her mother, and I all think he should be forgiven just as our Lord forgave us."

"Then I guess you are a free man, Carson. I hope you appreciate what these fine people have done on your behalf," Mr. Smythe told him.

"I can't express my gratitude adequately. I know it's more than I deserve."

When Carson walked away, Lexie turned to David and asked, "David, how much do you love me?"

"What brought this on? You know I love you more than anything in the world." He put his arms around her in a comforting embrace.

"Then would you marry me, right now? Tonight?" Lexie asked him, uncertainty showing in her eyes.

With love shining from his eyes, David replied, "If that's what you want, yes. Let's go see John."

The prayer meeting was over, but before people had returned to their wagons, John called the congregation to order and said, "Folks, you are all invited to a wedding. This young couple has been disappointed time after time, but tonight we're going to get the deed done."

The old familiar words of the ceremony rang in Lexie's ears. "Do you, Lexie, take this man to be your lawful husband? As she watched David repeat his vows, love shining from his eyes, she thought the words were beautiful. *I never thought I'd be married with no wedding dress, nothing borrowed, nothing blue, no cake, nothing except David and me. But after all, that's all that matters, just as long as we're together.* She was surprised when David slipped a gold wedding band on to her finger.

"Where did you get this ring?" she asked when they had been pronounced man and wife.

"It belonged to my grandmother. She made me promise that my bride would wear it, so I've always kept it with me," David replied. "I've some other beautiful pieces for you, too."

They stood in line with Sarah and Tom, and Olivia and John while everyone wished them well. David was concerned about Lexie's standing so long. Drooping from the lack of exercise, she assured him she was fine.

When at last David and Lexie were alone, standing in the dusk of the evening, David enfolded Lexie in his arms and said, "Well, Mrs. Duvall, all we have to do now is to get on with our new life. We been through a lot together, and together, with our Lord's help, we can face anything."

Lexie looked at him with love in her eyes. "Oh, yes, darling, but just think, I never wanted to come to that old place called Oregon. It's hard to believe I felt that way."

"Never mind, you're here, I'm here. Let's not waste time," he said and kissed her thoroughly.

EPILOGUE

Lexie stood looking out of the window of the Duvall's white clapboard house. The house had been completed within the first six months of their arrival. It was a beautiful house with plastered walls and walnut paneling. Living room furniture had been shipped from Boston. Richard had made the rest for the young family.

No longer did the town of Stringtown fit its name. Besides the people who came on the first train in 1843, two more wagon trains had come that year. And now a year later, three more had arrived. Houses were no longer in a line on one street. The town boasted a number of streets with houses lining them.

The town was a beehive of activity. Now the town boasted a bank, a post office, a new Baptist church a Methodist church, two lawyers' offices, three general stores, and to Lexie's delight, a school.

Richard was the proud owner of a furniture store. Tom was contentedly running his newspaper office. Another doctor had arrived to help take the heavy caseload from David, who was kept busy in his new clinic that he had hired Olivia's father to build. James and Jane were prospering on their farm just outside of town.

"It's about time," Lexie said aloud. She had been watching for the birthday club to come. It was meeting day, and Lexie was to entertain them since it was her mother's birthday month. Now, they were beginning to arrive. She watched Jane, Lenora, Olivia and Sara climb down from Lenora's buggy and come up the concrete sidewalk to the house. Opening the door, she invited the women in.

"Where are the babies?" Lexie asked.

"James is waiting for the fields to dry up after the rain, so he said he would keep Sara Jane and little Jimmy," Jane replied.

"My mother has the twins," Lenora told Lexie as she bent and kissed her on the cheek.

"Mom has Jimmy Joe," Olivia said.

Each of the women entered the living room and placed a gift on a lamp table.

Lexie hugged Sarah and wished her a happy birthday.

"Well, daughter, when are you going to make me a grandmother?" Sara asked, smiling. She put her arms around Lexie and gave her a big kiss on her cheek.

"Well, Mother," she said surprising Sarah, "in just about eight months!" Lexie squealed delightedly and hugged Sarah in return. She carefully added a gift to the others on the table, only to be met with an onslaught of congratulations from her friends.

It was customary for the club friends to sew or just visit. Today they just spent the time catching up on what had transpired for each of them since the last birthday party. After cake and cider, the women prepared to leave.

Just as they were ready to depart, David returned home to be congratulated too. David kept a wide grin on his face until their friends were gone. He turned to Lexie who waved goodbye to the ladies until Lenora flicked the reins, and the team pulled away from the house. David put his arms around Lexie. "How is the little mother?" he asked tenderly.

"Getting bigger every day," she replied laughing.

"Are you happy, honey?" David asked her, planting a kiss on her nose.

"Ecstatic. Can't you tell? I can't thank God enough for bringing me here. When we left Missouri, I never dreamed I'd be this happy ever."

"Just remember that I'll do everything in my power to keep you that way. Oh, by the way, I got some very good news today. Mother and Dad are coming to live in Stringtown too. Dad finally convinced her that it would be a good place to see their grandchildren grow.

"I think it is a lovely place to see our grandchildren grow too," Lexie said.

"Amen to that," David said.

Printed in the United States
47331LVS00008B/109-123

9 781424 126842